Neal

Llwyncelyn.

2010

Cave

by

Hugh Bowen

STRATEGIC BOOK GROUP

ALSO BY HUGH BOWEN:

REVERSAL
WHY?
EDGE

Strategic Book Group
P.O. Box 333
Durham CT 06422
www.StrategicBookClub.com

ISBN: 978-1-60976-787-7

Printed in the United States of America

Book Design: Bonita S. Watson

Dedication

I dedicate this book to the whole Bowen tribe: my grandparents, Sir George and Lady Florence Bowen; my father, Air Commodore "Van" Bowen, one-time Lord Lieutenant of Pembrokeshire, and my mother Noel; Mr. Smith of Berry Hill farm; Essex Havard and the many people of Newport; the household staff of the ancestral home, long since converted into a hotel; and the innumerable Bowen family: brother and sisters, uncles and aunts, nephews and nieces, cousins galore, now scattered far and wide around the world. I particularly thank my cousin Joy Neal and her interest in the history of our family, and my niece, Joanna Bowen, resident of Haverfordwest, Pembrokeshire, who helped me in multiple ways and edited a draft of the book. Not least in my memory is my cocker spaniel, Topsy, who helped me shoot rabbits and birds, much needed in wartime, and loved to run with me all over the northern part of Pembrokeshire.

Finally, without my wife, Wendy, and her patient editing of the text, this book would be much less than it is.

Contents

Preface

The primary scenes of this story are set in the south-west coastal region of Wales in the UK. The small town of Newport, Pembrokeshire and its locality were important to me as I grew up and I have a deep affection for the area and the ways of the Welsh people who live there.

The folklore of those Welsh shores has been written about in historic novels, particularly and admirably those by Brian John.[1] His stories are set in Newport and its nearby countryside and my book follows in his footsteps, mixing fact[2] with fiction. In writing it, I have drawn on

---

1 *On Angel Mountain, House of Angels* and others. Trefelin, Cilgwyn, Newport, Pembs SA42 0QN

2 All the locations and place names in the story are true, sometimes with a slight variation, such as Llwyn for Llwyn-gwair. I have used this means to stay true to the geography and history of the region while avoiding the implication that

my family background stretching back to the 13th century and my knowledge of the place and region.

In my youth, I became acquainted with the people there when cycling along the roads, running along the coast and in the hills, fly fishing in the streams, and shooting rabbits with a little .410 shotgun. It was wartime, when every bit of food was valuable. I worked on the farms and after ten hours in the fields I would be brought along with the men to drink beer, underage as I was, in the public houses, the "pubs," in Newport, Nevern, Cardigan, Felindre Farchog, Crymych, and Eglyswrw[3], to name a few of the local places. I learned Welsh pronunciation and Welsh songs. Though little of a singer myself, I loved the spontaneous taking of parts by the basses and tenors, and the soprano parts sung by the few women who, in those days, came to the bars.

An introduction to the long history of smuggling in the region can be found on the Internet[4]. In 1983 there was yet another smuggling incident along the coast; this one close to Newport. I knew of it at the time from my relatives living there and a BBC program picturing the place and the

---

the present residents of these locations are those depicted in the book. One way to find a map of the region and the places mentioned is to go to *get lat long* on the Internet, then enlarge the hybrid map of the region.

3   Only occasionally have I indicated the pronunciation of Welsh words. In those cases, I've thought, the sound of the Welsh word, repeatedly said by the characters, helps the story along. The reader may consult http://britannia.com/celtic/wales/language.html to learn how to pronounce this inherently musical language.

4   See, for example, http://www.smuggling.co.uk/gazetter_wales_10.html

people. A prime player in the drama, and the discoverer of the place where the smuggling occurred on the coast, was the late Essex Havard, an acquaintance of mine from childhood. He kept the Ironmongers[5] shop in Newport.

An account of this incident from the police point of view is recorded in "Operation Seal Bay" by Pat Molloy published by the Gomer Press, Llandysul, Dyfed, UK. At the time, Pat Molloy was Detective Chief Superintendent, Head of Dyfed-Powys Criminal Investigation Department. The book provides a documentary account of the police work and the legal aspects of the case.

In CAVE I have used some of the actual events of this smuggling incident and, in the same manner, have used an actual visit by Queen Elizabeth II to St. David's Cathedral in 1955 for background in my otherwise fictional story.

As mentioned in the story, the word "cave" in Latin does not mean a cave as in English. It is pronounced *kay-vee*, at least by English school boys, and means "Beware!"

Hugh Bowen
Denver, Colorado
September 2010

---

5 My policy has been to use words natural to the indigenous people portrayed in the book and to allow word meanings to emerge from context in the story. However, here and there, I translate. Thus, an ironmongers shop in the UK is a hardware store in the US, and a torch in the UK is a flashlight in the US. For foreign words, I provide their meanings in parentheses.

Chapter 1

A Drowning

The blonde man cursed, but only in his brain. His voice had gone. His muscles had lost all power. The last of his feeling was being stolen from him by the cold water.

The life jacket was barely keeping him and his sodden clothes afloat. One of his shoes had disappeared. If he still had the strength, he would have kicked off the other. He had tried to put the pencil in a pocket, along with the numbers, but it had floated away.

He knew he would soon be gone. At least he had killed one of them. Perhaps the pencil would be found. Perhaps someone would make sense of the numbers. He'd done the best he could.

The water took him down. The pain in his chest was searing. His throat clenched shut in a spasm.

Then there was nothing.

Chapter 2

An Unusual Catch

Daisy was an old-fashioned, open-deck, broad-beamed, 18-foot, sailing boat, with a gaff rig and well-worn hull. Rhys looked after her lovingly. "There's a girl for you now," he would say in the lilting tongue of the Welsh.

Daisy was kept in the solidly built stone boathouse by the Cwm, the Welsh for a small inlet in the coast. Down at the end of the long slipway, the river Nevern flowed out to the sea. The owner of the boathouse and of *Daisy* herself was Sir James Owen, the local squire. He lived in the Owen ancestral home, Llwyn House, a mile and a half up the river, and he let Rhys have the use of *Daisy* out of a long habit between the families.

All her long life *Daisy* had been a working boat and she still was. Rhys used her for fishing and laying down and gathering up the lobster pots he set below the Morfa

3

cliffs. The Morfa headland was on the far side of the bay from their small town, Newport.

Daisy, with her retractable centerboard, could pretty much always go out to the bay over the sand bar at the mouth of the Nevern. Though, at the bottom of a tide, Rhys, and whoever was with him, might have to roll up their trousers and pull her over the gritty sand, or else attempt to navigate the narrow, swift flowing, channel under the cliffs. That was foolhardy, as everyone thereabouts knew. Some of the English, who came there with their smart modern boats on trailers, ended up with smashed in hulls.

On this day Rhys had asked his friend, Taf, to come out with him to take in whatever was in his lobster pots. The two men were of Celtic stock, dark haired and sturdy. Lobstering in Newport Bay was hardly a commercial endeavor; the lobsters were too few for that. Rather, it was a way to supplement the dinner table, earn a bit of money by selling the catch to the local pubs and lunchrooms, and cheat the Internal Revenue out of a few pounds.

Rhys and Taf had *Daisy* on the trolley. They trundled her down the stone slipway into the water. "Did you fill up the outboard with petrol then?" Taf asked, grinning.

He remembered, as they both did, when they were out by *Carregedrywy*, a rocky islet, always with cormorants and their droppings on it, and the wind had died. They were left to bob up and down on the calm sea, along with the empty tank of their little outboard. They had to row home. Not that they really minded and it was now a standing joke between the two men and their wives.

"Now, now, Taf. I'm only an idiot once in a while," Rhys told him, with a broad smile. They were good friends. Rhys owned the ironmongers shop in the town and Taf, a carpenter and handyman for whatever needed to be done, was always in and out to buy his supplies.

They pushed *Daisy* out into the Cwm and raised the mainsail and jib. *Daisy* pulled away in her stately manner on the rising tide, making for the sandbar. They let the centerboard down just a bit, enough to help *Daisy* sail a straighter course. Then they were over the shallows of the bar and making out through Newport Bay toward the open sea beyond.

They let the heavy metal board down all the way and now, away from the cliffs, the wind was steady. They romped along on a broad reach, making for the buoys of their lobster pots. It was nothing new to them; they had done it and enjoyed it many times. It always felt good to be sailing along in the fresh sea air and to look back at their small town with its ancient castle at the foot of their "mountain." Not that it was much of a mountain, only a little over 1,100 feet. But it was their mountain, and the gorse and the heather grew on it abundantly, painting the lower slopes in yellows and violets.

The men threw out fishing lines to catch the mackerel and sewin, the Welsh name for sea trout, that frequent the bay. Rhys was at the tiller, holding her steady. "We're probably sailing too fast to catch anything," he said; "but what the hell, eh?"

"Sure! Perhaps there's a whale out here, just waiting to be caught!"

"There better not be!" Rhys laughed. "Did you see that film Gregory Peck made, sailing out of Fishguard down the coast there, about the whale? It's from an American book called Moby Dick. The fellow's name was Ahab. He was all rapt up in his mind about this whale. It would kill him, if he didn't kill it. That's what happened, the whale killed him."

"I remember it. They had to make a rubber whale and tow it around to make it look real. Men do have their passions, don't they?"

"Here's our first pot coming up, Taf. I'll go up into the wind so you can bring it in."

There was nothing mechanical about lobstering with *Daisy*. It was all hard handwork. Taf snared the line of the lobster pot with a gaff and brought the pot up.

"Look at that, will you? A bloody miracle!" he exclaimed. There were three good-sized lobsters in the pot and two crabs. "Must be our lucky day!"

They went on to the next pot. It had just one lobster in it. Taf re-baited it and threw it back into the blue-green water, as he had done with the first pot.

They set off for the next pot. They would hardly expect more than half-a-dozen lobsters and a few crabs from their pots; though they could have lucky days to put beside their not-so-lucky ones when the pots were empty.

Suddenly one of their fishing lines went taut. *Daisy* slewed round and stopped, almost as if they had dropped anchor. The thick line was holding. It was over the gunwale and was forcing that side of the boat down, almost to the water.

"*Diawl!*" Taf gasped, using a Welsh expletive meaning devil. "What the hell is that?"

Rhys struggled to bring *Daisy* up into the wind. The sails flapped as he succeeded in doing it. "We must have caught that whale! Can you bring it in, Taf, whatever it is?"

Taf hauled in the line, hand over hand. Whatever it was, it was heavier than any fish he'd ever caught.

"It's a bloody monster!" he cried out.

"There it is!" Rhys said, looking over the stern of the boat.

"What is it?" Taf queried.

"Christ! It's a body!" Rhys exclaimed. Now he could see its long white face.

Daisy had seen all sorts of flotsam and jetsam brought up out of the sea, but nothing like this. Nor had the men. They had the body alongside the boat, their faces almost as pale as that of the corpse. It was a man, quite a young one. He had dirty blonde hair and a clean-shaven face, though with a day or two of bristles. His body was a bit bloated - not a pleasant sight - and he was wearing a water-logged life jacket.

"What do we do?" Taf queried, shaken by the sight.

Rhys, a Volunteer Coast Guard, knew what to do. "We'll get him aboard, Taf," he said gruffly, "over the transom back here. Else we could swamp the boat."

Rhys secured a rope around the body, under its shoulders. With a struggle, lifting and pulling, the two men got it on board over the stern.

"That's a horrible thing to have to do," Taf said, breathing hard.

"It is indeed, Taf. He must have fallen off a boat; probably a small one. The life jacket has no name on it. Have you heard of anything, Taf?"

"No, indeed I haven't."

Rhys had his mobile phone with him and called the police station at Fishguard. He told the constable at the desk what had happened and that they were going back to the boathouse at the Cwm.

A vehicle could only approach the boathouse through the small fields and gates cut into the earth and stone fences on the hillside above. The land belonged to Ethan Jones, a crusty old curmudgeon, very jealous of his rights of ownership. If he let anyone through, they had to pay for it. He would try it even with the police.

An inspector came on the line and said he knew the place. They would have a police car and an ambulance there as soon as they could. Yes, he would deal with Ethan Jones.

The wind was now against them and, rather than tack back, Rhys and Taf lowered the sails and, after a few tugs on the starting rope, had their little outboard going.

Daisy didn't travel very fast with it and that gave them time to get over their first shock.

"Cover his face, Taf. He looks a decent fellow. We should respect him."

Approaching the Cwm, they saw the police car and ambulance picking their way through the fields and gates belonging to Ethan Jones. He stood glowering at the top. The vehicles stopped by the boathouse and the inspector and paramedics went to the top of the slipway. Some people had gathered round, curious about what was happening.

Daisy chugged into the Cwm. The local police constable had arrived and told everyone to stand back. The corpse was taken out of the boat and put in the ambulance. The paramedic noted in his log that the man was dressed in light clothing with only one shoe on, had two euro coins and a bit of paper with numbers on it in a pocket, and no identification. The Inspector listened to the account that Rhys and Taf gave him. He told them they should come to the Station House in Fishguard the next day to make a formal statement. He would send a car for them.

* * *

The Llwyn Arms was crowded that evening as the "celebrities," Rhys and Taf, recounted their experience. The people listened with avid interest. Taf was the raconteur, careful not to leave out any gruesome detail, with Rhys sitting back and adding some comments.

Taf expounded, "All we were doing was fishing, see you, on the way out to the pots. We were talking about whales. So when the line went stiff like a ram rod, it was like we had foreseen it. Strange it was. Well now, I thought, we have the catch of the century. Indeed I did! But I was fearful. The devil might be in it. There was a chill in my spine. And then there it was! A man as drowned as ever you could see!"

Rhys noted, "He certainly was very drowned, been in the water for some time."

"And you didn't recognize him?"

"No. He couldn't have been from around here. We would know a tall man with blonde hair and a long face. He just had light clothes on, nothing to keep him warm; and he had lost one of his shoes, poor fellow."

"Yes, poor fellow, I wonder who he was," Eirwen, the busty bar girl said, drawing down the beer handles to fill the glasses with the locally brewed ale.

"Oh, they'll find out soon enough," Dilwyn Smith, of Penny Hill farm, said.

But who he was, it would turn out, was not so easy to ascertain.

Chapter 3

The Conspicuity of the Unusual

The sandbar *Daisy* had negotiated was accounted something of a blessing by the people of Newport, *Trefdraeth Sir Benfro* in Welsh. With limited access to the sea, big yachts and much of the rest of modernism, stayed away from the little town tucked away on the southwest coast of Wales. Their low stone buildings, with gray slate roofs and small rooms with small square windows, had withstood the southwest gales that came in over the Irish Sea from the Atlantic for centuries. The natives liked their town, with its narrow steep streets and blind corners around the edges of buildings. If others found it difficult to negotiate, so much the worse for them.

Newport, and its sea frontage, Parrog, had a few B & B lodgings and the Red Dragon Inn with its new set of rooms. They catered to the summer visitors and the few who came at other times of the year. In the summertime, the Browne family at the grocery were kept busy and Rhys at the ironmongers sold a good few buckets and spades for young children to take to the beach. For the older ones, he had shrimp rakes with their mesh nets. They were pushed along in the shallow surf and could catch enough shrimp for a boil-up on the beach.

Some say the Welsh have more heart than head and the boathouse, a feature of the Parrog shore, would not disprove that contention. It had been built at the end of the 19th century to house a lifeboat. The enterprise hadn't worked out due to the mouth of the river Nevern, the estuary into which the lifeboat had to be launched, becoming more and more silted up. For the period around low tide, the life boat could not be launched. From the start the nearby Fishguard life boat turned out to those in need. So the ownership of the boathouse had reverted to the Owen family on whose land it had been built.

The Welsh are not a retiring sort when it comes to opinions, enterprise, and curiosity. It's said of the people of Dyfed, where Newport is situated: "If you want to find a dull bugger around here, you'd better bring him in with you." Their curiosity about strangers was proverbial. When there were "foreign" boats close to shore or in the harbor, they were quickly noted. Talking of them in the pubs helped flush the beer down. Visitors, especially those who came there after September, did not escape notice. In the sparsely populated farming country beyond, a stranger was as notable as a black sheep among the flocks.

Newport Bay, with its long sandy beach and dunes rising to the farms inland, is bound by high cliffs on either side. Under these cliffs, the small pebble beaches and the caves the sea has burrowed out, are mostly inaccessible except from the sea. A few routes up and down the sandstone and shale cliffs are possible to climb, taking one's life in one's hands. The path along the top of the precipitous cliffs gives fabled views along the rocky coast and, on a clear day, one can see Ireland. Inland, the rolling fields lead to farm houses and barns.

Rees Llewellyn occupied the farm of Ffynon, above Morfa head. He was renowned as a local character, full of tales of mysterious happenings, eerie strangers, and ghosts of ship-wrecked sailors. His stories became noticeably more dramatic and improbable with the amount of rum he had in him.

Every year there are accidents along the cliff path. People approach too close to the edge in spite of the warning signs. Coast Guard boats, from Milford Haven to the south, are called in to retrieve the bodies. Some float out to sea and sink, never to be recovered. Other victims are those who capsize when sailing single-handed away from the coast. Most also disappear into the depths. The drowned man could be one of those, it was thought; except that he had been kept afloat by his life jacket, though only barely. In any event he could hardly have fallen off the cliffs. No one hiked the path with a life jacket on.

The corpse was the topic of curiosity for a week. Sensible thoughts gave way to far-fetched speculations. He was a Russian off one of their submarines, come to spy on what the Navy was doing down there around Pembroke with the Americans, was one suggestion. Soon, however, attention turned to the harvesting of the oats and barley crops. It could not be left too late; sunny days would soon give way to autumn rains.

Another concern was the shortage of lobsters in the pots. Some attributed the scarcity to the curse that St.

Tryn, their fisherman saint, had made a thousand years
ago. He had declared, so it was said, that a drowned man
laid a curse on the lobsters.

Rhys disagreed. "That's not what Taf and I found. We
had a pot next to the corpse and it had three lobsters in it.
There now! There's a poke in the eye for your curse."

The vicar at Newport said the curse was all nonsense in a sermon he gave to the thin congregation in
his church. He said St. Tryn had blessed fishermen and
given them his protection and that all else was the too
vivid imagination of the Celtic storytellers.

The people of Newport didn't mind having a fisherman saint in their history. They would, half-jokingly,
call on St. Tryn to give them a good catch when they
were out fishing. In any event, it was a bit of local
folklore, good for telling to visitors; as were all the local tales, like the one about St. Brynach and the angels
on their mountain.

Their conical *Carn Ingli*, the Mount of Angels in
Welsh, was the remains of a long extinct volcano and it
was not only beautiful, but sacred to those who believe
in such things. By tradition, St. Brynach came there in
the fifth century to rest in a cave and commune with angels, giving the mountain its name. It had been inhabited
long before by Neolithic people and around the summit
there were the remains of small round buildings and de-
fensive walls.

If you fell under the spell of the mountain, when you
were up there all alone, you might see visions of the angels. And that was not all. The Neolithic people, it was
believed by some, had worshipped Oestre, a goddess of
fertility. Devotion to her could aid a barren wife. By
spending a night on Carn Ingli, she would become pregnant. One woman declared a man-devil had chased the

goddess away and had taken his way with her. It was bad seed. She gave birth to a stillborn monster and that, some said, by some curious logic, proved the story.

* * *

The first clue as to the drowned man's identity, for what it was worth, was the two Euro coins in his trouser pocket. The constable heard it from his friend on the Milford Haven police force and told it to Mr. Mathias at the Newport garage.

"He could have been French then," the constable proposed. "We used to have a few of them here, in their berets, selling their strings of onions; good onions too they were. They came from Brittany and some of their old boats were not so sea-worthy, I can tell you. Perhaps a boat sank out there and all that was left was the drowned man."

"Maybe," Mr. Mathias nodded. "In the old days there were a lot of French and others here. They had regular smuggling runs up and down the coast. There was no one much to stop them. There were the Portuguese too. They brought in their wines. Some say that was the start of port wines becoming popular in England."

"Well, well, is that so?" the constable grinned. "I wouldn't mind catching a smuggler with some bottles of port."

Except for people getting drunk and the occasional fights in the pubs, his life as the local policemen was mostly a pleasant routine. He scratched his head. "Whoever he was, it's strange no one has claimed him. Have you any ideas about it, Mr. Mathias?

Mr. Mathias frowned. "I have better things to think about. I leave it to others."

Then a shrimper, a young girl, came across a man's shoe washed up on the beach. Her father was with her and, knowing the story of the drowned man, brought the shoe to the constable. A police sergeant arrived from Haverfordwest to take possession of it. He gave his opinion, over a pub lunch and a pint of bitter at the Red Dragon, that it could be a valuable piece of evidence. It was soon known, in the mysterious way that information flows in the countryside, that the shoe was French and matched the shoe on the drowned man's other foot.

"Oh, he was a Frenchie for sure," was the considered opinion and that, for them, settled the matter.

Life continued as usual in the town. It did not escape notice, of course, that two large vans, full of equipment, had been parked at the back of the Red Dragon. The five men with the vans had taken rooms there. They had told Myfanwy Thomas, the keeper of the Red Dragon, they were on a project and would be staying for a while.

Taf Jenkins was a good friend of Myfanwy. He did whatever needed to be done for her at a good discount. That evening, Taf brought back the two chairs he had re-glued for her and then sat down by the bar for a pint. As it happened, Rhys came in too, so they had their pints together.

A tall man sat down with them. He had a "posh" English accent; been to one of those classy "public schools," Rhys surmised. After introducing himself as Trevor Howe, he said, "The bar girl told me you are Rhys Jones and have the ironmongers here. So I thought to have a word with you. We'll be needing a good bit of stuff."

"I'll be happy to help you, then," Rhys told him.

Trevor Howe took out a notebook and began detailing what he wanted. It wasn't so much that the items were unusual, it was their quantity. Among other items, he wanted 1000 feet of 20 millimeter polypropylene rope and a large quantity of stainless steel bolts and washers.

"I'd have to send away for them, Mr. Howe; to the warehouse in Swansea."

"How long would it take to have it here?"

"They swing by twice a week as a rule, when they have a delivery, that is."

"We're in something of a rush on this project. You say the warehouse is in Swansea? That's what? Sixty miles from here? Could you send a van there tomorrow? I'll make it worth your while."

Rhys was not an easy man to diddle. "It's possible. Yes. It's possible, Mr. Howe. But unusual, you see. Tell me how much is 'worth my while' for me to go to Swansea, pick up the items, and have them back the same day? That is what you want, if I understand you right?"

"Yes, that's it. As to the money: first, a fair price for the goods. After that, I pay for what I want, Mr. Jones," and he drew £50 notes from his expensive polished-leather wallet.

Taf Jenkins' jaw dropped as the £50 notes mounted up.

"That's four hundred pounds for your trip there and back, Mr. Jones. I'll go through the full list with you and then you have the lot back here tomorrow evening. Is it a deal?"

Rhys looked at him quizzically. Trevor Howe returned his gaze. "Are you doubting me, Mr. Jones? Here, take the money. I'll trust you."

Rhys did not pick up the money immediately. He still wasn't sure about the man. "Yes. I'm trustworthy, Mr. Howe. Ask around. Everyone knows that. May I ask what your project is?"

"Oh, yes! It's no secret. We're doing research on the marine life along the coast here. We'll be photographing the seals and keeping counts on them, and the porpoises and dolphins, too. Some American billionaire wants them fully protected. It's a spare-no-expense deal. My job is to manage the operation."

"So that's it," Rhys said. "Well, Mr. Howe, I don't see anything against it. What do you think, Taf?"

"I'm not sure what I think. But I know what I'd do! Take the money!"

They all laughed. Rhys told Mr. Howe that Taf was a carpenter and an all-round handy man. "Very useful, he can be."

"I'm sure. Glad to know you, Mr. Jenkins. That's settled then. Here's my list. Let's go through it."

Rhys asked the bar girl for paper and pencil so he could copy the list. Taf could hardly contain his astonishment. It had to be worth thousands of pounds.

They were finished. Trevor Howe stood them a round of drinks. He paid with a £50 note. Marianne, the bar girl, had seen £50 notes before, but not often. It was unusual. Even Myfanwy said so.

The unusual is, of course, conspicuous. Mr. Howe, it seemed, did not understand that elementary fact about human perception and curiosity.

Chapter 4

Starting a Sabbatical

Van and Ava Bentham were glad to be finally leaving New York for Van's sabbatical year. They were off to England, Wales, and France. Van had been born in a big old house at Trewarn, close to Newport in Pembrokeshire. He had been part of the "brain drain" leaving England in the 1950's for enviable posts in the US. Now he was a dean and professor of psychology at New Jersey State. He had just finished his end of term activities, among them dressing for the commencement in the distinctive Cambridge doctoral gown, cape and hat to which he was entitled. He had gained his M.D. and Ph.D. at Cambridge University.

One of his specialties was Forensic Psychology and he would be a visiting lecturer at the universities in Aberystwyth, Cambridge and Paris on that subject. In Paris he would renew his acquaintance with his friends at *La Sûreté*. He had worked with them and the FBI in tracking down a serial killer who had taken refuge in Paris[6].

Ava had come to terms with Van's inability to do nothing. His hours had to be filled. For him, a sabbatical was not time off; rather, it was an opportunity to do something different. Knowing she would be resisted, she had, nevertheless, proposed a cruise.

"Oh, God, Ava! You know what I think of cruises. Voluntary imprisonment! You eat and drink too much with unknown people, most of whom you'd rather not have met."

Ava didn't press the point; the suggestion was more to open the subject, not to expect agreement. Persuasion was needed. She would pick the right moment. It came as they were sharing a dish of *moules marinières,* at the Jubilee restaurant on East 54th street.

"Be calm, my love, and listen. A cruise will be something new for both of us and it's a reasonable thing to do at our time of life."

"I hardly think 'reasonable' the right word," Van objected.

"All right, 'sensible,' if that suits you better. You need some time off, Van. You really do. Actually the cruise line contacted me. They'd heard about me being a 'Charm Ma'am' pushing *'Manners, Fashion, and Etiquette'* and giving seminars on how to eat peas with a fork. So I talked with them."

"And … ?" Van queried, apprehensively.

"Oh, they soon came around to my requirements when I told them I was married to a famous author, professor, and forensic psychologist who would be coming

---

6 See EDGE by author.

with me. So you are signed up for whatever chit-chats you want to give and do book signings, too."

"What? Good grief!" Van cried, clamping a hand to his forehead.

"Now keep calm, dear. We go free. In fact, they will pay us! How about that?"

"Great balls of fire, Ava!"

"Now, now, darling." Ava said calmingly. "I know how you hate to be idle, though that's not a crime, you know, and you hate the heat, too. So we're going north. It'll be fascinating. There'll be icebergs and things like that. We're going on a Norwegian boat, the Asta, leaving from a pier here in New York, so you don't have to have your legs cramped up to your chin in an airplane. Our first stop is St. Johns in Newfoundland."

"H'mm. St. Johns, eh! I've never been there. In WWII it was where the convoys formed up to cross the Atlantic and it was the last point that Lindbergh saw on his way to Paris. Its Cape Spear is the most eastern point of the North American continent. It has a fascinating history, full of intrigue."

"Yes, dear. You'll have plenty of opportunity on the boat to talk about it."

Van finished the last *moule marinière*. "All right, my dear. Where to next? The north pole?"

"Not quite, my love. Here's a map of our route," and, taking a small map from her handbag, Ava showed it to Van. "Next we go to Nanortalik in Greenland, then a couple of stops in Iceland, and on through stopovers in the Faroe Islands and the Shetlands to finish up in Southampton. From there we catch a train to London. Then we take a taxi to the Franklin Hotel in Knightsbridge, the one you've told me about. I've booked us a Deluxe Garden Room. So what do you think?"

Van raised his glass to his wife. "Though I almost hate to say it, considering you have cut through one of my favorite prejudices - cruises - I say you're a wonder girl! I would never have dreamed up such an outing."

"I bet you can think up something vitally interesting to say about Norsemen's psyches."

"Now that you mention it, I was chatting with a Swedish psychologist the other day and we were talking about the so-called warrior gene and ... "

"Save it for the trip, dear."

* * *

They were dining at the Captain's table the evening before arriving at St. Johns. Ava had begun her presentations on how "Manners Makyth Man" and Van had given an overview history of the Norsemen and their culture. The conversation had taken many turns and now they were talking about the mystery of the brigantine sailing ship, the *Marie Celeste*. A hundred and forty years ago, she was found sailing, all shipshape and undamaged, off the Spanish coast, with no crew or passengers aboard.

Laura Manning, a middle-aged woman, bright and sophisticated, declared in a humorous manner, "They were sucked up by an alien spaceship! What do you think, captain?"

"I hadn't thought of that," the captain laughed. "What do you think, Dr. Bentham?"

The other diners were looking at him. "OK. I've always liked mysteries and this one is particularly mysterious. It is usual, you know, when there is no good explanation for something, that our minds fill in the blank with fancies. These days our imaginations turn to extraterrestrial aliens," he grinned.

A man suggested, "It's possible, isn't it?"

Van smiled. "If you wish it so. Depends on your cosmic view. Laura's supposition follows in the footsteps of others who have suggested alien abduction, time travel, and various otherworldly explanations. Conan Doyle, the man who wrote the Sherlock Holmes stories, was a spiritualist and wrote a fanciful story about the Mary Celeste mystery. Incidentally, he gave the ship the name *Marie Celeste*, when her actual name was Mary Celeste. I suppose he thought *Marie* was more romantic than just plain Mary."

"Well, professor, what do you think happened?" one of them asked.

"The evidence points to a hurried departure. Under duress people can do strange things. It appears the people got off voluntarily. There was no sign of violence. My guess is that they feared something."

"What could that have been?" Laura quizzed.

"It had to be something seen as dangerous, like a bomb. But that's just speculation and does not explain why the lifeboats were still aboard. I can't see them all diving off the ship."

The captain broke in. "I think another ship was involved, possibly a pirate ship. Though why pirates would take the crew and passengers, and nothing from the ship itself, makes no sense."

Another in the group put in, "You'd think a corpse or two would have washed ashore. But that didn't happen, as I remember the story."

The captain nodded. "Yes, that's right. Nothing was known to have come ashore."

Laura asked, looking at Van somewhat too admiringly, Ava thought, "Don't some corpses stay afloat, Dr. Bentham? I've heard you can become bloated like a balloon. Perhaps they were eaten by sharks and that's why nothing was found."

Van didn't really want to go into the subject, but they were curious about it.

"Well, if you insist. Yes, bloating can happen. Most often, the corpse just sinks and, in time, goes to the bottom. If a person has a life jacket on, he'd probably die of hypothermia first, that is, becoming too cold to sustain life. When a person is wearing a life jacket, the body would float for a time. In some cases, the lungs retain air due to a laryngeal spasm that closes the throat. Then the body may stay afloat or be semi-submerged for a longer time and bloat and decompose to some degree before sinking. When a body is recovered after being in the water awhile, it will often have nibble marks from fish, and crabs when it is near to shore, especially on the appendages."

"What a morbid subject," Ava cried. "Don't ask my husband questions like that! You are liable to learn more than you want to know!"

"It's so interesting though," Laura exclaimed. "It must be wonderful to be married to a man who knows so much."

Ava gave her a barracuda look.

"I don't like to think about such things," a woman said. "Let's talk about why most men care little about fashion, at least if they're heterosexual, and women go crazy about it, shall we?"

The talk took off on that tack, with good-humored bantering between the sexes.

* * *

Van was having a good time. In Iceland he spent hours in the library examining the Edda chronicles and

reading translations. They are centered on Norse mythology and legends of Norsemen heroes.

The Norsemen, he told his audience in one of his
"chats," were brave and able, but unmerciful, and believ-
ers in monsters and spirits of all sorts. A saving grace
was that the Norsemen married native women. In France
they became Normans. The Normans invaded England
with the result that probably all Englishmen, and all those
who emigrated to America from England, have some
Norse blood in their veins. Norsemen must have had an
overabundance of the 'warrior gene' that, in muted form,
Van suggested, produces some of the assertiveness in our
make-up. After some questions and quips about "blaming
it all on the Norse," Van ended and was about to leave for
lunch when Laura Manning came up to him.

"A great talk! Somehow I'm going to put that stuff
in one of my books. I write so-called Romance Novels
under the name of Pilty Downs; you know, after the Pilt-
down mystery of the missing link that was really a big
hoax." She laughed. "Sort of amuses me."

"Forgive me if I admit I haven't read any of your
books."

"I'd be surprised if you had. My readers are almost
all women. Probably most of them lead dull, frustrated
lives. But it's a pretty good living. I've been in New
York and around New England to soak up stuff."

"I congratulate you on your success. I'm afraid my
books are more prosaic than yours."

"Not a bit. I couldn't put down *Why?*[7] I lost half-a-
night's sleep over it."

"I suppose I'm glad to hear that. Will you join Ava
and me for lunch?"

---

7   See WHY? by author.

Over lunch, in which Laura and Ava hit it off surprisingly well, Laura told them she lived in the Chelsea district in London. Chatting about where they were spending their sabbatical, Ava told Laura they were going to where Van had been born and lived as a child.

"Oh, where's that?"

"It's a little place called Newport. Not one of the big Newports of the world. It's almost unknown and off by itself on the coast of Pembrokeshire in southwest Wales."

Laura admitted she didn't know where Pembrokeshire was.

Van smiled. "You're a typical Londoner. Outside of London, the UK hardly exists!"

Laura laughed. "There's some truth to that."

Ava suggested, "You should go there. Historically the place was full of fair maidens in castles and gallant knights riding to their rescue, with a few witches and various kings thrown in. Or so Van tells me. I bet you could write a great book about it all!"

"That's a thought!" Laura exclaimed.

The ship reached the Shetlands and they picked up London newspapers.

"Well, well, look at that, will you?" Van exclaimed to Ava. "My little Newport is in the news. A couple of locals fished a corpse out of the bay. It was semi-submerged and bloated when they hooked it." He laughed. "Do you think we had a premonition to have been talking about drowned corpses the other evening? I'll tell Laura about it. It's more up her street than mine. The authorities there don't know who he is. A mystery corpse! What fun!"

"Really, Van! Don't be so macabre. Poor man! I bet he found it no fun to be drowned."

"Yes. Very true. I shouldn't make fun of it. Drowning is a painful way to die."

Chapter 5

London

"You just write Pembs for Pembrokeshire," Van told Ava when she asked how she should write their Welsh address on the letters and postcards she was sending around the world. They would soon be occupying the cottage they had rented above Newport on the slopes of Carn Ingli.

After their northern cruise to reach England, Van was happy to be in London. The small five-star Franklin Hotel had been excellent five years ago and it still was. Their room looked out onto a well-tended English-style garden through high French windows. Breakfasts were brought to them in the room and Van had his much-beloved Scottish kippers every morning. Ava thought they were the stinkiest fish she had ever come across and, as the days were warm and sunny, almost unnaturally so for

September in England, she went out on the patio to have
her grapefruit and scrambled eggs.

Being from California and newly married to Van,
Ava found London a novel experience; not least, the
swirl of traffic coming from every direction. Van took
her to the Tower and identified the exact spot where
Anne Boleyn had her head chopped off. It was more
than she needed to know, but it pleased Van, as she
knew, to be up on such things.

Leaving Van to spend time at the British Library, Ava
explored Harrod's, a short walk from the hotel. It lived
up to its reputation of being the up-scale mega-store of
the world. Among other items, she bought the latest
fashion in sturdy raincoats, rain hats, and hiking boots.
She would need them in Wales, Van had told her.

Among the people they looked up was Heddy Stridewell, the daughter of a man who had been at Clare College, Cambridge with Van as an undergraduate. The
young woman had joined the Metropolitan Police Force.
Now she was a Special Inspector stationed at Scotland
Yard and immersed in the Intelligence Division, one arm
of Britain's fight against terrorism.

Van invited her to dine with them at Wilkinson's, a
great fish restaurant in the West End.

"My goodness, you look so like your father, Heddy!"

"You knew him well?"

"Oh, yes! We shared the same staircase in the old
court at Clare and we did some cramming together. I'm
so sorry he's gone."

"Yes. He was a good father to me. He encouraged
me to go in for police work. I was a bit of a tomboy. He
thought it would suit me and it has."

Ava had been studying the menu. "I'm choosing between a Dover sole and a lobster," she announced.

"Oh, we'll have fresh lobsters in Newport," Van told her. "I advise the Dover sole. The sole caught off the white cliffs of Dover is something unique. Don't you think so, Heddy?"

"Yes, indeed. I'm down that way near Folkestone every now and again, working with the police to catch the illegals hitching a ride on the Chunnel trains."

"Oh? How do they do that?" Ava asked.

"They find some sort of lodgment under the cars in their effort to reach England. Then it gets too much for them. The train travels close to a hundred miles per hour in the tunnel. They fall off and are killed. We work with the French police in trying to stop it. But these people from Eastern Europe and Turkey are desperate. They think it's worth the risk."

Van nodded. "Poor fellows. But immigration into England, legal and illegal, has gone on for centuries; more so lately, I suppose. Look at the many foreign faces you see here in London."

"Yes, and it's hard to find the few dangerous people among them; not all of them are illegals," Heddy told him.

"I imagine so. How do most of them make it here? There can only be a few riding the Chunnel trains."

"Most of them get in with passports and visas, some legal, some false. We spot most of the false ones. We get tips from foreign police forces and custom agents, like we do for the smugglers."

"Yes, I've heard about that. Another item that's gone global."

"Right. Then there are the few who do incredible things, like parachuting into the highlands of Scotland! The man shouldn't have landed there. The locals spotted him immediately! Actually, we rely on locals to spot the unusual and suspicious to a great extent. We can't be everywhere. So we count on the sharp eyes and, I suppose, a bit of the natural suspicion of strangers, to help us. My boss calls it 'the xenophobia asset.' The people he works with often have to look up the words he uses," she laughed.

Van was amused too. "It's a good point, Heddy. People are far more aware of the unusual than the usual. Hang a picture on the wall and, after a week, you hardly see it. Habituation. The xenophobia asset, eh! I like it."

Ava interjected. "How about swimming in?"

Heddy laughed. "It would be a long swim! Twenty-two miles across the Channel and that's the shortest route."

"But suppose you were let off by a boat close to shore. You could swim in then."

"I suppose," Heddy agreed. "It has probably been done."

They were served with crab bisque and stopped talking to savor the chef's skill. In between the last spoonfuls Van said; "I think I know what Ava may have been thinking about. Isn't that so, darling?"

"Yes, that man washed up on the coast of Wales. Did you hear about it, Heddy?"

"I think so, but just as an item. A man drowned. We have daily dockets of such happenings. But I don't think there has been any follow up. Not with us, in any case. I imagine the local people are taking care of it."

"It was just a thought," Ava said.

"My wife comes up with intuitions, Heddy. Sometimes they are right on. An ancestor of hers lived in Salem, Massachusetts. So she may have witch's blood coursing through her."

"Now, Van! Don't be naughty! When he has one of his forensic cases, Heddy, I chip in with some ideas; that's all."

"Some damn good ideas, too," Van affirmed.

Heddy was interested. "You mean that whoever it was down there in Wales could have been trying to get into the country?"

"It seems possible to me," Ava said. "If you are a good swimmer, it seems preferable to being killed under a train. The bit in the paper said they hadn't identified him. Now who goes around with absolutely no identification?"

"It's a good point," Heddy agreed.

Ava continued, "If that happened, trying to swim into the country illegally from a boat, there would have been other people on the boat. They must have known about it, but they didn't report it. That would mean they were in on the scheme, whatever that was. It couldn't have been just an accident. And if he had been sailing along all alone, and fallen overboard, I would think the boat would have shown up, like the Mary Celeste did, with no one on board. We were talking about the Mary Celeste mystery, Heddy, on our cruise boat on the way over. It's really quite obvious, something fishy was going on! There!" she grinned.

Van laughed, "That's wonderful, my dear – something fishy. Oh! The joys of the English language!"

Heddy became thoughtful. "You know, you may be on to something. Heaven knows what. You told me you were going down there. Here's my card. If you come across anything out of the ordinary when you're there, let me know."

And that was how Van and Ava started being assets to the British police and MI5 in the matter of the unidentified, fished-up and fishy corpse at Newport, Pembs.

Chapter 6

Plans

Intelligence - *Intel* - that is good, solid, to the point, information - is the basis of success in any operation. Major Trevor Howe, retired from Special Forces, understood that very well.

Leaving his men to work out how to build a waterproof chamber under a stony beach, a cache for the stuff to come, Trevor put on his hiking boots. Leaving the Red Dragon Inn in Newport, Pembrokeshire, he left the small town and walked northward along the cliff path of the National Coastal Park of Wales. A mile out from Newport the path climbed to the top of the high cliffs of Morfa Head.

Trevor spent the day scouting the place. As he had expected from studying maps, and from the report of the north Pembrokeshire coast from Geery Schrotenboer, the skipper of *Mother Hen,* their survey boat, there were a number of stony beaches that would suit their purpose. The cliffs above the beaches were all steep, some vertical, and the beaches below them inaccessible except from the sea. The most promising beaches were those that were difficult to see from above, unless one went dangerously close to the edge of the cliff, which Trevor didn't care to do. The invisibility of most of the beaches from the path was a positive feature for their plan. It much lessened the chances of being seen by hikers or the few locals.

The full length of the beaches could be seen from passing boats. However, during his hours of walking the cliff pathway, Trevor saw only two small boats out to sea and a lobster boat attending to its pots a few hundred yards out from the cliffs. To the extent that lobster fishermen might wonder what they were doing along that part of the coast, they would be discreet and stick to their cover story.

Planning to use this part of the coast was right on. Provided they were careful and not there for more than a week or two, it would be unlikely that anyone would discover that anything nefarious was going on. Sure it had its risks; but all their operations had a measure of risk. As long as they all were aware of that fact, the risk could be minimized. He would have his men damp down their activities overall and keep the critical ones out of sight. At all times they must act consistently with their cover story; that is, they were photographing and recording the seals, porpoises, and dolphins along the coast.

On returning to Newport in the late afternoon, Trevor picked up the message that Lief, in *Mother Goose*, had arrived at Aberystwyth and was tied up in the harbor.

As Trevor would learn when they met, Lief had put *Mother Goose* to sea at Kuwait, sailed through the Persian Gulf, around Arabia, through the Red Sea and the Suez

Canal, and then the length of the Mediterranean, until stopping at Gibraltar. *Mother Goose* was a fast sea-going yacht, 80 feet in length, equipped with powerful engines and a stack of electronic navigation and communication gear.

Lief had stopped at Gibraltar to obtain a clean bill of health from H.M. Customs and Excise. His two passengers had Kuwaiti passports. They were finely dressed in traditional Arab style. They had chartered the boat, Lief told the British authorities, to take them on a tour of Northern Europe. The Brits had not searched the boat after Lief swore he was carrying no contraband. Even if they had, the likelihood of their finding the keel compartments on their own was virtually zero. They would need a pointer from someone about the construction of the keel, put the boat in dry dock, and disassemble the keel to find the stuff. The difference was that Lief had a skilled diver on board. Oscar Flavio knew how to open the concealed compartments from underwater and float the containers up on their safety cords.

Lief was aware that Gibraltar reported all boat comings and goings to London. By stopping there he had effectively inoculated himself from having any trouble at British ports. He and all his crew had legitimate passports. He was Norwegian, born in Oslo, thirty years old, blonde, slim, and athletic. Lief could dazzle women, but only when ashore. It was far too risky to have a woman aboard *Mother Goose*. Lief came from an upper-class background, was well educated and spoke English fluently, as many Norwegians do; it was nothing exceptional.

Mother Goose had continued up the coasts of Spain and France, and then put in at St. Malo on the northern coast of Brittany. There they picked up Geery Schrotenboer from *Mother Hen*. She was a smaller boat than *Mother Goose*, but similarly equipped.

The next day, following his reconnaissance of the coast, Trevor drove north along the coast road to Aberystwyth. It was raining and misty. It was another point in favor of the location. The autumn weather, more often rainy and cloudy than sunny, would not entice people to go out in their boats or encourage hikers to walk the cliff path.

Trevor had no difficulty in spotting *Mother Goose* in the harbor and gaining their notice. Lief sent a dinghy over to pick him up.

Lief and his number two, Hans Fleigel from Hamburg, the captain of *Mother Goose*, were there as well as Geery. Trevor sat down with them to have coffee in the lounge of the well-appointed yacht.

Lief told them he was going to take his two passengers ashore in the morning and put them on the train leaving at 7.35. A common sight was to see dinghies taking people ashore. This excursion from *Mother Goose* would be no different. The men would be dressed in casual clothes and their light skin coloring would attract little notice. In any event, putting them on land and getting them on their way had to be done; and this seemed the best way to do it. To Lief's relief there was no sign of Customs and Excise men or Coast Guards at Aberystwyth. The harbormaster had only been concerned that they operated safely in the small harbor.

"Still, I'm not entirely happy about doing this, the truth be told," Lief told the others. "It's an extra risk. But the money is exceptional and we are in the business of making money, as I don't need to tell you."

The men smiled their agreement.

"These two men, whoever they exactly are, are exceedingly well funded and, frankly, those bastards down there in the Gulf and up in Pakistan and Afghanistan, had us over a barrel. We do this for them or else they go back to using the land routes. Our supplies would dry up. So that's how it is. Like it or not. But I struck a good bargain with them," Lief grinned.

Trevor interjected, "Those men should be able to stay below the British radar, there are so many of their sort in the UK now. I doubt you have much to worry about."

"I hope so. But I don't want to hang around here any longer than I have to. Now, Geery, update me on the drowned man. Who was he?"

Geery waved his arms in the air, with the smoke from his cigarette making blue trails about his bearded face.

"Damned if I know!" he said in his Boer accent. He was very much a Boer and despised the English. "Claude, the corpse in Newport bay, had been recommended by that man in Paris, DeBouef. He said Claude had worked for him in Marseilles and was reliable. I was relaxed about him. There was nothing wrong with the work he did. Then he was caught at the entrance to the radio shack. It was suspicious though, frankly, nothing for sure. We punched him up a bit, but he didn't say anything. We stripped and searched him without finding anything on him or in his belongings. So we gave him back his clothes and locked him up with a guard at the door."

Geery stopped to drink some coffee. Lief demanded impatiently, "But you must have some idea who he was?"

"Only that he might have been a bit too good for us. He spoke English and French well. I just took the word of DeBouef that he was a right guy."

"That was a mistake, it seems. What happened then?"

"He may have thought he could swim to shore. As you know, we'd been reconnoitering the coast, finding Morfa Head a likely spot, as I have passed on to you, Trevor. We were not that far out from the coast. Somehow he got the guard to unlock the door. He killed him by putting some kind of spike through his eye and churning it around in the man's brain."

"A spike? What sort of spike?"

"I don't know. Whatever it was, he took it with him. A dangerous customer."

Lief muttered, "So it seems. He had a weapon that you didn't find. He lures the guard to unlock the door. He kills him in a peculiarly professional way. He has all the signs of a trained agent." Lief paused. "And there has been nothing in the media to say who he was?"

"Not so far as I know."

"It adds up. He was on the other side. Let me emphasize the importance of no one carrying identification with him, like this guy, except for special purposes. You, Trevor, need your proper identification. It's part of your cover story. But, for the men, no tags on clothes, nothing. It has worked well in this case, it seems. See to it with your men, Geery. You must strip them of any I.D."

"Yes, I understand. Their clothes, the whole lot. That's what I do."

"Good. And Trevor, that applies to your men too."

"Heard and understood," Trevor said.

"Here's what I think," Lief continued. "The man was an agent, either British or French. When in a hole he acted decisively and skillfully. That there's been no publicity about him strongly suggests that the Brits or the French, whoever was running him, want it that way. But more importantly, if I'm right, it means they are suspicious of *Mother Hen*."

Trevor Howe exclaimed, "Keep *Mother Hen* out of my operation. We will have a hard enough time keeping tight security as it is."

Lief agreed. "Geery. You will cool your heels in St. Malo for the time being. We have another assignment coming your way. OK. We'll move on. Trevor, where are you going to put the cache?"

"That's not much of a problem," Trevor said. "There are several good sites that meet our requirements. Let me speak up, and then have done with it. You all know I thought it a good idea to move the stuff into the UK by a route like this. But there are special risks, to put along-side the plusses, in operating in an out-of-the-way place. Strangers are more obvious. We have received a 'correct' signal from the Boss, one of his super-terse ones. I'm not sure what it means. Does he want us to reconsider?"

Fleigel shook his head. "No. I'm sure the signal re-ferred to that snooper. The Boss wants us, Geery and me, and you too, Trevor, to make sure we don't have any other pigeons on board. Speaking for myself, that's taken care of. My crew is warned. Anything out of line, and I told them I meant *anything*, will result in their departure from this world. They know it. But I know this crew pretty well. I believe I can trust every one of them."

"You will remain on your guard," Lief warned him. "The Boss, as you know, does not tolerate mistakes. All right. Back to you, Trevor."

Trevor poured himself a coffee. "You all know as well as I do, no route remains secure forever. In due course it's bound to be compromised. This operation is open to discovery, especially if we stay for any time. We have a good cover story, about marine research, that will do for the short haul. But long term ... no way."

Lief nodded in agreement. "That's right, Trevor. A quick hit and then out. It's a typical risk/benefit issue. Keep the risks low and gain the maximum benefit possible. If we do it right, be quick about it, with good concealment and a good cover story, we can do it and then get out of there. That's what I expect of you, Trevor - to make that happen."

"OK. I just wanted to be sure we were all on the same page. I've not been wasting my time, you'll be glad to hear, Lief. I've started to assemble the hardware we'll need."

"Good, Trevor," Lief said. "All of you, listen. I run an either/or operation and I think you all know what the 'or' is. OK. Enough said. You're intelligent people and are amply rewarded."

Lief turned to Trevor. "I want the site chosen and the cache built as quickly as you can. It has to be hidden and well disguised. I leave that to you. We will do a dummy run first and, assuming there are no problems, we'll bring the bulk in."

"OK," Trevor agreed.

"We'll be setting up security signals with you, Trevor, ship-to-shore, using a transponder. You understand that, once we start to move the stuff, you'll have to move fast. You will set up your arrangements that way and plan ahead for any emergency."

"Sure. I don't plan on having an emergency, Lief. I plan on doing it right, from start to finish. But I'm used to contingency planning. It's what they teach you in the army," Trevor chuckled drily. "If necessary, we'll either conceal or get the hell out of there. As you know, I'll have my small landing craft, actually glorified inflatable boats. On the map there's a cove up the coast with a narrow little road leading up from the beach. It's called *Kybor* and has that crazy Welsh spelling, C-e-i-b-w-r. That will be our get-out-of-there route."

"All right, Trevor. It's your call. The bottom line is - do a first class job. We give you the assets and you employ them - employ them for success. Do I make myself clear?"

"Very clear."

"Very well then, it's a go. I will tell the Boss that. Keep me informed. And, Trevor, if you need any incentive just think about what the Boss has promised you for a successful operation with no hitches. Was it half-a-million pounds or half-a-million dollars?"

Trevor smiled. "It's good pay either way. I'll move fast. We'll make the cover story stand up by spending time photographing the seals there. Tomorrow I'll purchase the landing craft we need along with the outboards to suit. I know what I want, the Zodiac military style inflatable with a 200 horse power Yamaha. They are seagoing, carry a good load, and move fast. An outfit in Swansea has them. They'll bring them to Newport for the right price."

"Good," Lief exclaimed, "that's all settled then. Anything else, Trevor?"

"I don't think so. It just needs doing."

Trevor said he would like to get going back to Newport. They shook hands and Trevor left. Lief turned to Hans Fleigel. "Have Oscar Flavio step in here, will you? We have a problem in London he can help us with."

Hans Fleigel frowned. "I have him training the men on getting the stuff out of the keel, then off this boat and into the carrier boats. As you know, it's not the simplest thing in the world to do."

"I understand. Work it out with Mark England in London. Give him a phone call. Be discreet. Remember that it's always possible our phone calls are being intercepted."

"Don't worry. I'm aware of that."

Oscar Flavio was a squat, muscular man of forty, a swarthy Serb who, if he had been in the Mafia, would have been a top *Capo*. He was renowned for keeping a tight rein on his men.

Lief stood by the window of the cabin looking out over the harbor and the seaside town. It was still pouring with rain, but there were breaks in the clouds.

Oscar Flavio entered. "Hello, Oscar. A pleasant spot, isn't it? If you like rain! But I'm afraid I have to take you away from it."

Oscar's English was not his strong point. "I'm not afraid! Never!"

"No, no. I know that. Listen. You are to go to London to our house there: number 12 Surrey Gardens, a small hotel, close to Paddington station. You've been there before. You remember your way there?"

"Yes, I know."

"This is what you do. You book in. They'll have a room for you. Stay in the room until Mark England comes to fetch you."

"Mark England, yes"

"He will explain to you what has happened."

"You blame me for something?" Oscar growled.

"No. Mark needs your help. A disposition."

"A disposition, uh."

"The Frenchman, Yves Mateur, the man you had working the Eurostar train between Paris and London. He had grown careless. He was found with cocaine on him. The police had him in custody, but he escaped."

"I not trust him," Oscar snarled.

"That's right, he was untrustworthy. That's why he was only a carrier. Now he's on the loose and threatens us. He blames you, Flavio, and swears he will kill you."

"Kill me, uh! Him! He a chicken!"

"I agree. But we don't want any complications."

"How I find him?"

"After you arrive, Mark England will tell you the plan. I don't know the details. Then you do what you do."

"It be pleasure. Pouf! He gone."

"Yes, pouf!" Lief agreed. "You will take the sleeping

car train to London from Fishguard. We will reserve you a first class cabin. You'll have a good night's sleep."

Oscar Flavio left. Lief poured himself a Scotch and sat down on the plush settee. He ran his mind through the items on his agenda. The two men would be on their way tomorrow. The charge was £100,000; that was: £50,000 down in the Gulf and £50,000 on delivery. The men had paid the second £50,000 in cash out of their money belts. The Newport operation was proceeding well. Trevor Howe was a man to be trusted. Yves Mateur would be taken care of.

Lief finished his Scotch and looked out the window again; the sun was breaking through.

Lief rose early the next morning. He was going to see the two Arabs on their way himself.

The dinghy with its little outboard was tied up beside them. The two men, dressed casually with peaked caps on their heads, let themselves down into it followed by their large cases and a long narrow one. Lief asked what it was for, but they didn't tell him. Lief steered to the landing and tied up to a bollard. He walked, with the men pulling their wheeled cases behind them, up the road the short distance to the station. He carried the long case for them. It was quite heavy. They passed only a few men, going to work. Lief exchanged "Good mornings" with them. They reached the station without incident. The ticket office was open and Lief bought the two men tickets to Leicester.

Going to the platform where the 7.35 train was waiting, they saw the stationmaster in his uniform and half-a-dozen men boarding the train. Among them were businessmen with briefcases. They paid little attention to their surroundings. No doubt they frequently took the train.

A couple of minutes before the train left, a fashionable older woman appeared. She met up with the stationmaster. Speaking with her, he pointed to the flower pots placed along the platform. She scanned them with a sharp eye while taking in the scene on the platform. She was slightly surprised at seeing two rather swarthy men with large cases and a blonde man seeing them off. He was helping them with a long narrow case. It was nothing so extraordinary, just unusual at that time and place. It would be a tid-bit to tell her husband about.

She boarded the train and the stationmaster blew his whistle. The train started on its way up the coast to Machynlleth and then on to Shrewsbury. The men would change there for a train to take them on to nearby Leicester.

Lief walked back to the dinghy satisfied he had dispatched the men safely and without attracting attention. In that he was wrong. Women are into the details of life more than men.

Chapter 7

Sir James Gives His Help

The following day, Trevor Howe, having learned about the boathouse and seen the small green field next to it, phoned Sir James Owen. He was invited to Llwyn House. He had learned from a local that Llwyn is pronounced *Thloo-in*.

Sir James told him, "Don't worry yourself, Major Howe. All the English people who come here have difficulty with it. I'm used to it being called *Loo-in* house. And we do have some loos in the house!" he laughed. "So, it's the seals you're after."

"Yes. They are our main objective. The grey Atlantic seals. We'll be counting porpoises and dolphins too. Others, sponsored by the Cardigan Bay Marine Wildlife Centre, have been doing the same thing. But not on this particular part of the coast. It's too secluded and difficult to observe from the land-side. Actually, its seclusion makes it a good place to look for seals and the birthing of their pups. That's what I've been told and it makes sense."

"And you're being sponsored by an American?"

"Yes. I don't know much about him. He must be filthy rich and he knows what he wants. Our first job is to photograph every seal we can find between here and Cardigan and identify all the locations with GPS coordinates. A marine biologist will be helping us, but she hasn't arrived yet. She's in London seeking a license to tag the seals."

Robert Heath, the butler, discreetly entered the study. "Sir James, the cook wishes to know whether the gentleman will be staying for lunch. It's lamb chops, sir."

"Splendid! Yes. Major Howe, please have lunch with me."

"That's most kind of you. Thank you."

"Robert, tell Mrs. Evans we will be two for lunch. Will you join me in a whisky and soda, major?"

"Thank you again."

"Whisky and soda, Robert. And choose a Beaujolais for lunch."

"Very good, Sir James."

Over lunch there was opportunity to exchange reminiscences of their military lives. Then the talk returned to the major's project. He said he would choose a spot on the coast to set up his equipment so they wouldn't have to haul everything there and back each day.

"Well, you don't want that to be where the seals are. You would scare them off and interfere with their life styles. We'll look at some maps after lunch and I think I'll be able to guide you to a likely spot."

Robert served them coffee in the study. Sir James spread some maps and satellite photos on a table. "It really is miraculous what you can see these days on these satellite photographs. Quite unimaginable when I was a boy. Look here. This is Morfa head. A small stony beach right here," and James pointed to it on the satellite photograph, "could suit you very well. I've never seen seals there. They pup on the beaches further up. Lots of animals are creatures of habit like that."

"How accessible is that beach?"

"No way you could climb down to it right there. There is a place a bit further along that is possible to climb. But I don't advise it. The cliffs here are danger-ous. In places they are too soft, shale rather than sand-stone or granite. You think you have a handhold, then it breaks away. Anyway that little beach could be just what you are looking for, secure and lonely. Look here. On this Ordnance Survey map it is indicated by the word Cave. It's the only place nearby so designated. I suppose there must be a long cave back there."

"If we set up there, I'll call it Seal Cave to go with our Seal Project."

"Very good. You'll be bringing in equipment?"

"Oh, yes. Quite a bit."

"You'll need to stop people from pilfering."

"I've thought of that. I plan to leave a man there to guard our things once we are set up."

"A good precaution. I can help you in other ways, major. I expect you know about Lord Lieutenants. It's mostly an honorary position, but with some influence. I'm the one here, for the county of Pembrokeshire. I'll be glad to let the authorities know of your project. Other-wise they could possibly cause you difficulties. A word from me and they will leave you alone."

Trevor Howe could hardly believe his good fortune and thought he could push his luck a bit further. He thanked

Sir James profusely, and then told him, "I have a bit of a problem of where to keep and launch my boats. They are the landing craft type. I've seen where your boathouse is. Would it be possible to park my boats in the little green field next to it? It would only be for a short time."

"Glad to help out, major. There's a gate with a lock to get you into the field. I'll give you a key. The gate is set in an old stone wall, probably been there a hundred years. Your landing boats will be safe in there, though I advise you to cover them with a tarpaulin so that they'll attract as little attention as possible. Otherwise you may have kids climbing in, you know."

"Thank you again, Sir James; that's good advice. I'll need to get my supplies down to the boathouse and then for my boats to take them to where I'll be set up; no doubt, at the beach we've talked about."

James frowned. "There's a bit of a problem there, major; getting vehicles down to the boathouse. I don't own the land between the boathouse and the road at the top of the hill. A miserable old fellow, Ethan Jones, owns the land and he is very jealous about giving any right of way over it. He has refused me any access except for an exorbitant sum that I refuse to pay. So I do without. You say your American sponsor says 'no-expense-spared'?"

Trevor nodded. "Yes. I am fortunate about that."

"I suggest you negotiate an arrangement with Mr. Jones to let your vehicles in. But don't expect it to be cheap."

"Thank you again. You are being a great help to me."

"Don't mention it. Glad to help a fellow officer. If you need any other help, just let me know. Where are you staying?"

"At the Red Dragon."

"Ah, yes. It's been done over. You are quite comfortable there?"

"Yes. Very well set up. Thank you again, Sir James, for your time and help."

Trevor took his leave. Robert Heath saw him out. "Excuse me, sir. May I advise you to keep Sir James well informed about your project. He always wishes to know what is happening in the locality. That way he can help out best."

"I'm sure," Trevor Howe replied, curtly.

As he drove down the driveway from the house, he felt put out by the butler's remark. No doubt he had overheard some of their conversation over lunch. But he should know his place and not intrude in matters above his level.

On the main road, Trevor simmered down. A butler necessarily knows about his master's doings. It's part of his job. He himself had known that with his batmen in the Army. The world was changing. No doubt it was archaic to take umbrage these days over a thing like that. Trevor put the thought aside. That would prove unwise, though in a quite peculiar way.

Driving without delay to the house of Mr. Ethan Jones, Trevor found him the surly bastard Sir James had led him to expect. He was full of cuss words and, evidently, had no time for the "gentry" like Sir James. "Bloody parasites, living off the rest of us," was one of his less offensive remarks.

"I'm an army man, Mr. Jones, with a job to do," Trevor told him. Being an army man earned him the grudging acceptance of Ethan Jones.

"It'll be five hundred pounds a week. That's what I'll do for you. And if you damage the gates or the land, that will be extra."

The price was exorbitant, but necessity was driving Trevor Howe. Time was not to be wasted and he needed the space right then and there. He handed over ten £50 notes.

As promised the boats and the extra gas tanks arrived in Newport that afternoon. Major Howe's men had them on the ground next to the boathouse that evening, covered over with the tarpaulins Rhys Jones had sold them.

Chapter 8

French Letters, German Cigarettes, and Codes

Van and Ava were installed in their rented cottage on a lower slope of Carn Ingli. It was an easy walk down to the town and to the beach along the Parrog shorefront. The walk up the hill on their return was a guarantee of a good appetite. Their garden was stocked with late summer flowers, blooming colorfully, and Ava delighted in cutting a few and bringing them into the house. This was the part of Van's sabbatical that, she insisted, would be pure R&R. No computers, no case work, no lecture notes, just roam around and relax - if that was possible for Van. He had once said he would like to run, or ride a motorcycle, into his grave.

To Van's pleasure their landlord had lent them a telescope with a tripod. From their mountain perch, as Van put it, even though it was only 300 feet above sea level, he could make out the 3,000 feet peaks of the Wicklow Mountains in southern Ireland and the smudges of ships plying their routes on the Irish Sea. To the north the coast was well delineated past Morfa head and up toward Cardigan, and south down to Strumble Head, the lighthouse there emitting its super-bright flash every twenty seconds, day and night.

The morning sun was shining invitingly. "OK," Van announced, "we climb to the top of the mountain this morning!"

They were thankful for the telescoping hiking poles they had brought with them as they made their way upwards. They walked up Mill Lane, a narrow alley sunk between high embankments, and then pushed on, hiking along a path used more by sheep than people.

On the summit the wind ruffled Ava's clothing and hair as she scanned the all-around view. Van thought her utterly beautiful.

After drinking from their water bottles, they compared the archeological map of Carn Ingli, that Van had brought with them, with the remains of the Neolithic walls and hut circles spread out before them.

Van contemplated the scene. "It doesn't take much imagination to see them here: the men, women, children and livestock, even though it was 5000 years ago. It was the first age of agriculture and the herding of sheep. It was an age, too, of tribal warfare. This place was a fortress. On one side it's a steep drop, difficult to climb for attackers, especially when defenders are rolling rocks down on their heads. Along the flatter parts they built a wall and we can see the remains of the angled entrance to their fortress village over there. It was probably only inhabited in the warmer months or when marauding tribes

threatened them. It seems too exposed to the elements
for permanent habitation."

Ava was listening while looking around. On this occasion she was thankful for Van's penchant to provide
mini-lectures on whatever was before them. After all, he
was a professor!

She butted in before he could begin a disquisition on
ancient habitations and fortresses. "Look, Van, over
here is a little circle within a bigger one. Could have
been a fireplace in the hut; the stove where they cooked.
What fun! What a marvelous place!"

"It is, isn't it? We are descended from them or maybe we
are a slightly different hominid branch. Especially myself.
I was born over there in the white house you can just see
among the trees. I may be more Celt than Anglo-Saxon."

"But I doubt there's much of a Neolithic man left in
you, Van," Ava grinned. "I haven't seen you running
around with a spear for your dinner."

Ava wandered off. Van continued to compare the map of
the stone walls and circles with the ground around him, and
searched to see how much he could recreate of the lifestyle of
the people who had lived there. One thing for sure, they had
a magnificent view of the coast and the surrounding countryside. It would be very difficult to surprise them.

Descending a steep slope Van spotted an entrance
to a cave. He scrambled down to it and found a small
cave formed by rocks falling on top of one another. Van
peered inside, but could see little, just a good-sized re-
cess going back some ten feet.

Ava turned round, but didn't see Van. "Hey! My
Neolithic man! Where are you?"

Van appeared at the top of the steep rock wall, a bit
short of breath. "That was quite a climb! There's a little
cave down there. I don't remember it from when I was

exploring this place as a boy. Perhaps it has been formed since. I liked to run up here, take in the view, catch my breath for a minute, and then run down again with my cocker spaniel, Topsy. I loved it."

He walked over to where Ava was peering at something on the ground. "Van, it wasn't only the ancients who had a good time up here. Look at that," she said, pointing to a couple of used condoms and a small area of flattened grass and heather.

"You're right. It's not exactly surprising, is it? I'd say it's a wonderful place to enjoy sex." He looked at Ava with a suggestion of a leer.

"Behave yourself, Van. There are people coming up the path."

"OK. Another time, my dear." Van said with a chuckle. "The lads and lassies who were up here may have had a good time, but they broke the golden rule: Take Out What You Bring In."

Ava wrinkled her nose. "So we have to clean up? Not me, my dear!"

"Hey! Children may come up here and find the condoms and think they are balloons. God knows what infections they might be carrying. I'll find a stick. Hold on."

Looking around Van found a small stick and jabbed the two condoms onto it. He brought them up to his eyes. "Well I'm blowed! They're French! French letters, eh! You know that's an English name for condoms?"

"No, I'm strictly American and don't know about the competitive name-calling you Europeans do."

"Yes, they're French all right. Quite distinctive. I recognize them from my work at the American hospital in Paris. Of course, they could have been brought in here by anybody. But, at least it's possible that French people were up here and were overcome by love or lust."

"I suppose lust is more usual, but I'll plump for love; it's more endearing," Ava said. "Let's go!"

"Just a moment, Ava. There are some cigarette butts here too. They probably had the traditional post-coital smoke. While I'm about it, I might as well clean them up." He bent down and picked them up, looking at them. "Well, the people may have been Germans. They were smoking German cigarettes. These are the HB brand, very common in Germany."

"I don't see that proves much. They could be tourists from God knows where and picking up things as they traveled around."

"Very possibly, I agree. But, you know, most smokers, besides being idiots, tend to smoke their chosen brand."

"Does that apply to condoms too, my dear?"

"Maybe. I don't know. But it wouldn't surprise me. It's a long time since I used one."

"I'm glad to hear that, darling," and she gave him a friendly kiss on the cheek

Having nowhere else to put the distasteful items, Van wrapped them in his handkerchief and put them in the pocket of his hiker jacket. He looked around for any other litter, but the top of the mountain, often swept by wind and rain, was pristine.

Ava was becoming impatient. "Come on, Van. It's time to go. I told Myfanwy at the Red Dragon we'd be having lunch there at one o'clock. She said she had fresh lobsters."

On the way down, Van chatted about his relationship to Sir James Owen. Van had written to him that they would be visiting and Sir James had invited them to dine with him that evening.

"We have a common great-grandfather, Sir George Owen. He had a daughter who married a Bentham boy.

The Benthams were from Picton in the south of the county, the part of Pembrokeshire that is known as 'Little England beyond Wales.' It has an interesting history dating from the 9th century when Norsemen invaded and laid down some Norse genes, as they did everywhere they went."

"Yes, darling. I think you have proved before, on the boat, that we are all mongrels with a bit of Norse blood in us. I'm deciding whether I'm happy about that or not. From what you said, they were an enterprising but aggressive lot. Not the sort of people you'd have to dinner. They would steal your silver! Look! The Red Dragon is in view over there. Now we have to concern ourselves with how to eat lobsters politely. I bet the queen has hers broken down. I'll ask Myfanwy to have the cook do the same for me. No one can eat them politely just as they are."

"I respectfully disagree. I find half the pleasure is to face the beasts whole and then skillfully crack them open and work hard to find the meat."

"That's a character difference that could be grounds for divorce. I'll make a note of it in my secret book!"

"Along with all those things that make these days the happiest of our lives, isn't that so?"

"No one would believe my professor is such a romantic," and Ava put her hand in his.

After their lobster lunch, that Myfanwy told them they were lucky to have considering the dearth of lobsters in the pots, they returned to their cottage for a siesta.

* * *

They were preparing for the evening. Ava, though determined not to show it, was slightly nervous. "Having never met a Sir before, are you sure I don't curtsey?"

"For heaven's sake, Ava! No! Just be yourself! I'm sure my cousin is an agreeable fellow. He's younger than I am. I remember him only as a toddler. I'm keen to meet him now."

In the bedroom Ava muttered to herself, "Striking but casual," as she went through her limited wardrobe. She stopped at a Galanos suit with a glittery vest.

They drove through the extensive grounds to the square-faced Georgian-style house, and parked on the gravel by the impressive front door. Van had told Ava that the original building dated back to the early 12th century, about fifty years after the 1066 Norman Conquest. It probably consisted of a small building situated where the hall is now. The house came into the Owen family about 1450 and successive generations enlarged and restyled the house a number of times.

The butler opened the car door for Ava and showed them into a hall where a log fire roared in a large fireplace. Sir James, a tall man of 50, with a well-chiseled face, rose from his wingback chair and greeted his cousin and his wife enthusiastically.

"What would you like? I have the English habit of sherry before dinner, but I think my butler can fulfill any taste you have."

They settled for sherry. The thin-stemmed glasses were brought to them by the butler on a silver salver. Ava tried not to show how impressed she was. No one she had ever known had a butler!

"Please excuse the absence of a lady," Sir James said, speaking to Ava. "My wife died and my daughter, who lives in London, is only down here occasionally."

Van reminded James how many members of the family had sailed boats out of the boathouse.

"When I was a boy, James, there were some pretty

smart boats there. One of them was a marvelous old boat that we could cram people into. What was her name?"

James said, "Was it *Daisy?*"

"Oh, heavens, that's right! *Daisy!*"

"She's still sailing, you'll be glad to know. Mostly now I let Rhys Jones have her. He's the ironmonger in Newport and uses her to go after his lobster pots."

"And she's in good shape still?"

"Just a bit older. Rhys keeps her well."

"I'd love to go out in her again."

"I'll arrange it for you," James assured him.

Robert appeared to announce that dinner was served.

Jugged Hare, a dish that Ava had never had before, was the main course. Ava gamely tried it and had to admit it was very good, especially when accompanied by a well-aged bottle of Nuits St. George. There followed a gooseberry tart with cream supplied from the Home Farm. They repaired to a drawing room to have coffee and port.

Ava found Sir James quite enchanting. He had a reserved British manner out of which a sudden twinkle of his eye and a lilting laugh would emerge.

For the most part Van left the conversation to Ava. "Your family goes back a long way, doesn't it, Sir James?"

"Yes, it does. Van and I have oceans of ancestors. Some were awful. A couple were hung at the gallows in Haverfordwest. But most were pretty good, some quite noble in the *noblesse oblige* sense. They did a lot of good round here."

"Van told me that some were members of parliament and a couple were Lord Lieutenants. What is a Lord Lieutenant?"

Van broke in. "You've asked the right person, Ava. Just yesterday I read that James is the current Lord

Lieutenant of Pembrokeshire. There was an article in the Western Mail describing who would be doing what during the queen's visit to St. David's."

"Oh, my," James sighed, "I'm found out. Yes. It's quite a distinction; one of the things the queen bestows, with advice from all and sundry, of course."

Ava was fascinated. "The queen! What do you do? Imprison people in towers and things like that. Oh, gosh! Van! Why didn't you tell me?"

"Truthfully, I didn't know it myself until yesterday. Then I thought we could both find out more about it this evening. It's been quite recent hasn't it, James?"

"Yes, just this spring. Usually, I don't have much to do, but that has changed. As you've read, the queen will be visiting here shortly. It's to do with the founding of St. David's Cathedral in the south of the county. It's the oldest cathedral in the UK and it will be quite an affair. If you are still here, I hope you'll come and be a part of it."

"Van!" Ava cried, "Don't you dare not be here for it!"

"I have choices for whom I present to the queen," James told them. "If you like, I'll put you down."

Ava's jaw dropped. "Wait a moment. Do you mean that Van and I would be presented to the queen?"

"Yes. I would present you."

For one of the few times in her life, Ava didn't know what to say. She gasped, "You're not kidding, Sir James?"

"Please call me James, Ava. Anything but Sir James. And stay away from Jim or, even worse, Jimmy. I won't answer to them," he laughed. "No, I'm not kidding. Actually you'll be helping me out. My daughter is very modern. She disapproves of royalty and has declined to be there with me. You are my cousin, Van, and you and Ava can have her place."

"Oh!" If Ava had been astounded before, now she was flabbergasted. "But ... but ... " she sputtered.

"Why don't you think about it?" James said.

Van sipped his glass of port. "That would be quite an honor, James. We'll get back to you. But tell me, I'm not up on what a Lord Lieutenant does."

"It's one of those old things that has been handed down to us. Nowadays it's hardly essential, but rather nice. Everyone likes a bit of dressing up and ceremony. Being a Lord Lieutenant is mostly honorary. It's both ceremonial and advisory; very much like what the queen does, but in a much smaller way. No real power, but influential. You are the queen's representative in the county. When the queen comes to visit, you are the person to welcome her and be, as it were, her lieutenant in matters of the county and local protocol."

"Is that all? Or do you do something more?" Van asked.

"Sort of yes and no. I had a Major Howe in here yesterday. He's in charge of a project to 'Save the Seals', or something like that, off the coast here. I told him I would help him with the authorities. He's setting up camp on a beach by Morfa Head and doesn't want any interference. I've let him park his boats by the boathouse. That's the sort of thing I can do to help things along. When you are on good terms with the local politicos and the police and so on, which I am, I'm glad to say, you are consulted about this and that and pick up on what's happening. Would you like to hear about a current item?"

"Yes. Oh, it's so interesting! Please tell us." Ava buzzed.

"I expect it may interest you, too, professor. A puzzle."

"So what is it?"

"Have you heard about the drowned man fished up in Newport bay?"

"Yes, we have," Ava said. "We read about it in a paper when we reached the Shetlands. We were talking about it with the daughter of an old college pal of Van's."

"Yes, we were at Clare together. Sadly, Haven died a short time ago. However, he left a splendid daughter whom we met. She works at Scotland Yard."

"Really!" James smiled. "She could be a useful person to know, if you get into trouble."

"I don't intend to do that," Van smiled back.

"I hope not. As you might imagine, the drowned man created quite a stir here for a few days. Soon after it happened I was over in Haverfordwest, talking to the police chief there. We were doing some planning for the queen's visit. The conversation came round to the drowned man. I'd heard there was nothing much on him except for a couple of Euro coins. The police chief confirmed that. A bit strange, I thought."

"What have they made of it?" Van asked.

"I really don't know. The police chief went on to tell me, sort of in confidence, that they had found something else on him. It hasn't been reported; they're keeping it quiet; though it may be nothing much."

"What is it?" Van asked.

"A piece of paper with a coded message on it. They had MI5 down here to look at it. The Police Chief told me they took it away with them without saying anything. Since then he's heard from a pal in Scotland Yard they can't make heads or tails of it," he laughed.

"Baffled, eh!" Van grinned.

"Apparently so. I asked the police chief what sort of message it was and he gave me a copy. It looked like something you'd need a code book to decipher. He said to show it to one of our witches! In jest, you understand. He said a sorcerer might have better luck deciphering it than the cryptographers. He has quite a sense of humor."

"Have you still got it? I've always been interested in spy stuff. I'd like to see it."

"Yes. I have it in my desk. Just a moment."

James returned and handed Van a piece of paper with a line of writing on it. "The original was water-logged, of course. But the letters and numbers were plain enough."

Van took it and read it aloud. "52Y017   04M832 161216   072018   040707   201809   240716   260000. Well, it's obviously a cryptogram. I imagine the boys in London have been whirring their computers trying to decipher it."

"That's what the chief told me," James nodded.

"And they haven't solved it?"

"Not so far as I know. The chief told me a short message is usually impossible to decipher. They need more messages and longer ones. He told me that, as yet, a similar message has only shown up with our troops in Afghanistan. They found it on another dead body, a Taliban man killed in a bombing raid on a village there. How's that for something bizarre!"

Ava was excited. "Isn't this wonderful, Van! An international something or other. What do you think? Can you decipher codes?"

"H'mm. There's not much to go on, but … well … as I told you, I've been interested in spy stuff. We used a simple cipher when I was flying with the RAF and I much admired Alan Turing. He was the master mind in solving the German Enigma codes. He and his colleagues at Bletchley Park outside London created the first programmable digital computer to do it. By means of that computer, Churchill could read the German signal traffic as fast as the Germans could. A magnificent achievement. Incidentally Turing was a talented runner. When he was called to London, he sometimes ran the 40 miles to White-hall. He would have made a great marathoner. He came to a sad end, committing suicide by poisoning himself. He was arrested for his homosexuality. They did that back then and he was forcibly given hormone injections. Not long since the British government made a public apology for their outrageous behavior toward him."

Ava turned to James. "Please forgive the professor. These preliminary chitchats are warm-ups to tackling the question."

Van smiled. "Ava knows me very well. Well, this code. I doubt it needs a codebook or a deciphering machine. You don't usually find those things in Afghan villages. The drowned fellow here may have been wandering around Europe and possibly some of his pals were German from the cigarette stubs we found on Carn Ingli," and Van described what they had found. "I'd guess the decoding procedure is something fairly simple, something compatible with the everyday functioning of the human mind. We also know, from what you've told me, James, that the computer boys have had no luck with it as yet, so it's probably unlike the ciphers they can decode with their computer programs. At the same time, it must be some form of substitution code; that is, it must yield a message in a language that can be understood by, evidently, a wide variety of people. That implies the code translates into English."

James exclaimed, "That all sounds very logical, at least with your explanation. You always had a reputation for being brilliant, Van. I was thought more the dunce in the family."

"That was very unfair, James, and, by everything I see, you've proved them wrong." Van was lost in thought for a moment. "You know, codes are seldom solved by brilliance. They all have a logic behind them, plus some kind of trick you have to see through. If they are too complicated, ordinary people can't use them. They would forget the routine and make mistakes. Ultimately a code has to be simple to be usable. Do you mind if I copy it?"

"I suppose not. But keep it to yourself. I don't want to run foul of the Official Secrets Act!"

The butler appeared to ask if he could do anything else for them that evening. Sir James told him, "No, we're all right, thank you, Robert. I showed that coded message to Professor Bentham and he can't make much of it either, just like you and I!"

"It is very obscure, sir, very obscure. Good night."

"Good night," James said after his departing form. "He's ex-military and excellent at his work. He had to face a court martial over something he was blamed for. I don't believe he did it. But he was found guilty and discharged. I'm trying to help him get over it. Anyhow, he's a good butler, a valet when I need one, a chauffeur too, and a handyman around the house."

As Van and Ava drove down the driveway, Van exclaimed, "That was quite an evening. I didn't know my cousin was such a big man in the county."

"He needs a wife as well as that butler fellow," Ava declared. "I think he sees it; that he's kind of incomplete as he is. I wonder why he hasn't remarried. He seems a hell of a good catch."

"Maybe. Unless he has something hiding in his closet."

Chapter 9

The Cache is Built and an Apparition is Seen

The inflatable Zodiac boats and powerful Yamaha outboards were exactly right, Trevor found, after he had examined them and tested them out. With the extra gas tanks, they would have quite enough range to be sea-going; and they were sturdy enough to take the timber and hardware out to Seal Cave.

Seal Cave was ideal for their purpose. The cave itself was quite wide at the entrance, then narrowed as it went inland for about fifty feet with a gradual upward slope. It was large enough for the men to use as a daytime shelter and a place to sleep in at night in their sleeping bags. Just in front of the cave mouth the beach, under a layer of stones, was sandy earth, easily workable with spades.

His big man, Ernik Kristol, with the help of the others, would make short work of excavating it.

Trevor had his men up well before dawn to get the day's work started. He told them: "The faster we get this thing built, the less chance anybody will see it."

They excavated a square hole, some 10 feet deep and 12 feet on either side, in front of the cave mouth. Their working was mostly hidden behind a rocky promontory coming out from the cliff face at an angle and sloping down into the stony beach. They carried their diggings of sand and stone to the water's edge and dumped them into the beach and sea. It all disappeared quickly. When a boat passed, they went behind the promontory to avoid being seen.

They brought in the planks on the boats, loading them at the Cwm. They told the few persons who saw them, that it was part of their project to study the seals. With the planks they boarded the inside walls and the floor of the chamber. They used sturdy planks to form the roof, with posts to support it. They covered the roof with thick polyethylene sheeting. Then they moved the stones back over the roof to make it look like it had before, the end portion of a small stony beach. The entrance was a trap door that would be covered with stones when not in use.

To stop water seeping in from the walls and floor, they used more polyethylene sheets and drums of fiberglass resin. The resin was sticky and tough and stuck to their clothing, particularly their boots and gloves. They discarded the gloves and the worst of their clothing. Their boots were impossible to clean. They picked up some of the resin from the floor whenever they descended into the chamber. To be sure to keep the cartons, when they arrived, out of any water that might come in, they made a raised floor above the actual floor.

Though his team understood the need for security, that didn't always translate into what they actually did. The big man in particular, Ernik Kristol, had more muscle than brains. He went up the hill to the Post Office from the Red Dragon and bought a postcard of Newport Bay. He sent it to his mother in Copenhagen. "This is where I am," he wrote on it. He was proud of himself for being there and doing important work, even if he didn't understand it very well.

Now, after moving tons of earth and rocks, Ernik decided he would climb the cliff. The tide was low and he waded along the foot of the cliff until he could see a way up.

It was a difficult, dangerous climb. At the top of the cliff, Ernik was elated by his success. He waved his arms and punched the air in triumph. He gazed out over the sea. He couldn't see far. It was dusk and cold and misty. He set off along the path toward Newport.

For a person to be on the path was not, of course, unusual. But it was unusual at that time, as night was falling. Rees Llewellyn, of the Ffynon farm above the Morfa headland, was herding his cows into the fields after he and his farmhand had milked them. He used the short-legged Welsh corgi dogs to help drive the cattle. They nipped at the cows heels and, in spite of their diminutive size, made excellent herding dogs.

The sun was almost set when, as Rees looked westerly through the misty air, he saw the figure of a huge man-like beast at the top of the cliff. The giant, after shaking itself, raised its arms in triumph and punched whatever it was in front of it. Then the monster turned in the direction of Newport and vanished down the slope in the mist and dark.

Rees's jaw dropped. He could hardly believe what he'd seen. There was no doubt in his mind he had seen an apparition. His farmhand was at the gate at the top of the field. Rees went to him. "Did you see it, then?"

"See what?"

"That ghost or spook or whatever it was?"

But the farm hand had seen nothing.

Rees went to the farmhouse and fortified himself with a glass of rum, then another. Shaken by his experience, he got into his car, a worn out Morris Minor, and drove it more or less steadily to Newport. He parked by the Llwyn Arms.

"It was as real to me as this beer I'm drinking, see you. I hadn't had a drop all day. Stone cold sober, I was. It appeared in the mist at the top of the cliff. I tell you, it was a spirit. Yes, it was. It seemed to fight someone or something and punch it back over the cliff. Then it raised its arms, like it was victorious."

"Oh, come on, Rees. You've seen strange things before."

"Perhaps I have. They come to me out of the world beyond."

Very likely the story would have been passed off as just another of the imaginative tales Rees brought to the pub of an evening. However, Mrs. Smith of Penny Hill farm came in for her glass of port. After a few sips she told Sheila from the drapery that there were strangers about. John Jones, their drover, reported he had seen the head of a big tall man behind a hedgerow of the field that led down to the bridge at Penny Bont. It was dark, so he didn't have a good view. But who would be walking about their fields in the dark?

"It was that ghost, the one I'd seen," Rees cried.

Eirwen, the bar girl, heard it all and she relayed it on to newcomers. For a while it was the topic of the evening. The vicar stopped in for a pint and heard the story

himself. "You'll have to choose between your eyes and
your imaginations," he laughed.

"Oh, don't be so fast, vicar. The devil has his ways
around here. We all know it."

Van heard about it from the loquacious postman who
came to their door. "Did you hear, doctor, about the
apparition that Rees Llewellyn saw above the cliff on
Morfa Head? Now he's saying it was the ghost of the
drowned Frenchman. Of course, it might just have been
the rum. Rees likes his rum."

"Tell me about it, if you have the time?" Van thought
it might be a story he could use to spice up his lectures
on Sensation and Perception.

"Well, now, I'm in no great rush and I certainly like a
good story." The postman told the story with a few em-
bellishments of his own, as is the wont of story tellers. "I
thought you would like to know, doctor, seeing you are
from here as a boy."

Van chuckled. "Yes and I heard stories like that one
when I was a boy here."

"It's hard to know what is in people's mind and what
is the truth of a matter, isn't it, doctor? Well, I must be
getting along. Good day to you."

Thumbing through the mail, Van told Ava what the
postman had told him. "Heaven knows what the truth of
the matter is. When I was a boy, living in the house near
here, I swore I heard ghostly sounds. They really scared
me. Then, of course, growing up, I put such thoughts
aside; in the same way as I had overcome my fear of
the dark. Years later I learned that a century or two ago
a man had hanged himself in that room. What do you
think of that?"

"You're the psychologist, dear. But, as you ask me,
I think our minds sometimes just run away with us and

we're left to think what we want. That man could have seen something on the cliffs and then his imagination took over. Where did he say it was?"

"At Morfa Head."

Ava thought for a moment. "Wasn't that the place where James told us Major Howe would be making his camp?"

"You're right. Perhaps he'll see some ghosts too," Van laughed.

"Improbable, is my guess. He sounds like a man who deals with realities."

"Well, if this ghost is a reality, which is the obvious thing to believe, he might see it!"

That's how they left it. But the thought percolated in the back of their heads.

Chapter 10

Kari Foss is Not Too Troubled

Kari swiveled round in her high-backed chair to look out over downtown Oslo and the harbor. She scanned across the scene through the floor-to-ceiling window of her pent-house office. A schooner was tied up in the harbor. Its tall masts were a pleasure to look at. She owned it. She also owned two of the merchant ships in the harbor. She would never, of course, compromise those ships. Not only were they profitable in themselves, but also excellent protection; they represented her obvious and fully legitimate business.

The new opera house, descending in a long slope to the waterfront, was also a pleasure to see. Its bare-bones style, with its long straight lines, was symbolic of the

Norse spirit: strong, adventurous, aggressive, enterprising, determined. The traits she had.

She, being a top benefactor for the opera house and a prominent business person in Oslo, had been awarded the Olaf Star. Long since she had seen that patriotism and respectability, tinged with religion, were excellent protections. However, she knew that Olaf, the 10th century warrior king and unifier of Norway before he became a Saint, was stubborn and rash, and lost as many battles as he won. In that, he was no role model for her.

She doubted the incident off the west coast of the UK was any big concern. Who was he? Did it matter? Lief, her young brother, had said the man could have been a government agent. It was also possible he was a plant from the competition. Either way he'd had little chance to learn anything and what he had learned, if anything, had drowned with him. According to press reports he was just another unknown. No doubt the matter would still be alive on some police docket, but it would be shifted to a dead file before long. There were too many corpses to spend time on a seemingly inconsequential drowning of some unknown. It was one of the many things she knew from having worked for Interpol. Though she was young then and only an assistant, it had been invaluable in terms of knowledge and experience.

Right now, Lief had his hands full with folks around the Middle East. To keep Lief and his boat in the chain from the poppy fields to the consumer they were demanding that he transport individuals to the UK. They would pay large sums in cash for the service. Lief had assured Kari he would take care, minimize the risk, and make it as safe and profitable as possible. Rather against her better judgment, she had put her doubts aside and told Lief to go ahead.

The Welsh expedition, as she called it, was under way. She had suggested to Lief that he use the harbor at Aberystwyth for refueling and as a temporary base. She had been there when she was a university student in Britain and liked the place and the verdant hills enclosing it.

The operation further south on the lonely Welsh coast had to be a quick hit. She had stressed that. Her purpose was to make an end run around the usual routes. She understood, of course, that the Brits knew the main import routes and were successfully intercepting about 40% of the goods. It irked her, even though she could live with it. Now she would bring in a large load by a brand new route. The Brits would only be aware of the sudden flood on the street, but have no idea how it had got there. She smiled. Even after all the expenses, she expected to make about $7,000,000. That is, provided all went well. It damn well better! Her passion was success, not failure.

She felt confident that Lief would manage things well. She never micro-managed an operation from a distance. But there was a lot at stake. She had advised Lief to send in a dummy shipment first. If the Brits were onto the scheme, they would only succeed in finding some canned food or whatever.

Kari was not exactly cynical, but the fact was, as she well understood, her covert business was heavily dependent on the conflicts of the day. She'd only been down there once. It was too dangerous to make a practice of it. The fields of red poppies towered over by high mountains were quite awe inspiring. They had an esthetic quality, quite apart from their value as a commodity. She mused over it. The spiritual quality of the poppy fields in that setting was an appropriate underpinning for their *jihads*. Religion was an ever present excuse for anything, no matter what. That's what made it occasionally beneficial. But it was also the source of much of the world's miseries and a gross impediment to peaceful cooperative progress. Though that was not a major concern of hers. Rather, she simply accepted that the more fanatic and the better farmers the people were down there, the more she profited. It was not in her make-up to flinch from that reality.

She shrugged her shoulders. The irony of it appealed to her. The very people who were fighting against the source of the drugs, the USA, the UK, and some Europeans, were also the main users. The Afghan farmers gave a percentage of their take, perforce, to the Taliban. The money funded their fight against the Americans and the others. She, in effect, was the link that completed the circle. Such is the way in this imperfect world.

To move the stuff through mosques, temples, churches and brothels was simply common sense. The East was full of officials waiting to be bribed and Europe of priests open to pressure. An amazing number of them had abused their choir boys and not a few girls, too. The public outcry was only the tip of the iceberg. What was seldom realized, in Kari's estimation, was that abuse was systemic in a belief system based on hierarchies, faith, and irrationality. It would continue until change was widespread in the human psyche. Religion was a false solace arising from ignorance, as a friend of hers said. Ah, well! But that also was not her affair, beyond using it to her advantage.

Churches had crypts to store stuff in, all sorts of people went in and out, and charity bundles were loaded on and off trucks. It was almost too easy! Each waypoint knew nothing of where the stuff was coming from or where it was going. All they knew was that the *Boss* knew their perversities and they did as they were told …

or else. Brothels, with their flow of men going in and out were equally advantageous for her purposes. Hamburg, in particular, was a readymade conduit.

There were always problems to be understood and solved. She was suspicious that DeBouef in Paris was a double. He seemed to be too good to be true. Undoubtedly, he had been in a racket in Marseilles. The question was, had he been turned? He hadn't been with them for long and nothing untoward had happened so far. The information he supplied was good, up to a point; but little of it was actionable or new to her. He had brought that drowned man, Claude, into the work. Was it a pointer or not? Perhaps she should go to Paris and size up the man for herself. Perhaps it would be just as well for Lief to dispose of him. Then she would have no further need to worry about him.

Kari was at a lull point in handling her usually busy businesses. She folded her arms as she continued to gaze out the window and let memories flood in to remind her of issues considered and decisions made. For the most part there was no need to revisit them. Years ago she had reconciled herself to the fact that people abused any number of substances and wantonly drove themselves to perdition. It was their choice and her libertarian philosophy was not troubled by the fact that some died. Pestilence, earthquakes, wars, traffic accidents - more than a hundred deaths a day in the US alone - killed far more people.

To be a Norwegian was an asset to her. Norway was a minor player in the world drug scene and had few problems itself. What little there was existed side-by-side with the sex business and that, in turn, was a small blip on the map.

Norwegian culture is resistant to being inquisitive in other's affairs. Kari knew about the Resistance during the German occupation in WWII. Her grandfather and father had been players in it. They had made use of the social taboos against meddling. She had spent long winter evenings listening to their exploits and their system of security against the German Gestapo and the indigenous Norwegian traitors led by Quisling. She learned of the imperative to disconnect the parts of an organization. When the Germans discovered a resistance cell, that was often all they discovered. They could torture and kill, but it was more for revenge and sadistic pleasure than to succeed in unearthing genuine information.

She had sent Geery Schrotenboer a message to have him aware that she knew about the drowned man and that she required him to improve the security arrangements on *Mother Hen*. At the same time she had indicated to her British team the steps they should take with respect to the Eurostar route and its temporary suspension. The British authorities needed to be diverted. Her messages were always terse and meant little except in the context of the operations being conducted. She relied on her team to know her intentions, then act as they saw fit to execute them. Even if a message was decoded, a most unlikely contingency, little would be given away. They would just be words with no context.

Kari had written the message out herself and sent it out by her special e-mail distribution system. It would appear to have multiple senders and be untraceable to anyone who chanced upon it. The code was an adaptation of the one used by the Norwegian Resistance during the war. The Germans had never cracked it, though it was simplicity itself once you knew it: the message had an address, some significant words, and a sign off. It needed no code book or machinery and could be learned and used by anyone.

She used Irak, her name spelled backwards, as her sign off. Only her brother, Lief, knew her identity. She would laugh about it. All those macho men being handled, unknown to them, by a woman!

Kari believed in incentives. However, every so often it proved necessary, if distasteful, to dispose of someone and let the moral sink in, as might be the case with De-Boeuf ... for safety's sake.

At times providence stepped in, as it had done in disposing of the snoop who had drowned himself off the coast of Wales. No doubt it had been unpleasant for him, not only the physical pain of drowning, but the disappointment of not making it. She even felt sorry for him, sympathized with the plight he had found himself in, and admired the action he had taken in taking out his guard. She could use men like him. Pity he was dead. He could have been recruited, not unlike how Trevor Howe, for one, had been brought aboard. Usually it was a mix of finding the dirt in their past, uncovering their weakness, and making them an offer impossible to refuse.

Standing by the window, Kari continued to gaze out over the Oslo scene. About equally she enjoyed the arousal her covert business stimulated in her and the quiet satisfactions of accomplishment, success, and reward.

Chapter 11

A Crab, a Pencil, and a Call to London

Van and Ava went wading along Newport beach. Coming to the start of the cliffs and the caves at their base at low tide, they entered the caves and had fun making echoes inside them. Along the rocky shore there were pools the tide had left behind. Ava called to Van, "Come and look! There's a big crab in this one."

Van came over. "Do you want it for lunch?"

"Can you get it out?"

"I could when I was a boy. I was quick enough then to put my hand in and catch them. But there's another way."

Van took off his shirt and tied the ends of the sleeves together. "There's bound to be a stick washed up on that little beach over there, Ava. See if you can find a longish one."

77

Ava came back with just the right stick. Van put his shirt in the pool and spread it out underwater on the bottom while keeping hold of the ends of the sleeves. He took the stick and gently nudged the crab over the shirt. He had to do it three times before it stopped on the shirt. Putting the stick aside, Van slowly put his hand in the water to gather in the tail of the shirt. He edged it toward the surface. When he was ready, he snatched the shirt out of the water, the crab flying out with it. He'd caught their lunch.

"Wow! I've never seen anything like that before, Van. You've kept your crab-catching skills to yourself, my Neolithic man! I think I'll love you a tiny bit more!"

After tying up the crab in his shirt, Van's eye caught something glinting at the edge of the pool. He knelt down and grabbed what turned out to be an ordinary lead pencil. At its end was a rubber eraser circled by a shiny metal band. He turned it round and then stopped. Looking intently, he saw there were letters crudely scratched on its side.

"Come here, Ava. What do you see there?" and he showed her the scratches.

"They're letters, aren't they?"

"I think so. Maybe a child did it. I think the words are *'mother hen dope.'* Do you see that?"

"Yes, I think you're right. Would a child write dope?"

"Oh, I think so. To a child 'dope' would mean a silly fool. It's an odd thing to find, whatever its origin. I'll take it back and have a look at it with my magnifying glass."

Back at the cottage they boiled the crab and shared its meat. Being so fresh, it was very tasty. After putting his feet up and reading the Western Mail paper, Van turned his attention to the pencil and the copy of the code James had passed on to him. He put them side by side on a table.   In his brief case he found his never-to-be-forgotten magnifying glass and examined the pencil.

Ava laughed.   "You're like Sherlock Holmes.   Wasn't he always examining things with his magnifying glass?"

Van took no notice.   "Yes, someone scratched *mother hen dope* on the pencil.   The thin scratches could have been made by a pin or something with a small sharp head."

Ava looked over his shoulder at the pencil and the code.   "You know, one is a mysterious phrase in plain English and the other is a mysterious message in code."

Van put them close together on the table.   "You're right about that, quite a coincidence."

"Oh, I can do better than that!" Ava cried.   "Something fishy was going on out there, as I've said before. Now we have a code on a piece of paper in the pocket of a drowned man and some odd words on a pencil, both found in the bay here.   Coincidence?   Coincidence my foot, if you ask me!"

Van sat there with a dumbfounded look on his face. "Goddammit! You could be right.   But where does that lead us?"

"Oh, that's for you to figure out.   I've done my bit. Put that big brain of yours to work."

Van picked up the piece of paper with the code on it. "It's like those war time codes, Ava.   I suppose they are much updated now and probably nearly impenetrable. But this one, as I said when we were with my cousin, wouldn't be like those.   Probably it's quite simple."

"Do you think you could solve it? I know you can do those damn convoluted crossword puzzles."

Van laughed.   "Yes, and they get harder and harder for me every year.   I would like to see the other message, the one they picked up in Afghanistan."

Ava had gone over to the window. "Gosh, it's such a view from here. I love it. Thank you for bringing me here. You can see so far out. But not as far as Afghanistan! Why don't you phone your friend's daughter, Heddy, about the code? She might help. Maybe she does that kind of thing."

"That's an idea. She told us to keep our eyes open. I'll find the card she gave me; it has her phone on it."

Scrambling around in his briefcase, Van found the card. Heddy answered the phone. Having greeted each other and had a moment's chitchat, Van said, "I've been hearing about the body fished up in the bay here. It turns out that a cousin of mine is the Lord Lieutenant of the county and he is sort of in-the-know with the authorities here. He showed me a copy of a coded message that was found on the drowned man ... "

"He did what?" Heddy almost screamed down the phone.

"Yes, it's a cipher . . ."

"Jesus Christ! So much for our security fence! Have you got it there?"

"Yes, I have it in front of me."

"Read it to me."

Van read it to her.

"All right. That's it," Heddy said, very soberly.

"I guess you are saying I shouldn't have it."

"That's the understatement of the year! Who knows you have it, beside your cousin, the mad Lord Lieutenant?"

"Just Ava."

"Well, keep it that way. You have no idea what you have stumbled into."

Van got up from his chair and paced up and down in some agitation, holding the phone to his ear. "There was nothing intentional about it, Heddy . . ."

"What else do you know?"

"Let's see. My cousin told me it was hush-hush, that the code hadn't been cracked yet, and that a similar message was found on the body of a Taliban fighter in Afghanistan."

There was a pause, then Heddy responded. "I can't tell you how much that dismays me. Have you anything else to tell me."

Van was rattled. "Hey, Ava! Heddy is asking whether we've noticed anything down here. Have we? If you can think of anything ... here's the phone ... tell her about it."

Ava took the phone, "Hi, Heddy!"

"Hi, Ava. I'll talk again to Van. Don't hang up. Have you heard about or noticed anything else."

"I'm not sure. What sort of thing?

"Anything ... anything at all . . ."

"Well, Myfanwy at the Red Dragon has some men staying there who have equipment in vans and they've asked for a lot of stuff from the hardware store - that is the ironmonger."

"Anything else?"

"Yes. She also said they are throwing fifty pound notes around. And ... let's see. Van found two used French condoms along with stubs from German cigarettes on top of the mountain here and today we found a pencil in a tide pool with the words *mother hen dope* scratched on it."

"What was that? What was scratched on what?"

"*mother hen dope* was scratched on a pencil."

Heddy drew in a long breath. "All right. Give me back to Van."

"Van. I want you and Ava to come to London. Bring the code and the pencil with you."

Van told her, "I have those condoms and cigarette butts in my hiking jacket pocket. I forgot to clean them out, shall I bring them too?

"Yes, do that. Give me a minute. Stay on the line."

Van looked over to Ava. "See if you can find a little container we can put the condoms and cigarette butts in, will you?"

Heddy came back on the line. "OK. A train from Fishguard leaves for London, Paddington station, this evening at ten-fifteen. It's the boat train serving the passengers who have come over from Rosslare in Ireland on the ferry. They have first class sleeping cars on it now; they've just been reinstated. You're in luck. I have a bedroom compartment reserved for you in the name of Bentham. Be on it. I'll meet you at Paddington in the morning. Don't talk to anyone about what you've been telling me or that you are coming here. No one!"

Van was concerned now. He shook himself like a wet dog. There! That felt better. Heddy was still on the phone. "One more thing, Van. Do you know anything about codes?"

"Yes, a bit. I have some opinions about this one."

"Right. Bring your opinions with you."

Ava had found a small plastic container in the kitchen. The condoms and cigarette butts were still in the pocket of Van's hiking jacket wrapped in his handkerchief. He put them, just as they were, in the container.

"Ugh!" Ava wrinkled her nose. "Disgusting!"

Chapter 12

Interrupted Sleep

Ava had never traveled in a sleeping car. There are sleeping cars in the US, operated by Amtrak, but she'd never been on one. Like most Americans, she flew to the places that were too far to drive to. So, arriving in Fishguard, and after having a good dinner at the Royal Oak pub, being ushered to their first class sleeper compartment on the train, was a novel experience for her.

Van told her, "I was used to the old sleepers. As a boy I went up to London with my father overnight. I would sleep well and always enjoyed the experience." Van looked around. "My goodness, this is much better. We have a shower, a toilet, hand basin - the works."

Ava was taking in the amenities with wide eyes. Everything had been designed to fold away cunningly. "I love it already. I'm going to take the lower bunk. That's a woman's privilege."

"You mean I'm ostracized to the upper bunk?"

"Well - not the whole night ... "

Van grinned. "There's a buffet car. Do you want anything?"

"No, we had dinner only an hour ago. And look! There are bottles of water by the table and some mint candies."

"I told the steward he should wake us at six-thirty and we would have breakfast at seven. He brings it to us. Nothing fancy, but sufficient. We arrive in Paddington at seven forty. This isn't a fast train and it stops quite often."

Ava sat down in one of the chairs. "What fun we are having, Van! We are now special agents, like 007! You can be him and I'll be the gorgeous mysterious woman. Did you see *From Russia with Love*? Some of it happened in a sleeping car, just like this one. She was a double spy and he had to fight a man who was also a double spy. It was quite complicated, but good fun."

Van laughed. "I hardly think we will have anything but a prosaic trip to London. Sorry to disappoint you."

"In that case I will concentrate on having dreams of being rescued by that handsome young man who is playing 007 now. Though I don't think he's as good as the old ones. In the meantime, my darling husband, you will have to do."

"Thank you, I suppose."

"Over dinner you were telling me about how the French landed in Fishguard when you guys were fighting Napoleon. Tell me more."

"It's quite an amusing story, something of a fiasco. A local peer, Lord Cawdor, was in charge of the Welsh troops, such as they were. He set up headquarters at the Royal Oak, where we've just had dinner. I will spare you the details. However, a curious one is that the French were under the command of an Irish American from

North Carolina, a Colonel William Tate. He had fought in the Revolutionary War and now, in February 1797, thought he could induce the Welsh to rise up against George III. He was sadly mistaken.

From our family's point of view, the hero was Major Owen. He was in charge of the Newport *Fencibles*, a volunteer militia force. The alarm being given that four French warships were landing troops just south of Fishguard, Major Owen gathered his volunteers with whatever small arms they had and marched them to Fishguard along the road we just drove along from Newport.

Although the French had a few good troops, most of them were a rag tag mob; rejects from Napoleon's regular troops engaged in Italy. As soon as they landed, many mutinied against their officers and deserted. Moving inland these men found stashes of Portuguese wine that had been commandeered by the Welsh off a shipwrecked Portuguese boat. The boat belonged to smugglers and was one of the many boats smuggling wine, salt, and other commodities into Britain. These men sat out the two-day war in a drunken stupor.

The Welsh heroine was Jemima Nicolas who, with her pitchfork, went out single-handed and rounded up twelve French soldiers who, like the others, were quite the worse for wear from the wine. She brought them to the church in Fishguard and locked them inside.

However, the tale most often told is how the local farmers' wives rounded up all the women they could find. They told them to wear their high Welsh hats and cloaks and gather with their brooms and pitchforks along the cliffs. This they did. The French, looking up from the beaches, mistook them for a regiment of Grenadiers and, feeling hopelessly outnumbered, surrendered unconditionally."

"Is it true?"

"Absolutely! The invasion was defeated by a mix-
ture of smuggled Portuguese wine and Welsh women in
their national costume. 'Oh!' they cried, 'We swept those
Frenchies out to sea where they belong!' The festivities
went on for some time, as you may imagine."

Soon they were in bed and by the time the train had
chugged to Carmarthen along its twisty path, they were
fast asleep. They remained that way until they were approaching Reading, the last stop before London. They
would have been awakened by the steward, but they
were actually startled out of their sleep by sharp noises
and a commotion down the corridor.

Van started up in the upper bunk, hitting his head on
the low ceiling, so he was seeing a few stars.

"Ava! That sounded like gun shots!" he gasped.

"They can't be," Ava said, sitting up. "We're in England now … "

The commotion was continuing outside their door.
The train slowed down, then stopped.

Van had clambered down from the top bunk. "Stay
where you are, Ava!"

Van went to the sliding door, unhooked the latch,
and pulled it back. He thrust his head out and then
stepped out into the corridor. Other people were doing the same, all in various stages of undress. There
was turmoil at the end of the coach. Van heard shouts,
"Where did he go? Did you see him?"

Two trainmen, conductors in uniforms, came burst-
ing up the corridor.

"Get back! Get back inside! Lock your doors," they
shouted and they pushed people, Van included, back into
the compartments.

"Well, here's a how-do-you-do!" Van exclaimed, re-
covering his balance.

Ava was trying to get herself together. "What's happening? And what in heaven's name is a how-do-you-do?"

"Oh, it's a rather out-dated English phrase meaning some sort of rumpus. Rather quaint."

"Van! Stop it! This is no time for quaint English phrases. Somebody may have been shot, if those were real gun shots."

Van went to the window. "It must have been something like that. There are two police cars, with their lights flashing, speeding toward us. That's quick reaction."

"Let's get dressed, Van. If we are to be featured in the Great Western Train Shooting, I want to at least look good."

They were glad when the steward knocked on their door with coffee. All that he knew was that there had been a shooting and a man had jumped from the train.

The train re-started. There were policemen in the corridor, checking each compartment. The man showed them his ID, a Chief Inspector. His companion walked in and pulled down the blinds over the window of the compartment.

"You are Dr. and Mrs. Bentham? You are American?" the inspector asked.

"Yes," Van replied.

"May I see your passports, please?"

Ava and Van found their passports. The Chief Inspector looked them over carefully and returned them. "You are all right? You have not been harmed in any way?"

"No."

"No one has been in the compartment or tried to get in?"

"No."

"Has your luggage been with you all the time?"

"Yes."

"Please look in your cases and tell me if there is anything not your own in them."

It took Van and Ava a couple of minutes to do that. They found nothing unusual. They both said it was all their own possessions.

"Very good, doctor. You and your wife are to stay in this compartment with the blind drawn until we reach Paddington. At that time, do not descend from the train. Remain here. Government officials will meet you and escort you out. These measures are precautions for your safety. Please obey them closely."

Van said, "Yes, of course. Can you tell us what happened?"

The Inspector asked, "You heard gun shots?"

"Yes."

"A man was shot. That's all I can tell you. Direct your questions to the officials who will be meeting you. Good day."

Van sat down with a thump in one of the chairs. Ava was beside him. Van wiped his forehead. "No, Ava, I don't know what's happening. We'll have to wait. We should be in Paddington quite soon. It's not far."

Ava's hands were trembling as she repacked her case. "Van. I'm scared."

Van tried to comfort her. "I think we are all right. We are being protected. We'll sit down and wait."

As the train slowed down and stopped in Paddington station, Van saw, round the side of the blind, that there was a small army of police and others on the platform. An ambulance drove up to the door at the end of their coach. In the same moment there were hurried footsteps in the corridor and Heddy's anxious face appeared at their door. Behind her were two men.

"Thank God you two are all right! The first news

was so garbled that we couldn't make out who had been shot. I was so scared for you!"

She turned to the two men. "Pick up their bags, take them to the car. Then return and search this compartment with a tooth comb."

She swiveled round to Van and Ava. "We can't be too careful. You might have been the target. Now you will come with me. We are taking a car to our destination. Hold your questions until we get there. Let me know this. Who would have known you were going to take this train and had a sleeping compartment?"

Van looked at Ava. "No one," she said. "Isn't that right Van?"

"No one, I agree; unless someone was following us and saw us getting on the train. We didn't tell anyone, just as you told us."

"OK," Heddy nodded. "I guess it's another of those damn coincidences that we don't know whether to take as real or not."

Leaving the train Van and Ava were surrounded by police, some in uniform, some in plain clothes.

"Keep your heads down and move quickly," Heddy told them. "We've kept the media at a distance. But you never know. I don't want you to be known about."

Their guards shielded them as they hurriedly took the few steps to the car. Ava rolled her eyes. "Jeepers, Van! I feel somewhere between a celebrity and a criminal!"

Chapter 13

An Invitation Accepted

"We are going to Thames House," Heddy told them. "It's the HQ of MI5. MI5 is responsible for domestic intelligence."

"I am familiar with that," Van said. "I consult with the FBI, as one of their assets. MI5 is a sort of sister institution."

Heddy was astounded. "You are full of surprises, Van! Do you know Dr. Phillippa Crest at the FBI in Washington?"

"Sure do. The last case I did was with her. A great person. Very tenacious."

"What a small world it is! She's been over here, working with us on the new profiling techniques. My director will be fascinated, I know, to learn you've worked with her."

Heddy took her mobile out of her bag. "Yes - FBI - ID - asset" was all Van heard.

Heddy put her mobile back in her bag. "Let me explain that my division at Scotland Yard works with MI5. It's sometimes a bit snarly. They can't arrest people like we can. So we are the ones in the limelight. You'll meet David Crick, who is my director at MI5."

Though the windows were dark tinted in the car, Van could discern they were skirting around the back of Buckingham Palace and making for Horseferry Road leading to the Thames Embankment and Thames House. The building is one of those heavy, stone-faced edifices governments like to build. It had been taken over by MI5 because they had been doubling in size to contend with the many threats bedeviling the UK.

The car pulled through an electronically-operated security gate. After entering the building they passed through security and were given badges. They walked to a lift and emerged on an upper floor. Heddy led them to a large impressive room with gilt decor. In the middle was a long polished table with chairs around it.

"We'll be meeting David Crick here," she told them. "There's a toilet down the hall that you may wish to use. You have the code, the pencil, the butts and condoms, Van?"

"Yes, they are in my briefcase."

"Put them on the table, will you?"

David Crick was a young man of about 35. Somewhat belying his outward light manner, he had a PhD. in Political Science and was one of the brains of MI5.

"Hello there," he greeted them on entering the room. Heddy made the introductions. David went to the table. "So these are the bits and pieces I've heard about. Fascinating! Little things in themselves, but possibly part of the evidence we need to catch the bastards and put them away."

A man came in. David Crick told him to take the items down to the lab. "I've told the lab to do a micro on the pencil and recover the DNA from the condoms and cigarette butts. With a bit of luck, we may get a DNA match on our data base. Let's sit down. I've asked for coffee and biscuits to be sent up. Now, tell me about yourselves. From what I know to date, you are a very interesting person, Dr. Bentham. Just now the FBI sent me your CV and your open file. I saw you are a Cambridge man. I expect you know the university is celebrating the 800th anniversary of its founding."

"I know," Van chuckled, "and they are having a full court press for contributions from alumni around the world. I'll be going up to Cambridge to join in the festivities and give some lectures. Ava hasn't been in a punt. So I'm hoping my punting skills will come back to me."

David smiled, "You'll be glad to know, Mrs. Bentham, that it's the punter who falls into the water, not the passenger. She's left adrift on the river Cam. But don't worry. It's a little slow-moving stream. Other punters will come to your rescue while your swain flounders about. It's an old Cambridge tradition. Please call me David. May I call you Ava and Van? I saw, from the papers the FBI sent me, Van, you had top secret clearance at one time."

"Yes, on a need-to-know basis. I can't talk about it unless I get specific clearance."

"Understood," David looked at his watch. "Give me a quick rundown on what you've done, seen, and heard in Pembrokeshire."

"Realize, David, it's been the two of us, Ava and me. Often she sees things that I don't. We'll tell you about it together."

David listened intently to their story. A man brought in maps and charts of the Pembrokeshire coast. With them they pinpointed locations, including Llwyn House. David asked, "Who is in the household there, besides Sir James."

"A butler. He's sort of an all round fellow, I gather."

"And there's a cook, a Mrs. Evans; a good cook too," Ava added. "Van, you should tell David about the butler seeing the code."

"Oh, yes, that's right."

David quizzed. "The butler saw the code?"

"Yes. James had shown it to him."

"Good God! What could he have been thinking of?"

"I doubt that it is of any importance, David. The butler just said something about it being very obscure and left the room."

David was not so sure. "What's this butler's name?"

"Robert; we never heard another name."

"Good enough," David said. "Heddy, just in case, run a check on this man, Robert whoever."

Ava spoke up, "If it helps, James said he'd been in the army and was court-martialed."

David thanked her for the information. "That gives us a direct line to him. Now, I'm sure you want to know about what happened on your train this morning. The reason why Heddy was so concerned was that it was possible you were the targets. You'd been discovering items that may be related to an insurgency scheme or an international smuggling operation, possibly both rolled into one. Actually, I doubt that they, the bad guys, know of your existence. But I couldn't chance it. Hence the precautions. I still think you are unknown to them. In our trade, that is a major, major plus."

Van looked at him enquiringly. "You are suggesting, David … ?"

"That you may continue to help us by simply being there as vacationers and keeping your eyes and ears open."

Though Ava had been tense, she had recovered her composure and was now relishing the adventure they were going through. So when Van asked her, "What do you think, darling?" she replied, nonchalantly, "I've never been a spy before! I think it'll look good on my résumé."

David grinned. "Perfect! Just be yourselves. I'll reserve the cloak and dagger stuff for your next assignment, Ava. Do the usual things that you'd do in any event. Then, if you see or hear anything out of the ordinary, let us know. If that's OK with you, I'll tell you in the morning how you'll communicate with us."

"So you want us to stay overnight?" Van asked.

"Yes. Please accommodate me. Heddy! Arrange something for them. OK. Now, I'll tell you what happened this morning on the train. Yves Mateur, a Frenchman, was shot and killed in the end compartment of the coach you were traveling in. He was a smuggler, an operative for the large organization we are gradually unearthing. He worked the Eurostar train from Paris to London. We knew about it and kept him under observation. The amount he brought in was tiny, but he was leading us to bigger game. Then we had a breakdown. Following a tip, he was apprehended by our Excise and Customs people. They didn't know he was what we call 'a bird on the wing.' They thought they had made a genuine bust. That's the way it goes sometimes."

Van nodded. "The old problem of the left hand not knowing what the right hand is doing."

"Yes, and it can be difficult to avoid it happening while maintaining compartmentalized security. That's what happened here. They got a tip and acted on it.

However, we are suspicious of the tip. We think Yves Mateur was a sacrificial lamb. By giving him to us, they could have hoped to divert our attention from something more important. It happens. These people are ruthless. However, Yves got away. Evidently he had not been searched thoroughly and managed to slip his handcuffs in a train toilet. He had a long history in crime and knew all the tricks. He half-killed the guards, jammed them in the toilet, and jumped the train. Now he was on the loose and, we assume, hell bent on revenge."

"But that all happened before, not this morning?" Van queried.

"Yes, that's right. That was the lead up to what happened this morning. We think Yves knew who had betrayed him, his immediate supervisor, a man called Oscar Flavio. We have had Oscar in our sights for some time. He pops up around the world and seems to be a 'hit man,' among other roles. Yves, we think, knew that his life expectancy was not good and that the man most likely to be called on for his disposition was this Oscar Flavio. So, basically, he wanted to be ahead of the game.

The next piece of this jigsaw puzzle is a woman working in the booking and reservations office of the Great Western Railway. We know about her. We also know about her accomplice in a parallel position on the Eurostar trains. In due course they will be quietly arrested and then we will turn them. They'll begin working for us, letting us know the travel movements of the people we are interested in."

"Good work!" Van exclaimed. "As you no doubt know, during the war we caught about two hundred German spies and turned all but two of them, greatly to our advantage. The Germans never suspected. The two hold-outs were shot."

"Yes, and it was a good lesson for us. Be smart before being merciless. In our present case, Yves Mateur probably learned, through these connections whom he knew personally, that Oscar Flavio was traveling to London on the night train from Fishguard. Oscar was in a compartment in the same coach you were in. That's why we were fearful for you. Yves Mateur boarded the train at Slough. He went to the compartment that Oscar Flavio was in and that ended up with Yves Mateur dead from gunshot wounds and Oscar Flavio jumping off the train. He's now on the loose."

Ava had been listening attentively. "Seems to have been a lot of jumping off trains. These days, with the speed the trains go, it must be almost suicidal. Does this Oscar Flavio know about us?"

"He'd only know if his seniors were on to you and, as I've said, we don't think that's so."

"So being on the same train was just coincidence?" Van asked.

"Yes. That's how it seems. But one can never be absolutely certain. You have been on the edge of their activities. Not that you intended to be. It just happened. So it's not entirely surprising that this coincidence should crop up. You are in the same part of the universe as they are. We see that kind of thing quite often. It's all part of the small world phenomenon. You are aware of that, I'm sure, Van."

"Oh, yes. I teach about it when I'm trying to have my students understand probability theory. What happens now?"

"First, just keep your eyes open. At the slightest sign of any threat, let us know. OK?"

Van grasped Ava's hand. "Yes, OK." He looked at Ava. "Yes, OK," she agreed, in a rather shaky voice.

"Right. Look. If you don't like it, pack up your bags and fly back to the States and we'll forget the whole thing."

Ava spoke up. "No. I don't like people killing other people. If we can help, we will. Isn't that so, Van?"

"Yes. That's who we are, David. Let's slay this dragon together!"

David's face brightened. "That's good to hear. So we go on to the next item. Heddy told me you had some opinions about the code. Is that right?"

"Yes. I think I recognize the type of code it is."

David looked over to Heddy. "I'd like Carruthers to hear this. Dig him up, will you?"

The coffee and biscuits arrived and they helped themselves. The tall windows of the room looked out over the Thames. David pointed out the London landmarks they could see, starting with Tower Bridge in the distance. Van, a lifelong runner, had run the London Marathon twice. "It was quite an experience to run over Tower Bridge, as it is any bridge, when you have a few hundred runners with you. The thing bounces. Some people are really shook up."

"You're a runner too!" David exclaimed, "A 'Renaissance' man! Did you know about Alan Turing, the great code breaker, being a runner?"

"Yes. He's one of my heroes."

"Mine too."

There was a knock on the door. David opened it and greeted a silver-haired gaunt man. He introduced him to Van and Ava. "Dr. Phil Carruthers is our cipher man. He's the inheritor of our old MI1. They were doing cryptography in World War One. Now we all live under the same roof, MI5."

They seated themselves round the table again. "I've asked Phil to join us to hear your impressions of the code, Van."

"I feel flattered. I'm not a code man. Though being a psychologist and doing crossword puzzles may help," he grinned. "I haven't seen the code you people found in Afghanistan. But, to have a Taliban fighter able to use the code, it must be a simple one. It can be decoded, I suggest, without a codebook or a deciphering machine."

Phil Carruthers nodded. "Yes. It's in the class, I'm sure, of quite simple substitution codes. I doubt it is a single substitution, that would be too easy to break. We've tried it and our decoding programs come up empty. These days you can run a million combinations and permutations in a minute or two. So it's almost certainly a double or a moving substitution. To go to a triple would negate its usefulness in the field, as people would become confused. Our difficulty is that we have only two examples of it. We need an inspiration from heaven or more messages, or both," and he let a smile crease his pale aquiline face.

"I don't know whether I can come up with your inspiration from heaven," Van said, "but let's consider this. These people are apparently dotted round the world. How would they direct a message to a certain person? The obvious answer is by name. But suppose you wish to suppress names. What would you do then?"

Phil Carruthers wrinkled his brow. "You are stirring up memories. You can have codes based on location. As I remember, the Norwegian resistance during the war developed one that the Germans never cracked. H'mm. It's an idea."

Van continued. "I was a navigator in the RAF and identifying positions was part of my trade. There are several ways of doing it. You start with names, when a location has a name. After that you use bearing and distance, latitude and longitude and, these days, GPS coordinates and grid chart locations."

"You are intriguing me, Dr. Bentham. What makes you think location is the underlying key?"

"Just inspiration from heaven! I don't know."

Ava interjected, "'Location, location, location', those are the three most important things for knowing where to put a shop and other things. I would think that, if you are running some kind of spread out operation, that location would be one of the most important things to know. I mean, you can't send a package anywhere without an address!"

David nodded. "True enough; it might work in some way like that here. Let me suggest, Phil, that you have your computers buzzing on these ideas. It may be some time before we intercept other messages and, perhaps, you can go further with the ones you have."

Ava was still musing about the problem. "You know, billions of e-mails are sent every day. You don't have to know where the other person is. Perhaps it could be something to do with e-mails?"

At that moment a woman entered the room and spoke quietly to David. He rose from his chair. "I have to leave you. There have been developments. Heddy, please see to the accommodations for Van and Ava. Arrange to have them back here at ten tomorrow morning, if that's all right with you, Van?"

"No problem," Van assented.

Phil Carruthers stayed for a moment. "You know - and it was stupid of me - I hadn't got around to e-mails. It's not going to be easy because we don't know anything about their origin points. But we are on good terms with Google and others. I'll get my fellows to look into it."

After he had left, Heddy asked, "Have you anywhere to stay tonight? The town is yours! Does the Ritz or the Dorchester tempt you?"

Van looked at Ava. She said, "We have our favorite little hotel, the Franklin, just next to Harrod's. If they are not filled up, we would like to stay there. I've got their card somewhere," and she opened her voluminous bag to find it.

They were in luck. The Franklin could put them up. They took a taxi there and collapsed on the bed.   They had lunch sent up and relaxed as they went over the remarkable night and day they'd had.

"I'm going to phone my cousin, Malcolm FitzRoy," Van said. "He's a wheel in the financial world here and terrific value as a person. Outwardly a Falstaff character, inwardly as sharp as they come. Perhaps he and his lady can join us for dinner."

Yes, they could. They would meet at Malcolm's club on Albemarle Street in Mayfair and then step over to the Al Hambra, a Lebanese restaurant in Shepherd Market.

Van told Ava that Malcolm had a little house on the Nevern river estuary at Newport. It had once been a fishery and now, after extensive re-modeling that, in time, got rid of the fishy smell, was their holiday place.

"So this is your new bride, Van," Malcolm greeted them. "I approve instantaneously!"

Over their dinner they talked of Newport and Carn Ingli and the many stories told about it. Van recounted what he knew of the seal-watching operation being run by a Major Howe. "They've built a hut up the coast for their gear, I believe."

"Would this Major Howe run you out to it?"

"I imagine so, if I asked."

"Don't worry. We're down there every other weekend and I'll run you out in my boat. She should really be in an antique museum, but I like her. We have to go out on an out-going tide and come back after the tide has turned. Otherwise my Lame Duck can't make it."

"Your Lame Duck?"

"Yes - that's my boat's name, the Lame Duck! Ha!
Ha!" Malcolm roared, almost tipping off his chair as he
leaned back. As he usually was, he was in good spirits.

Chapter 14

Happenings - A Mixed Bag

Van and Ava met with David Crick and Heddy the next morning. They said they would keep their eyes and ears open.

"OK. That's fine," David said. "Your contact person is Heddy. You will have one of our special mobile phones to communicate with her. It has all the latest stuff: phone, e-mail, camera, video, GPS and so on and it has a security guard making it a scrambler unit, too."

Van had rented standard mobile phones for Ava and himself, but they wouldn't be secure.

David's mobile rang. "Excuse me." He listened to the phone. "So he's safe in hospital?"

Van and Ava couldn't hear what was being said, but they could see the gratified expression on David's face. He put the phone away.

"Good news! We've got Oscar Flavio. He jumped off the train and broke his leg. Ava, you were saying it was a bloody dangerous thing to do; evidently it was for him. But Oscar is a tough fellow. He hobbled as far as he could and reached a ditch. He collapsed at that point. He tried to set his leg with a stick and bindings he made from his shirt. He thought to wait until nightfall, make it to a road, and hitch a ride."

"What happened?" Van asked.

"An interesting little story. The farm where he was belongs to a woman who was walking with her dog. The dog picked up the scent and went to the man. The woman couldn't move him herself. She went back to the farm building, attached a chain harrow to her tractor, threw an old mattress on it, and returned to the man. She bundled him, with whatever help he could give, onto the mattress and dragged him on top of the harrow back to the farm. She saw he was in a bad way and phoned the local hospital. They came with an ambulance and alerted the police. They phoned the Yard.

The man had no identification on him except the butt of his train ticket: Mr. Smith, for all that was worth. The Yard told them to finger print and photograph him. And that's how we know we've caught Oscar Flavio. We matched his prints and his picture."

"Congratulations!" Van said. "I imagine you will interrogate him pretty strictly."

"Yes; we will certainly interrogate him, using our methods. You know what a skilled interrogator says? 'Give me two chairs in a plain room and time. That's all I need. Sooner or later I will tell you everything the person knows.'"

"I've heard that," Van said. "Torture gets you nowhere, as we've learned to our cost. It's very much like
hate. It does more harm to the hater than the hated."

Ava had been sitting silent while the two men had
been talking. "David, you said the man had no identification on him except for the butt of the train ticket?"

"No, none; and that was a false name, of course."

"Does that include the tags on his shirt and other
clothing?"

"I don't know. I could find out."

"You remember the man fished out of Newport Bay?
Why not compare this man with him? He had no identifica-
tion on him either, other than he was wearing French shoes.
Is that another coincidence or, rather, non-coincidence?"

"Could be. We'll look into it."

* * *

Van and Ava caught the night train back to Fishguard,
this time able to enjoy an undisturbed night in their compartment.

Back in the cottage at noon, they took a deep breath,
hugged each other, and broke out laughing.

"This afternoon, Van, all I want to do is to buy some
shrimp rakes, take off my shoes, paddle along the beach,
and see if we can catch some shrimp."

"You're on, girl! You're on!"

They bought the shrimp rakes and a bucket at the
ironmongers and received valuable advice from Rhys
Jones about shrimping. "You hold the rake like this,
at an angle, and push it through the top of the sand in
the shallow water," he told them, demonstrating the
action required. "Remember, before you do that, you
kneel down."

"Why should we do that?" Van asked

"Well now, you haven't been shrimping before, you say?"

"Only a very long time ago, as a boy."

"So you have forgotten that you kneel?"

"I'm afraid so," Van told him, while seeing the twinkle in Rhys Jones eye. "You must tell Ava, my wife, who has never been here before, why you kneel."

"It's simple. We have our own saint of fishermen, Saint Tryn. You want to catch the shrimp and you ask for heavenly guidance from him, and anyone else up there, for where the shrimp are. So you kneel, just like you do in church."

After a moment of silence Ava burst into a gale of laughter. "And I suppose you say a prayer too?"

"It would do no harm, milady, no harm at all! In my experience it's a matter of 'God alone knows' where the shrimp are. My personal advice to you is, if you haven't caught any shrimp where you are, go to a different place."

Ava was laughing about it all the way to the sands. When they arrived there, she piously fell on her knees. "O Lord and Saint Tryn, let me catch as many shrimp as we need to have a good boil-up." She rose and told her husband, "There! I've done my part. Now the Lord has to do his - or hers - and Saint Tryn too."

They caught forty-seven small shrimp, Ava counted them. Van put them in the bucket with a bit of sea water and seaweed, as he'd done as a boy. "I think you had a direct line to up there, my sweet. That's a good catch."

When they reached their car, they stopped to look at the sunset. Next to the long gleam on the water, Van espied a boat moving quickly. He found his binoculars in the car and focused them on the boat. "I bet it's one of those rubber boats that Major Howe has, the ones that James has let him park by the boathouse. My goodness! That little boat is going like the dickens!"

Van continued to look at the speeding boat. "That's strange, Ava. It's going straight out to sea. If it keeps on going like that, it'll be in Ireland in a couple of hours."

For a while they watched the sunset and the sea gulls circling and squawking overhead. Then Van took another look for the boat. "That's amazing. It's disappeared over the horizon. What in the hell is that small boat doing out there? If anything happened, they'd be for it."

"Perhaps they have a date with a mermaid," Ava suggested

"The mermaid better have a life boat for them, just in case. Stupid fools."

They went back to their cottage and boiled up the shrimp. The shells fell off easily. Ava made a lemon mayonnaise to dip them into. "They really are tasty, aren't they, Van?"

Van agreed as he went to answer the phone. He was greeted by Laura, the Romance author, from their cruise boat.

"I got Ava's card with your number, Van ... "

Ava telegraphed across to Van. "Who is it?"

"Laura from the cruise boat."

"Oh, let me talk to her." Ava took the phone. "Laura! How are you? Lovely to hear from you. Are you in London?"

"Yes, I just got back from Scotland, gathering material about lairds and lochs and stuff. Listen. I'm giving myself time off from writing and I thought I'd come and see you and Van's Pembrokeshire. I've found it on the map."

"What a marvelous idea! We would love to see you. Our cottage is tiny, but there is a great pub close by with rooms at the back where you can stay. When might you come?"

"I'm thinking of the day after tomorrow."

"Are you going to drive down? It's quite far. Why don't you take the sleeper train from Paddington? We've just been up to London and back on it. The first class is super. You'll enjoy it. We'll meet you at the station. We have a car, but you can rent one in Fishguard if you wish. I'll reserve a room for you at the Red Dragon. How long do you think you'll stay?"

"I really don't know. Three or four days, I guess. I'll see when I get there."

* * *

Next morning, Van sleepily woke up. He went to empty his bladder. It was the usual mildly satisfying experience, one of life's minor pleasures, though a nuisance too. At the same time, it was an ongoing lesson in life's imperatives. When you have to go, you have to go.

He went back to bed, fell into a light sleep, and began to dream. His dream was about being at his navigator's table in their Lancaster bomber, dropping bombs on the hated Hun. He must find the exact latitude and longitude of their position. He was anxious; everything depended on him finding their position. The pilot was calling for a course to steer. Why couldn't he do it?

Van woke with a start, glad to find it was only a dream. He'd been only twenty then. The memories never went away. Van fell back, his head in the soft pillow. He was half awake, half asleep. The dream continued, now in a different form. He was finding latitude and longitude of a place to put in his small portable GPS. He could find it on Internet maps; but the maps gave positions in decimal degrees and he wanted them in degrees and minutes. The conversion was simple, but annoying.

Van woke up properly. Why had he been dreaming of latitude and longitude? It was pretty obvious. It was a remnant from talking about codes and lats and longs in London. The Norwegians may have identified places by lats and longs and used them in their code. H'mm.

It suddenly came together. Van quickly slipped out of bed, leaving Ava sleeping peacefully.

In his brief case Van found the copy of the code. Yes! Why was there a letter only in the first two groups? He wrote them down again on a separate sheet. 53Y017 04M832. If he substituted points for the letters, he had a possible lat and long in decimals. Wow! Grabbing his calculator he turned the numbers into degrees and minutes. 53^0 1.02' and 04^0 49.92'. He found his portable GPS and entered the lat and long numbers. They would give him the location on the GPS map. The map was small, but definitive enough. He yelped! The pointer was right on Newport! Where he was! The letters in the blocks, Y and M, were fillers in the lat and long. They might mean something or they might not. What he knew was that the first two groups, without the fillers, gave a place identification.

Van stood by the table, quite still in his Eureka moment. Then he ran into the bedroom and grabbed Ava. "Ava! I've got it! I've got it!"

Ava opened her eyes sleepily. "What . . what have you got, sweetie-pie?"

"The code, the code! I've got some of it. It's a simple position code, in plain sight! I knew it would be something like that. It's so simple! No need for anything but a map. Easy to get at with a GPS. The GPS becomes a simple deciphering machine! What do you think of that?"

Ava rubbed her eyes. "I'm going to the bathroom. You can explain it to me over breakfast. I always knew you were better than those computers, darling. That's why I married you."

Over breakfast Van tried to explain the intricacies of latitude and longitude and how they could be expressed. Ava grimaced. "I was never any good at math, darling. If you say it gives a place on the map, that's enough for me."

"And the place on the map is right here, at Newport. Can you believe it?"

"You mean someone is sending a message to someone right here?"

"Could be - could be. I have to figure out the rest of the code … "

Ava picked up the dishes and took them to the sink. Van followed her. "You know the rules, Ava. When in the UK, the man does the washing up."

"A very nice rule, too. I'll leave you to it and solving the rest of the code. I'm off to Browne the grocer. Anything you want?"

"He's got a little fish counter; ask him if he has any kippers … and mango chutney and crumpets. Those are my soul foods," he laughed. "Can you imagine? I'm beating those guys at MI5. Yippee!"

Van cleaned up the kitchen, something he liked doing, and made another pot of coffee. He returned to the living room and looked out over the bay, lost in thought.

He muttered to himself, "It's got to be a substitution code. That means the numbers have to be substitutes for letters. If it's that simple, then those six 0's in the next five groups are likely to be the letter e, the most common letter in the English language, and the 1's could be another vowel. But that would give very strange words, too many e's. Shit!"

Van settled down at the table and wrote out the code using various substitutions. Nothing came to light. It remained a jumble. He was discouraged and put it aside. It needed more thought. But what thought?

Ava returned and Van helped her in with the groceries.

"That Mr. Browne is such a nice man. It's so delight-fully old-fashioned there. You ask for something and Mr. Browne runs off and gets it for you. There were other shoppers there who were helping themselves, but Mr. Browne stuck with me. He told me I had to have something very Welsh and he gave me some laver bread. It's made out of seaweed that is gathered on the Gower peninsula, somewhere south of here. You eat it with '*cockles*' and Mr. Browne had a new batch in, so I bought some. You fry the laver bread and boil the cockles. I think that's right, not the other way round. So that's what you are having for lunch, my Neolithic Welshman! Sea-weed and something that looks like a slug inside a small snail shell!"

Van was laughing. "Another bit of soul food from my youth! But laver bread is good stuff. Make up your mind you are going to like it and you'll find it's delicious. And it's highly nutritious, too. It was a mainstay during the war down here. And the cockles are like tiny *escar-gots*. Anything else?"

"One of those men from the Red Dragon came in. He took a cart and loaded it up with canned foods. I mean - loaded! Mr. Browne told me he was one of them and rolled his eyes. He didn't say anything more. He didn't need to. With all the good fresh food around here, why load up with canned stuff? Mr. Browne said, 'That's a lot of tins.' Tins are what we call cans at home, right?"

"Yes, that's right. As G.B.Shaw said, 'Two peoples divided by a common language.' What Major Howe's men are probably doing is provisioning the hut, or whatever it is they've built along the coast. Major Howe told James he would be having men out there."

"Men!" Ava declared. "Too lazy to make a decent meal for themselves. Anyhow, darling, how did you get along? Have you solved the code yet?"

"No. For the moment I'm stuck. Dammit! I'm frustrated. I know I'm nearly there but I can't do the last step"

"Why don't you tell me about it? That can help sometimes, just to hear yourself think."

"OK. Here we go. Codes are some form of substitution. That is numbers stand for letters, sometimes in a very complex way that is impossible to decipher without computer help or a bulky code book. I am convinced that this code is not like that. I think it's a simple substitution, but I can't get it. Maybe it's a shifting thing. That is, in one block a number stands for a certain letter and in the next block that number stands for a different letter. Working only with this short message I couldn't hope to solve a shifting code. But it may not be that."

Ava finished putting away the groceries. "Let's assume it's solvable, sweetie. Otherwise why waste our time trying to solve it? Don't you think that's sensible?"

Van had to laugh. "Yes. Eminently sensible. But I don't see how it helps."

"I think your problem is that you are too brilliant, Van. That big brain of yours doesn't function so well on simple problems. So, let's see. There are 26 letters in the English alphabet. If each is expressed as a number, then you have the numbers 1 to 26. Isn't that right?"

Van grasped his forehead. "Goddammit, Ava! How could I have been so stupid! It makes perfect sense that each letter is represented by two decimals. One would become 01, 2 becomes 02 and so on up to ten. After that each number has two decimals. That would explain the number of 0's in a short message. I'll write out the code again starting with the third group. Now we have 16, 12, 16, 07, 20, 18, 04, 07 and so on. If it was a direct substitution 01 would stand for A. That would be too simple. Let me work on it."

Van disappeared for an hour. Ava was in the kitchen, wondering whether she could possibly eat seaweed bread and cockles, when Van dashed in. "Ava! Ava! We've done it! Look! The message reads *'Newport',* that's the lat and long, then *'aware correct Irak'.*"

"How did you do that?"

"It's so simple, it's laughable. All you have to do is slide along 12 letters so that L equals 1; M equals 2 and so on through the alphabet until you get back to K equaling 26. Anyone can do it, provided they know how many letters to slide along. When that number changes the whole code changes. It's a shifting code, very clever and very simple. Now we must find out how a person knows how many letters to slide along before assigning that letter with the number 1. I think it's hidden in the message. It must be in the numbers of the lat and long. Ava! Help! We're looking for the number 12."

Ava leaned over with Van. "The number 12 isn't there, so perhaps it could be two or more numbers adding to twelve."

"All right. Let's start with just two numbers. There's a 5 and a 7 in the first group and a 4 and an 8 in the second group. They add to 12." Van pondered for a moment or two. "It's a guess, but it makes sense. The trick is to add the first and last numbers in the first group to arrive at the number you want. It's simple and easily memorized."

"Oh, Van! Do you really think we've solved it?"

"I do! The last group with all those 0's is a sign off. The Y and M in the first two groups, the lat and long groups, may be just fillers or they might mean something."

Ava joined Van in thinking about it. "I know!" she suddenly bubbled. "That man who was killed. His name was Yves Mateur. There's your Y and M!"

Van cried out, "That's totally brilliant, Ava! The first two groups give the place and a person. But why Yves Mateur? He's never been to Newport, as far as we know."

"I don't think that matters. The message is about Yves Mateur, not to him. It says 'correct.' That could mean to take care of him. And that was done. Possibly Irak means someone who is or was in Irak. It's still a coded message. You have to be in the know to properly translate it."

Van was enthralled by what Ava was saying. "If you're right, Ava, and I think you are - we've smashed this code to smithereens! Between us we've done it!"

"So we're both geni or whatever the plural of genius is!"

"Nothing less, my dear! Nothing less! And, if I remember my Latin, you have to add another i to make it *genii*."

"I'll stay with geni, it's easier."

"I'll call Heddy on our new super-duper phone and give her the good news."

He did it using the speaker-phone option, so Ava could hear.

Heddy was suitably astounded. "I'll try it on the Afghanistan message. Hold on." In a minute she was back. "It works! It works! You should get a medal for this."

"This is Ava, Heddy. Please tell the queen that. We may be meeting her down here."

"I'll see what I can do," Heddy laughed.

"Incidentally, Heddy, if you spell IRAK backwards you get KARI. I saw it in the bathroom mirror when I wrote out the message. It's a woman's name. So perhaps the sender is a woman called Kari."

"Could be. Thanks. I'll see what we can make of it."

* * *

Van and Ava picked up Laura at the station at Fishguard after her overnight train ride from London. Van suggested they drive her around for the first day or two. After that she could rent a car.

"But, I warn you, if you get off the main road, and there is only one main road here, you are in a maze of narrow lanes with high hedgerows that you can't see over, and they twist and turn in whatever way the old mules and donkeys chose to take."

"I'll let you be my guide with pleasure," Laura said.

They drove on, fiddling their way through the narrow streets of the old Fishguard Harbor and climbed the steep hill on the north side. They were on top of the high cliffs and able to see along the rugged coastline.

"Gosh! That's a view, isn't it" Laura exclaimed.

They passed the headland of Dinas and the few houses and farms dotting the countryside. Laura leant back in her seat. "I love it; just love it."

Van grinned. "I knew you would."

"And you may love it more this evening, Laura," Ava told her. "Tonight, we are invited to dine with Van's cousin at his gorgeous home, an old family mansion with a butler. Fabulous! He's Sir James Owen and quite unfairly handsome and charming. He's also a Lord Lieutenant, the representative of the queen down here. You'll like him. We're planning to go sailing in a day or two in Newport Bay and along the coast to see the seals. Sir James has a boathouse where we start from. It's all small boat sailing here, nothing luxurious. So be prepared!"

Laura, for all her London *sang froid*, began consulting with Ava, rather desperately, about what she should wear to meet Sir James. "You didn't tell me I'd be meeting a Knight of the Realm, Ava! And a Lord Lieutenant to boot! Oh, God! I brought hardly anything with me!" she wailed.

Turning off from the main road, Van steered the car past the lodge at the start of the drive leading to Llwyn House. He slowed down as they went over a hump-back bridge over a little stream and then stopped at a cattle grate leading to the gravel area in front of the house. To their right was an interestingly shaped ditch.

"That ditch, Laura, is called a ha-ha. It's a way to keep animals from crossing over without a fence. On the house side, as you can see, the wall of the ditch is vertical and goes down five feet. On the field side it's a gentle slope. Animals can go down into it from the field without being trapped or harming themselves, but can't get out on the house side. It's too deep for them. All you need is a spade and a strong back to make a most ingenious and almost invisible means of blocking animals from coming onto the front lawn. It works like a charm. I remember when one of us boys was roaring around the field on a dirt bike and turned toward the house. I suppose he didn't see the ha-ha ditch and went full tilt into it. The bike stayed in the ha-ha and he was air-lifted onto the lawn." Van laughed. "It still amazes me that we didn't kill ourselves with all the tomfooleries we got up to!"

It was a sunny evening and Sir James met them by the front door. He was casually debonair in slacks and shirt with a loose ascot round his neck. They went to the patio by the conservatory. Robert hovered in the background and served them with cocktails or sherry according to their choice. He re-appeared with a dish of the local shrimp, lightly glazed with ginger.

James said, "Whenever I'm in the States, everyone seems to serve shrimp with the drinks. So I hope you like these, Ava."

"They're yummy, thank you. Tell us what's been happening, won't you, since we saw you last?"

"Well, not too much happens down here. We're in a bit of a backwater … "

Laura interjected, "An absolutely beautiful back water, Sir James."

"In its own way, it is, isn't it? People come this way to replenish their soul, or whatever you like to call it. Please call me James and I will call you Laura. All right?

"With pleasure, James," Laura responded, failing to hide that she found him a most attractive man.

Van said, "We've been to London and back on the new sleeper train and Laura has just come in on it."

James exclaimed, "I've been on it too, though I almost didn't. Did you hear about the shooting on the train? It happened the night before I was due to take it. They weren't sure if they would run the train. But they did and I had a decent night's sleep. And that was just as well. I had to go to Buck House - Buckingham Palace, you know - to meet with an equerry and someone from the Lord Chamberlain's office about the queen's visit here. It's years and years since the sovereign has been here and there's a lot to catch up on in terms of protocol."

With drinks in their hands, they strolled in the garden. James showed them his monkey puzzle tree. "Its proper name is *Araucaria Araucana*, though I'm not sure I'm pronouncing that right. The tree is a native of western Argentina and Chile and very long lived. This one was brought back

by one of my sailor ancestors, Frederick Owen, a couple of
hundred years ago, soon after it was discovered by Europeans. It's a hardy tree and the climate here is quite like its
native habitat. It has done well here, as you can see."
      "Why is it called a monkey puzzle tree?" Laura asked.
      "Go up to it and take a close look. Though be care-
ful how you put your hands on it. Those spikes are very
sharp. The story goes that a man in Cornwall had one of
the trees in 1850. He was showing it to friends and one
said, 'It would puzzle a monkey to climb it.' The name
stuck. In France it's called the *'désespoir des singes'*, the
despair of monkeys. This tree is a male tree. It really
should have a female tree with it. Then I could have lots
of young monkey puzzle trees!" James laughed.
      As they walked back to the house, Ava held Van back
to let Laura and James be ahead of them. "They make a
good couple, don't they, Van?"
      "Now, Ava! Hold back on your match making."
      "Well, James practically invited her to bed down
with him, with that talk of his male monkey puzzle tree
needing a female!"
      Van had to grin. "It was suggestive, wasn't it?"
      The dinner was excellent, starting with a traditional
Welsh leek and onion soup, followed by a savory dish,
'Angels on Horseback.' James explained to Ava, who
had not heard of it, that it was shucked oysters wrapped
in bacon, skewered, and lightly sautéed.
      "Heaven knows why it's called *'Angels on Horse-
back.'* It's like our folklore, lost in the mists of time,"
James smiled.
      "But deliciously up to date this evening, James,"
Laura enthused.
      Robert was the attentive, almost invisible, butler.
He kept their wine glasses filled with Chablis from

France and a Syrah from Australia. They were soon in a jovial mood.

Over the roast beef, carved by James with well-practiced skill, the conversation turned to their sailing plan. James explained, "Rhys Jones, our ironmonger, is a sort of boatman for me. I have a lovely old boat, *Daisy*; the best one to take for our expedition. Van remembers her from his boyhood. Rhys keeps her up and uses her to go after his lobster pots. He's a good fellow. He brings a couple of lobsters up to the house here for my cook, Mrs. Evans, to prepare. I'm really spoiled. I love them just plain and I like a good lobster Newburgh. I believe the dish originated in New England."

Laura told him, "I've just been traveling in New England and that's what they claim. But who knows?"

"Now there's a dearth of lobsters here," James continued. "The pots are empty. It has become worse recently. We all know the lobster catch goes up and down, and there are all kinds of beliefs about why it happens. But it has never been worse than this time."

"When we had a lobster at the Red Dragon, Myfanwy told us the same thing. They were becoming very scarce," Ava said.

James told them, "I was talking to Rhys Jones in his shop the other day. He's sure it's poachers. They've been on the lookout, but haven't caught anyone yet. So it's a bit of a mystery. Talking of mysteries, what about that code, Van? Have you solved it yet or has it baffled you too?"

Ava raised her glass and pronounced, with a slightly wine-helped lilt to her voice, "We, Van and I, made mincemeat of it. Didn't we, darling? A toast! Here's to us! Two *geni*!"

They drank from their glasses with broad smiles. James inquired what *geni* were. Ava gaily told him,

"Some of them come out of bottles, you know. But we didn't. They are the same as geniuses-s-s, if you can get round all those esses."

"You've really solved the code?"

Van felt he had to intrude. "Sweetheart, I don't think we should say anything more about it. It would be a burden on our host if he knew and I don't think the people in London would be at all pleased if we run off our mouths about it."

Ava sulked momentarily. "You're right. But, anyhow, we did it. Just us two!"

Laura quizzed. "What in the world is all this about? Sounds most mysterious."

James told her, "I'm afraid we've talked too much about it already. There was a message written in code found on a drowned man in Newport Bay. Very few people know about it. I have to ask you, Laura, to keep quiet about it until it is publicly known."

"No problem, James. But very intriguing. And you and Van, Ava, have decoded it?

Ava felt a bit shame-faced now. "Yes, we have; but we can't tell anybody."

"The plot thickens! How delightful! You will tell me all about it when it's over."

They went to comfortable chairs to enjoy coffee, port, and chocolate wafers. James and Laura chatted with each other. Van and Ava got up and strolled about the hall. Van told her about the family portraits hanging on the walls, interspersed with pikes and halberds.

"You see, Ava, they're long with nasty spikes at their ends. Various forms of them were used by infantry for centuries. And over here there's a replica of the Welsh long bow, the artillery of Henry the Fifth when he defeated the French at Agincourt. One of our ancestors was there with a company of Welsh archers."

"I think I'll sit down," Ava said, feeling slightly squiffy. "You can catch me up on your battles another time."

On the drive back to Newport, Laura turned to Ava and said in an excited, intimate voice, "Guess what? James invited me to sit with him in the family pew at his old church in Nevern on Sunday and said we would drive to see a cromlech afterwards. What in the world is a cromlech?"

"I haven't the foggiest, Laura. You'll have to ask Van. But you'll risk hearing more than you could possibly wish to know."

The two ladies, neither in their first youth, giggled to each other.

Chapter 15

A Guest at Llwyn House

"I'm not a great church goer but, being the top Owen, I pretty much have to come to church every now and again," James told Laura in a low voice as they sat in the ancient Owen pew behind the choir. "I have an understanding with the vicar that I'll be here once a month or so and, when I'm here, I read the first lesson of the day. It's always from the old testament, so I get quite a lot of who begat who."

At the lectern James read a piece from Proverbs. Returning to the pew, he whispered to Laura, "A sensible piece; it boiled down to saying 'don't be an idiot or a stinker.'"

The choir sang in both English and Welsh. As they were leaving, Laura said, "That Welsh singing is beautiful, liquid and strong at the same time."

"I'm glad you like it. Now let me take you to the cromlech. You can't come here without seeing it. It's one of our 'must sees.'"

They stopped to say hello to the vicar at the church door. People lingered to say, "Good morning, Sir James" and, "*Bore da*" (Good morning in Welsh) as Laura and James walked along the path under the ancient overhanging yews to the lynch gate and their car.

After traversing narrow lanes, they came to the sign for the *Pentre Ifan Cromlech*. James parked the car and they tramped along a muddy path. In a couple of hundred yards they came to the three tall stones sunk in the earth, with a cap stone across the top. It stood ten feet high, gaunt against the sky.

"It's a miniature Stonehenge, Laura; a burial site for the Neolithic people who lived here."

"It's like a tiny cathedral, isn't it? Whenever I see something like this, I try to see the people as they were then. Probably not very accurately. But, in some ways, I bet, they were not very different from us."

"Probably so, I agree. Take in the view from here. They must have liked it, too. It's hard to go anywhere around here and not see splendid views of the landscape or be down in intimate lush valleys."

Laura took some pictures; rather thankful for having something to distract her from her feelings about the man she was with. She found it a trifle absurd to have such girlish feelings. It must be the magic of the place and the sea air she told herself, unconvincingly.

James took her to the pub at Felindre Farchog where they ate a good pub lunch. At the church and now at the pub Laura had become fully aware that her escort was 'Sir James.' Everyone addressed him as such.

Dillan Davies, from the Pentre Ifan farm was there.

James invited him over and they chatted about local affairs and the barley harvest that had been the best in years.

"Well, Sir James, how is that butler fellow working out? What was his name now?"

"Robert - Robert Heath. He was from my old regiment, the Royal Welsh, a sergeant, and had been discharged after a court martial. But I'd heard that the charges against him for stealing were possibly false. A couple of the officers told me he was a good man, treated unfairly. So I took him on."

"You put your faith in him?"

"Yes, I did, and it's been justified. He has carried out his duties and learned what he needed to learn. He keeps himself clean and smart and does as he's told. I have no complaints."

"That's good to hear, Sir James. Some of the hands I hire - well, less said the better!"

On the way back James asked Laura if she was comfortable at the Red Dragon. She told him that it was fine; the room was sparse, but clean and new. "It's rather noisy though. I could be back in London!" she laughed.

"What makes it noisy? I wouldn't have thought it."

"It's those men doing the Seal Project. They're a rowdy lot, into the beer and whisky every evening. Myfanwy is having a time with them."

They came to the Lodge at the end of the drive to Llwyn house. "May I invite you in?" James asked her.

"By all means. I've only seen your garden in twilight, but it looked very interesting."

They strolled among the herbaceous borders and the trees down to the banks of the river Nevern. "It's quite good trout fishing here," James informed her. "Will you stay for tea? I bet Mrs. Evans will have some Welsh cakes for us."

The silver tea service brought in by Robert was English 18th century and worth a small fortune, Laura thought. James invited her to pour and she silently thanked her mother for having taught her the proper way to be the hostess at tea-time, even if she only had James to pour for.

James was silent, seemingly preparing himself to speak, but hesitating. At last he said, "Laura - I think you sense my difficulty. We've known each other for such a short time. This is a large house. Shall I continue?"

"Yes, please go on," she said, with an encouraging smile.

"All right. What we call the Rose Room has its own bathroom, a small suite. I have guests here from time to time and I hire in some staff. You told me about the Red Dragon being noisy. You would be welcome to stay here as my guest ... away from the noise."

Poor man! He was almost blushing. "As you say, James, we haven't known each other for very long. May I ask you a personal question? You had a wife?"

James clasped his hands together by his knees. "Yes. I did. She's buried at Nevern church, where we were. Three years ago."

"I'm so sorry. Perhaps I shouldn't have asked."

"No, no; not at all. Eira would have welcomed you here. Eira is the Welsh for snow. She was born in the middle of a snow storm in a rambling old house, like this one, in the Brecon Beacon Mountains." James found his handkerchief and dabbed his face. "Please excuse me. May I drive you back?" he said, getting up.

Laura stayed in her chair. "Won't you sit down, James? We can just be quiet together."

After a minute, Laura said, keeping her voice low, "I can come across as a rather aggressive over-sophisticated sort of woman, and at times I am. I've been doing life on my own. I write romance books that sell well, but are, frankly, trivial. They are glossy, but not real. In good part that's because, for a long time, reality was unbearable for me. We weren't married when John, a captain in the Guards, went off to war. He was killed in the Falkland Islands, one of the seven army officers killed there. You can read his name in the crypt of St. Paul's cathedral. We were to be married when he returned. It was all set. Everything. For a long time I secluded myself, not so much physically, as in my being, my soul, if you like. It's hard to find the right words, as I'm sure you know. It's only been recently that I've been out and about and meeting people, traveling around and slowly I've come out of my shell and living my life again. Perhaps my story can help you. We are quite alike, I think. In your case, if I may say so, you are the ideal of a gentleman who had his heart broken."

James was looking at her with relief, the tensions in his face melting away.

Laura gathered herself and stood up. "OK, Sir James. Stand up!"

They stood, facing each other. Laura carefully phrased her words, "I accept your invitation to stay here as your guest, James; if that is still acceptable to you?'

"I am not sure what to say, Laura. I haven't done this before. Is a simple 'yes' enough?"

"Perfect!" she smiled, "It is agreed. What now?"

James took her hand, saying, "Come over here."

He led her to the far wall of the study where an old map of the county and coast line, yellowed round the edges, was hanging. "It's a bit out of date, but it shows the essentials. We need to plan our sailing party for tomorrow. Here's my boathouse," he said pointing to the

Cwm, "and we'll sail into the bay and up toward Cardigan. The weather forecast is good, sunshine and a fair wind. With any luck it'll be a perfect day and we'll see some seals and their pups. I hope Major Howe has done nothing to disturb them. I informed the Coast Guard at Milford Haven and the Police Chief at Haverfordwest about what's going on and told them I would keep an eye on things. So we'll take a look tomorrow and hope to see nothing much except, perhaps, the hut or whatever it is that Major Howe and his men have built. They'll have to take it down again, of course, when they leave. Strictly speaking they shouldn't have built anything; the shore line is part of the Welsh National Park. But you make exceptions for good causes. If it's all right with you, I'll pick you up at nine tomorrow morning at the Red Dragon and we'll go on to the boathouse. I'll give Van and Ava a ring at their cottage to confirm the arrangement."

"That's great, James. Will the Rose Room be ready tomorrow afternoon?"

"I'll make it so," James declared, with a fervor that Laura had not seen before.

After taking Laura to the Red Dragon, James called Mrs. Evans and Robert to his study.

"Laura Manning will be staying with us. She will arrive tomorrow afternoon and will be in the Rose Room. We have not got very much time. Robert, you will clean the Rose Room and its bathroom within an inch of its life. Make sure everything is working properly. Mrs. Evans, please call your sister, Megan Lloyd, and see if she's available to start being in charge of the housekeeping and be able to continue, as she told me she would, through the time of the queen's visit."

"Yes, Sir James. When I last spoke with her she seemed quite available."

"Good. When those people were staying last spring, she brought two young women with her as house maids. I hope she can bring them again. Ten per cent up on wages. There will be a lot to do prior to the queen's visit. You'll have to make sure about the maids' uniforms and that the rooms upstairs are ready for them. All the linens ... "

Mrs. Evans held up her hands. "Oh, you don't have to tell me, Sir James. You can rely on Robert and me. Don't you worry."

As she and Robert left the study, she was telling him, "Give me all your butler clothes and your shirts and underwear. They all have to be laundered and ironed. Laura Manning is a London lady and knows what's what, don't you doubt it. Remember, she may want to serve the dessert at the table. Otherwise you do it at the sideboard. When there's a salad, she may wish to make the vinaigrette at the table; the one Sir James likes, with Colman's mustard and cream and sugar. You may mention it to her, Robert. I'll have my sister bring Sue to be your dining room and parlor maid, as she was before. We must do our best for Sir James. You understand? Our best!"

"I understand, Mrs. Evans. Indeed I do. I couldn't ask for a better billet."

"For the queen's visit we will have the house full, Mr. Heath. I'll have to talk to Sir James about the arrangements. Since his wife died ... well, housekeeping is really beyond him. So it's up to us. We must be well prepared."

Mrs. Evans liked Robert Heath well enough; though, she was sure, something was troubling him.

Chapter 16

The Witch's Cauldron

Laura was ready at the front of the Red Dragon when James drove up, with Robert sitting in the back with a large hamper.

"I've brought Robert along because we can't drive directly to the boathouse. We have to lug things along the shore-side pathway and Robert is a better lugger than I am. He will help us, too, to get *Daisy* into the water and out again. She's quite a heavy old boat. The hamper is full of Mrs. Evans best for our picnic."

"Have you a spot in mind?"

"Yes. It's called the Witch's Cauldon. The tide will be all the way out when we reach it and we will be able to go in and stay there for a bit. You enter through a tunnel, so we have to take our mast down. Don't worry. I've done it before," he grinned.

"The Witch's Cauldron! What next have you got to show me in your Pembrokeshire?"

"Let's see. We are due for a very high tide. The tide comes up the river to Llwyn House and beyond, flooding the low lying ground. You can bring a boat right up to the house and tie up by the tennis court. It's fun! Like nearly everything else round here, there is folklore about it. The extra high tides are attributed to a Moon Goddess. She does it to cleanse the shore of unholy things and evildoers. For a Moon Goddess to be involved is a curious bit of prescience. They had no idea that the moon physically causes the tides. The more mystical people here claim that revelations like that are in the Celtic blood. Believe it if you like."

At the boathouse they met up with Ava and Van. Van agreed that the Witch's Cauldron was a great place to go.

With Robert's help, they trundled *Daisy* down the slipway. Robert put the hamper in the bow and James showed them where the fishing lines were stowed. They put on life jackets and were off, making it over the bar, though with little to spare, with the jib and mainsail pulling well. Both the ladies had some sailing experience and knew how to position their weight on the windward side of the boat. Daisy spanked along on a southwest wind, with the sun shining and light spray coming in over her bow.

James stood out toward the Irish Sea. Soon the waves were long smooth rollers. Van and James were in the stern and Van told James about seeing a small inflatable boat disappearing over the horizon toward Ireland.

"If it was Major Howe's men, he had better tell them to back off," James said. "You can have quick storms out here."

"Yes, I remember that well," Van said.

After fifteen minutes James announced, "All right. We've gone out far enough. I'm going to let *Daisy* run before the wind on a starboard tack. You'll be able to see the coast from Strumble Head to the south, then Fishguard, Dinas, and Newport, and on to Morfa head and into Cardigan Bay. Running before the wind, will make us roll a bit, so hang on."

Laura broke out her camera. "I hope I can capture the nature of this wonderful place," she said, "and your windswept faces too!" she grinned as she snapped pictures of James at the tiller and Van and Ava taking out the fishing lines.

"I'll make for Seal Cave, as Major Howe is calling it, and see whether we can spot what is going on there," James told them. "Hey, you landlubbers, I've heard there are mackerel about, so get out those lines and spinners."

In a few minutes Ava's line went taut. "I hope I haven't caught a corpse, like your Rhys Jones did!"

"Reel in some more, Ava!" Van cried, as he saw the fish. "No corpse. It's a good-sized sewin. We're in luck!"

Ava was gleeful as Van put the fishnet under the sewin and hefted it aboard. Van had given the other line to Laura and she soon pulled in a mackerel.

James declared, "I should take you on as my fishing crew!"

They continued to catch mackerel as *Daisy* neared Seal Cave. They took the sails down and James started the outboard. They drew in close. It was a small stony beach. They saw a black polyethylene sheet secured around a mound at the top of the beach. There was no sign of a hut or anything like that.

James looked at the beach. "I don't want to take *Daisy* in on the stones. She's endured too much in her life already without adding that to her advanced years. I suppose that's some gear Major Howe has out here, under those sheets."

As he spoke a man stood up on the far side of the sheeted mound. Laura said, "Oh, I've seen him before. He's one of the men at the Red Dragon."

"Hello, there!" James shouted. "I know Major Howe. We're just here to have a look."

The man came down the beach, finding his way over the stones in his heavy sea-boots. "Well, there's nothing much to see here. The seals are up the coast. You should have a rubber boat to land here. Else you'll harm your boat on the stones."

"Yes, I quite agree," James said. "I was looking for the hut that Major Howe had built with that timber. Do you know where it is?"

The man didn't reply at first. "I'm just here to look after these things and see nobody pinches them."

"So you don't know where the hut is?"

"No, I don't."

With that the man turned round and clomped his way up the beach again.

Ava remarked, "Hardly a garrulous man, is he? All alone out here, too. You'd think he wouldn't mind a chat."

"It takes all sorts," James said, "and it's none of our business, as long as no harm is being done."

They set sail again and made for the coves up the coast. After a few small coves, they came to a larger one, with a good sized stony beach, and saw seals swimming by the shore. James scanned the beach through his binoculars. "There are seal pups on the beach," and he handed the binoculars to Laura. After taking a look, she passed the binoculars on to Ava and Van.

"Can you get closer, James?" Laura asked. "I want to take pictures."

"I mustn't go too close. The parents are looking after their young. It's important they are not intruded on."

Laura took a slew of pictures, doing her best to steady herself on the rolling boat. Van said, "I hope they come out well."

"I'm looking at them as I take them. They look good."

Van continued to scour the beach and the cliff above it with keen eyes. "Believe it or not, when I was a boy, I climbed the cliffs behind that beach, and I'm here to tell the tale," he laughed. "I rather think that someone has climbed up there again, disturbing the gravel and the few plants that are growing there. It may show up better when I take a look at your photos, Laura. Lend me your chip and I will blow it up on my lap-top." Van looked up at the tall cliff again. "It's a scary climb, I can tell you, especially to come down."

They sailed on and reached the mouth of the Witch's Cauldron just before the tide was at its lowest. Van helped James take down the mast. They went in, through the tunnel, keeping their heads low, touching the roof with their hands.

"It's mostly stones on the beach. But there used to be a sandy spot. Ah! There it is," and James beached *Daisy* on the little strand of sand. "We'll have to watch it. As soon as the tide begins to come in again, we must leave or we won't have headroom through the tunnel."

Van laughed, "When I was young and foolish, I did just that. I had a canoe and left it too late. There's a side tunnel over there and I could just get through it. On the other side there's a little enclosed pool where we kids used to swim."

"So what happened to my loopy canoeist?" Ava asked.

"I hauled the canoe out of the water and left it high and dry. Then I climbed up the steep pathway and made it back to Ceibwr bay where I had parked my baby Austin Six car. I came back the next day with a friend and we carried the canoe out."

They were at the bottom of a large impressive hole in the ground. On the landward side the curve of the earthen cliff rose up 400 feet or more. On the seaward side the cliffs on either side dipped down to a rocky land bridge over the tunnel by which they had entered. Gulls and curlews wheeled and dipped over their heads. James told them the place was a birdwatcher's delight, as were many of the places along the coast.

James turned to Van, "I'm sure you know about how this place was formed and its Goddess. I thought we would tell the ladies about it."

"You do it, James," Ava said firmly. "Being a professor, Van is prone to tell you more than you could possibly want to know."

James laughed. "I'll keep it short. The tunnel we came through was once a cave. Over the millennia the sea pounded away inside it, making it longer. Eventually it reached past the hard rock and went into the relatively soft ground beyond. That was easy pickings for the water. A chasm was formed that, in due time, collapsed and opened to the air above. The process continued with the sea taking out the debris through the tunnel. Thousands of tons of earth and stones went out through that little tunnel, until it became what we see today."

Ava said, "Fascinating! One more lesson about our ever changing planet. There's a Goddess here too?"

James took a piece of paper out of his pocket. "I can't remember this exactly, so I wrote it down. The cauldron here is the haunt of a Celtic Goddess, Cerridwen, also called the Dark Moon Goddess. She dates from about 3,000 years ago. A prayer to her goes like this, in English that is. The original is in Welsh, of course. I'll read it to you.

O Cerridwen, keeper of the cauldron
In your pot brews inspiration and divine knowledge
Thou, fecund Welsh witch
Thou, Mother Cerridwen of the divine cauldron."

"That's marvelous," Ava cried; "We'll be filled with in-spiration and divine knowledge just by being here. And there's the 'fecund' bit too. I bet they were fecund here!"

Van was laughing, "You have to be careful about how you pronounce 'fecund', don't you?"

Laura chimed in, "I just love all this stuff. James has told me about the Moon Goddess causing the high tides to wash out evil things along the coast. Marvelous stuff! I'm going to write a really good book and include it all. I'll hardly have to imagine a thing!"

Mrs. Evans had provided for them magnificently. They spread out the large blanket and feasted on a salad, ham and cheese sandwiches, cake and biscuits, washed down with red wine and coffee from a thermos. The sun beamed down on them and then was cut off by the lip of the cliff. "Time to go," James told them.

Under sail again on their way back to the Cwm, Laura sat close to Ava while the men were in the stern. "I have to tell you, Ava, that James has asked me to stay at Llwyn House. No strings attached or anything like that."

"And you've accepted?"

"Good grief, yes! Have you ever met a more eligible widower? He told me, sort of off the cuff, that he has a town house in Kensington in London and that he owns a lot of land down here. I mean - gosh!"

As they neared the Cwm, James told them, "Mrs.

Evans has dinner waiting for us at the house. We'll give her the sewin, so we'll have a fish course before the lamb from the Home Farm she has on the menu. I'll send the mackerel up to the Home Farm. Mrs. Roberts there has a slew of children to feed and the mackerel will be welcome."

Laura leaned over to Ava. "Ava, tell me if I'm making an utter fool of myself, but I think I'm falling in love."

"Not a fool at all! Van and James share the same genes and Van, with a fault or two, is an ideal husband. What you have to figure out, Laura, is what kind of love you're into. If it's a flash in the pan, enjoy the flash in the pan. If you think it's something more, let it develop. Don't push too hard. I'm sure you know as well as I do that money and possessions are not everything."

"True, but they go a long way," Laura grinned.

Van and Ava went back to their cottage to have a shower and change their clothes. James stopped at the Red Dragon to pick up Laura's bags and say hello to Myfanwy.

"Are you getting any lobsters in, Myfanwy?"

"No, Sir James; indeed not. Either the devil or the poachers are taking them!"

"I'm sure it's just a downturn; they'll be back."

"I think it's all that running up and down in those rubber boats with their loud engines. Rhys Jones is real ticked off about it. He thinks they disturb the fish and the seals. It's hard to know, Sir James, what exactly they are up to."

"I'll have a talk with Major Howe about it. I hear the men have been rather boisterous here at the inn."

"Yes, they have been. But they pay well. Never short of money, it seems."

Laura felt she had entered a nook of heaven when she went into the Rose Room. Robert brought in her bags and a pretty young girl in maid's uniform showed her about the room and bathroom, complete with a bidet. It was a country house room to perfection.

Over dinner that evening they talked about the day's outing, including the rather rude man at Seal Cave and that they hadn't seen any hut.

"They must have put it in one of those caves," was Ava's opinion.

The next morning Van sat at the table after breakfast making quite a long list of items to pass on to Heddy. He phoned her and went through the list. When he had finished, he said, "As Ava says, there is something fishy going on and it may have to do with the seal project of Major Howe. But what it is, I don't know."

Heddy asked if there was anything else. Van told her, "There's been a dearth of lobsters in the pots. It's making the locals mad. But we've been catching sea trout, they're called sewin here, and mackerel. We've also been in touch with a Celtic Goddess in a cauldron and, with any luck, we can invoke her as the local Moon Goddess of high tides to wipe out anything evil going on along the coast, I think you should know."

"Thanks. I'll pass it on," Heddy laughed.

Chapter 17

Turning Points

James phoned Van the next morning. "Van, something extraordinary has developed. I would very much appreciate you coming here."

"Right now?"

"Yes. I am sorry to be so urgent. But from what you've told me about your doings in the US, you may know better than I what to do."

Van told Ava he was going to see James about a problem he had. "I'll probably have lunch with him."

"I'll walk down to the Parrog waterfront and paddle around there."

Van drove to Llwyn House to find James standing by the front door. "We'll go to the study, Van, where my butler, Robert Heath, is."

Robert Heath was standing in the study, looking strained and nervous. James said, "Let's sit down. You too, Robert. I want you to tell Dr. Bentham what you told me. Start at the beginning and tell the full story."

Robert Heath sat forward in his chair, his face drawn. "I want to make a clean breast of it. I can hardly sleep of night. It began, sirs, when we were on maneuvers in the Beacons. We had to stay out at night in pup tents. It was winter time, rainy and cold. We'd been out all day since dawn and my men were exhausted. As the sergeant of my squad, I felt I was responsible for seeing that each of my men had put up their pup tents and bedded down properly, according to our training and regulations. It wasn't spelled out in orders, but I took it upon myself to go to each pup tent late at night and inspect the men. Then I bedded down in my tent."

"And the men were asleep?"

"Yes, sir. Most were snoring away, dead tired. Only a corporal was a bit wakeful and he had seen me."

"And what happened then, Robert?" James prompted.

"In the morning there was this great hue and cry. Someone had been round the tents and sneaked the men's wallets and taken the money from them. He must have seen me going round the tents and then done his thievery, thinking I would be blamed. He dropped two of the wallets in front of my tent. So that's how it was, sirs. I was accused and dishonorably discharged."

James told Van, "That's the story I heard. Then two officers told me the defending officer at the court martial had done a very poor job, and they hadn't believed Robert Heath was the thief. It was completely out of character for him to have done it. Continue, Robert."

"I admit I was bitter. I took a job down at Tenby where they have a lot of summer visitors. At a pub there, I would have a few beers and tell my story and use cuss words against the British Army and the government.

So, along comes this bloke and says I could make some money for myself if I would find out some information. They had a deal going and I'd be an agent for them. He said that Sir James knew the important people in the county and I should just keep my eyes and ears open. They knew Sir James needed a butler and with your generous nature, sir, it wasn't difficult for them to put me forward to you and for you to take me on. I told them I would never betray my country, but they said it was just a money making scheme. They were going to bring stuff in somewhere along the coast here and they didn't want the police or anybody interfering with them. Even then I knew it was wrong, but the money was good and I was still bitter over what had happened.

That's how I came to be here at Llwyn House. They gave me a mobile phone and told me to report twice a week or, if anything special occurred, I was to tell them immediately. Nothing much happened for a while. I drove Sir James to places and, now and again, I overheard conversations, but that was all. Then the body turned up in the bay. That, you might say, was the turning point. They wanted to know everything I could tell them about it and who was saying what. That was when, sirs, my conscience began to trouble me and I realized I was being involved in something a lot more serious than I had been led to believe."

"I can understand that very well, Robert," James told him, "Go on."

"The other turning point for me was when you, Dr. Bentham, were having dinner here with your wife and it came out that you had broken a code to do with the drowned man. As a military man, I know something about codes. I began to think the matter might be of some importance for the government and that I could be doing something against my country. Well, sirs, there's not much more to say. I realized I was in the wrong and came to Sir James to say I couldn't live with myself anymore." Robert Heath bent over in his chair, holding his face in his hands. "I am so ashamed."

James said, in a firm voice, "Sergeant Heath. Hold your head up. I am convinced your court martial was a mistake. You were unfairly treated. Then you did a foolish, if understandable, thing. I compliment you now on doing the right thing and I will retain you in your position here."

"Thank you, sir; thank you indeed."

James turned to Van. "So the question is, what do we do now?"

"The first thing to do is to have Mr. Heath make a list of everything he passed on, as best as he can remember." Van looked at Robert Heath, "You should also write down everything you know or guess about the people who employed you. You are to say nothing to anybody about this matter. When is your next telephone report due to be made?"

"Tomorrow evening, sir."

"Good, we have some time. James, can you spare Robert from his house duties to write out what I have asked?"

"Of course. Robert, you will do what Dr. Bentham has said."

After Robert had left the room, James exclaimed. "It's quite a pickle, isn't it? Just now it occurred to me, sort of like a bad dream, that there might be some plot afoot to coincide with the queen's visit. Do you think it possible, Van?"

"At this point, I think anything is possible; even that. James, I have a start on this thing that you don't know anything about." Van said grimly. "I'll give you a quick run-down on what has happened so far. It's confidential government business and not to be passed on. I'm sure you understand."

Van recounted the sequence of events.

James face drew long, "It's serious, isn't it?"

"It is, very serious. Ava and I have become 'assets' to Scotland Yard and MI5. We've been reporting to them. In fact, I made a report this morning bringing them up to date on what we saw at Seal Cave yesterday. I don't know whether it's significant or not. All I know is that it seems unusual, while possibly being entirely legitimate. I told my London contact about Major Howe and, no doubt, they are investigating."

"My God!" James gasped, "I told the police and the Coast Guard to lay off him and his project. What he claims to be doing may, in reality, all be a smoke screen?"

"Quite possibly. We don't know yet." Van looked at his watch. "I left the phone I use to call London at the cottage. I must get back there. Please stay here, James, and as soon as Robert has written his piece, warn him strongly to say nothing to anybody. Bring what he's written to me. Don't tell anyone else. I must consult London first."

Van was on the point of leaving when the phone rang in the study. James picked it up. "It's Ava. She's on her mobile from Parrog," he said, handing the phone to Van.

"Ava, what's up?"

"Have you heard?"

"Heard what?"

"Rhys Jones and Taf Jenkins found another drowned man off Morfa Head! They were in *Daisy* and they saw him on the surface."

"Ava! That's unbelievable! You're not kidding me?"

"No. Honest to God. Rhys and Taf brought him to the Parrog beach near the parking lot. I was there and saw it all. I'm still here, next to the boat. They're waiting for the police and ambulance from Fishguard. There are just a couple of people here, as yet. The body is in the boat still. A man said he had seen him at the Red Dragon. I'm pretty sure the corpse is one of Major Howe's men."

Van's mind raced. "Ava, there's been a major development here at Llwyn House. I'm going back to the cottage to talk to Heddy on the phone. You stay there. Find out everything you can. Did you see whether he was wearing a life jacket?"

"I'm close to him. No, there's no life jacket."

"What else can you see?"

"He has a big gash across his face. No blood though."

"No. There wouldn't be."

"I have my camera with me, Van. Should I take pictures? He's just here, open to view. Somebody has gone to find a sheet or something to cover him."

"Do that, Ava. Take pictures. Stay by him until the police arrive. If anyone interferes with you, kick their ass."

"Hey! You're talking to a Californian girl. I know how to kick ass!"

Van raced to his car and drove at top speed toward Newport, then through the streets, sending startled people running into doorways. He was about to turn up the side road leading to their cottage when his mobile phone beeped. It was Ava.

"Van! Quick! Come to the Parrog as fast as you can. We're being attacked! For Christ's sake be quick! We're holding them off ... " As Van listened, he heard

Ava shout, "Back! Back! You're not going to take him.
Rhys! Taf! Hold on! Help is on its way."

Van slewed the car round and skidded it through the
narrow opening between stone houses leading onto the
Parrog road. Taking the corners at full pelt, he arrived at
the parking lot in a cloud of dust and screeching brakes.

Van leaped out of the car and ran round the old ruined lime kiln toward the beach. He had been a runner
all his life and he went into his sprint mode. His strides
ate up the yards. Then he saw them.

Daisy was on her side on the beach above the water
line. Ava was standing at *Daisy*'s bow with Rhys and Taf on
either side of her, each grasping one of *Daisy*'s oars. There
were three men in front of Ava. They had, it appeared, retreated to decide what to do. The lead man shouted, "Get
out of our way, he's our pal!" and advanced toward Ava.

Ava had a round stone in her hand. She lifted her left
leg, raised her two hands and, in a whirl of motion, threw
the stone underarm. It hit the lead man in the center of
his chest. He fell like a stuck pig.

As Rhys would tell the crowd at the Lwyn Arms that
evening, "It was like a bullet! I've never seen anything
like it! Not a large person, she is. But that stone flew
like David's had, killing Goliath!"

Rhys did not know, of course, that Ava had been, in her
day, the star pitcher on the softball team at USC, University
of Southern California. She was famous for her fastball.

As Van continued toward them, he heard Ava yell,
"Ster-rike!" She bent down and found another stone.
Standing up, she glared at the other two men. "The next
one - - I'll aim for your head. Want to try me?"

The two men were kneeling by the side of the fallen man.
"You bleeding bitch, you! You could have killed him!"

"Not a bad idea," Ava told them.

Van came up to her. "Thank God, Ava! Are you all right?"

Ava was relieved to have Van beside her, while telling him, "Nothing to do with God, my sweet. We had the situation under control. They kept on saying he was their pal and would take him away. No way! I'll bet those men wanted to take him away because he has something on him, something they want to keep to themselves. Like that fellow at Seal Cave who wouldn't have anything to do with us. Rhys and Taf were great. We made a good trio; like the three musketeers."

Van was grinning with her now. They watched the two men help their companion to the parking lot. "That strike of yours was, if I may say so, very striking!"

"Not bad. I used to throw a good change-up, too. My curve ball wasn't so great. But you need a good fast ball when you have a smart-ass batter in front of you."

There was a crowd around now. "I am a doctor," Van told the people gathering around. He briefly examined the corpse, then took off his jacket and put it over the dead man's face. "The police and an ambulance are on their way. We must wait for them."

He took Ava aside. "Drive up to the cottage. Remember to drive on the left hand side, for heaven's sake! Call Heddy and tell her we need her here as quickly as she damn well can make it. Have her bring David Crick too."

Van was realizing they were uncovering what could be a large operation, even, possibly, in some way, threatening the queen. They had this new body. It had to be autopsied. The man hadn't died from a simple drowning. He had broken bones.

The police and ambulance arrived. Van told them he was a doctor and that the man had drowned and had multiple injuries.

"He hasn't been in the water long, probably not more than a day. He should be taken to a medical examiner to determine the exact cause of death," he told the police officer.

The officer took down Van's particulars. "We will wish to talk with you again, sir."

"I'll be happy to oblige."

The news spread fast and Van found himself confronted by a local reporter, a stringer for the Western Mail.

"Did you see the woman throw the stone?"

"Yes, I did. She's my wife."

"And you are a doctor, sir?"

Van did his best to cut the interview short and say as little as possible. However, the next day, the Western Mail headlined: "*American Woman Foils Attackers with Hurled Stone.*"

The lead was: *Ava Bentham, wife of Dr. Van Bentham, resident of New York and cousin of Sir James Owen, Lord Lieutenant of Pembrokeshire, was attacked by three men while guarding the body of a drowned man on Newport Beach. Eye witnesses said that Ava Bentham picked up a stone from the beach. As the men advanced toward her in a threatening manner, she threw the stone at one of the men with such speed and force that the man fell down, badly hurt. He was dragged away by his companions. The details of the attack remain obscure. Mr. Rhys Jones, the owner of the ironmonger shop in Newport, who was sailing the boat Daisy with his friend Taf Jenkins when they found the body in the water, said he suspected it was something to do with the 'Seal Project' underway along that section of the coast. We have no further details at this time.*

After the ambulance and the police had gone, Van phoned James. Robert had finished his writing. Van asked James to come to the Parrog and they would go on together to their cottage.

Arriving there the men found Ava on the phone with Heddy. "Van, you better take this. Heddy and David are coming in on a police flight to Haverfordwest. It's just a small airport, she tells me. Then they have a charter helicopter bringing them here. They have to tell the charter people where to land." She handed Van the phone.

"Hello, Heddy. Yes, it's pretty dramatic here. Where to land? Wait a minute ... "

James was tapping him on the shoulder. "Tell them to land in the field in front of Llwyn House. It's been done before."

"How will they find it?"

"I'll give them the GPS lat and long. I carry the numbers in my wallet. Hang on. Let me have the phone, Van."

"Hello. You can land on the field in front of my house. There's plenty of room. It's been done before. Are you ready to copy? Latitude 52^0 01.223' north, longitude 04^0 48.725 west. There's a hard driveway through the center of the field and that is the best place to put down. Phone me when you are close and we'll be there to meet you. Here's my mobile." James gave his mobile phone number.

Chapter 18

Facts and Inspirations

The helicopter put down in the field in front of Llwyn House. Van and Ava greeted Heddy and David and introduced James to them.

Robert had the car there. James said, "Robert will take your bags. We can walk to the house, if that suits you."

David said, "Good idea. My legs are cramped. There's not much room in those seats."

They went to the study where Laura was waiting for them with a tea service highlighted by cucumber sandwiches.

"Laura Manners is my house guest," James told David and Heddy.

"Let me pour some tea for you and then disappear," Laura said. "Sir James tells me you're here on official business."

"Thank you for understanding, Laura. I hope we won't be too long," James told her. He asked David whether he had made any plans for overnight for Heddy and himself.

"Heddy, have you planned anything?" David asked.

"The helicopter won't come back here to pick us up in the dark. Perhaps Sir James has some suggestions. We have to find a local place and we don't want to draw attention to ourselves."

James frowned, "If you put up locally, it will be known about soon enough and arouse some curiosity. That's the way it is here, especially now when the summer visitors have left. But here's a way to do it. I have empty rooms in the house here. May I suggest you stay here?"

It was a good solution. For him to have guests at Llwyn House was nothing out of the ordinary. It would draw no particular attention.

James took Laura aside. "The sister of Mrs. Evans is Megan Lloyd. She has arrived and will be the house-keeper here. Would you mind making her acquaintance and let her know we'll need two bedrooms prepared for our guests; and let Mrs. Evans know we'll be - let's see - yes, six for dinner.

"Glad to do it, James," Laura said, leaving the room.

At James' invitation the five of them found chairs to sit in. David opened the proceedings. "Sir James, let me start by thanking you for bringing your butler's tale to Dr. Bentham."

"You realize that when I did that I had little idea of the implications it had."

"Nevertheless it was the sensible thing to do. In the present case it also cleared the air about you, Sir James, as I shall explain. Before I go on, I must establish security. You must agree to keep your mouths shut. The FBI has given Van and Ava Bentham their clearance and you are in the clear with us, Sir James. I have the forms

with me that refer to our Official Secrets Act. Please
sign them after reading them through."

It took a couple of minutes for James, Van, and Ava
to scan the forms and sign them. David collected them.
"All right. We'll start with Robert Heath. Van reported
his name to us and Heddy discovered very quickly that
he had been in the Royal Welsh Regiment, the same one
where you had been a brigadier, Sir James."

"Yes, that's right."

"He had been court-martialed for theft and discharged. He was bitter about it. We knew that. Such
men are likely prey for the bad guys; may be just plain
criminals recruiting to rob a bank or subversives planning attacks against this country. However we didn't
know Heath had actually been recruited. We had vague
raw intelligence that your activities were being reported,
Sir James, and that made us think you were involved in
something. But we had no idea what it was or whether
it was illegitimate."

"You were snooping on me?" James exclaimed.

"Shall I say we were keeping an eye on what was
happening down here? For a time it all seemed normal.
Then came the matter of the unidentified drowned man
with French shoes. That pointed in a certain direction
involving an international operation.

I am going to put that aside. However, Dr. Bentham,
you have worked with the FBI and the French police
and you have lived in France for short spells. With your
medical knowledge and your experience in profiling,
which we know about from Dr. Phillippa Crest of the
FBI, we may be asking you to travel to France to help us
there. I will put that aside also for now."

David stopped to drink his tea and help himself to a
cucumber sandwich.

"Yum, delicious! Now, Robert Heath. He reported to his contact in an organization that is smuggling drugs and, very possibly, persons into this country. Now we will 'turn' him. That is, make him a double agent working for us. Therefore, Sir James, he will stay on as your butler and send out his messages. They will be controlled by us. He will also assist you with respect to Major Howe."

"Major Howe?" James queried.

"Yes. I want you to be undercover with respect to Major Howe. We believe he is in a position to lead us to the top people in the organization. He was in Special Forces in the army and fancies himself as a suave desperado. He also stands to make a great deal of money. I will be giving you more details and instructions, Sir James. You are to treat Major Howe as a fellow officer and provide all the courtesies. Van, my quick profile of him is that he has a big ego, thinks of himself as a valiant and clever fellow."

Van nodded. "That sounds right."

"OK. All of you, be clear about this. Undercover operations require absolute security. A breach could bring you personally into danger. If the other side cottons on to our game … it's known they will kill people. In effect they had Yves Mateur killed on the train, though not quite in the way they had planned. For your interest, I'll tell you we now think Yves Mateur was helped to overwhelm and escape from his guards, simply for the purpose of killing him. He had served his function of, supposedly, diverting us and was no longer of use to them. In fact he endangered them by possibly disclosing to us anything he did know; which, probably, was not too much. But that's still cloudy. We are interrogating Oscar Flavio and unearthing what he knows. It takes time, but we're winning his confidence, slowly but surely."

"These are not nice people," Van commented.

"They are not," David agreed. "They are organized by a ruthless and very smart boss. An important part of what we are doing is to get closer to this person and, finally, track him down. That's all I can tell you now and it's all you need to know."

David turned to Heddy. "Have I missed anything, Heddy?"

"Not in the big picture. Now we need to focus on Robert Heath. We think his next report is due tomorrow evening."

"Yes, that's right, Heddy. Robert told us that," Van said.

David nodded. "I'll obtain his formal agreement to work for us and then, Heddy, we have to work out what he'll say in his phone report." David looked around at the group. "Are there any questions?"

Sir James spoke up. "I have a bit of a problem. As I've said, Laura Manners is my house guest here. She knows nothing of this. I can ask her to leave, if you wish ... "

David thought about it. "No, that might draw their attention. These people are not stupid. They would expect Robert to report it and it might send a signal that Sir James was closing up his house to visitors. That could raise a red flag to them and wouldn't fit in with Major Howe being welcome here. Just be closely aware that Mrs. Manning must know nothing about what is going on. Heddy, bend your mind about us being here. We need a cover for Robert to report."

David's mobile phone sounded. He listened closely before ending the call.

"That was about the drowned man. They found no identification on him at Milford Haven. They examined his clothes minutely and in an inner pocket they found a scrap of paper. It had 'Billy had a grumpy pig' written on it." David laughed. "That certainly is strange!"

Ava held up her hand, "That might have been what those men down on the Parrog beach were after."

"How's that, Ava?" David asked.

"I was down at the boathouse when Rhys and Taf were putting *Daisy* in the water. Taf is quite a talker and was catching me up on local news. He told me about Rees Llewellyn, the farmer at Ffynon, seeing an apparition on top of the cliffs by Morfa head. Actually we'd heard the story before from our mailman. Taf believes he did see something, a big man who maybe had climbed the cliff there. The big man was seen again, in a field by Newport. That's what Taf told me. The dead man in the boat was big. I'd guess he's the same man."

David nodded, "It's possible. Actually he was a Dane. We know about him. We think him a bit of a simpleton. More muscle than brain."

Van was thinking about it, knowing his wife's intuitions sometimes hit the nail on the head.

"I saw a trail going up that cliff from sea level to the top. I had a better look at it by means of the photographs Laura had taken. It is quite well marked. That implies it has been used a number of times."

"Van, didn't you say the climb was difficult and dangerous? Why should anyone go up and down it a number of times?" Ava asked.

"It must be that someone had a reason for doing it."

"You would have a better view from the top," Ava offered.

Van considered for a moment. "Let's try to put it together. A large man was seen at the top of the cliff. We are supposing he had climbed the cliff. He was a Dane known to MI5. He was one of Major Howe's men. Am I right so far?"

"Yes," David said, "go on."

"The man that Rhys and Taf found in the sea off Morfa Head was big."

"I would say, very big," Ava put in.

"OK, very big and that helps to identify him. Now, here's the leap. Let us suppose he was the man climbing up and down the cliff. He fell off the cliff, badly injuring himself. That would explain the broken bones I found by a cursory examination of the body. The tide was in and he was washed out to sea, probably still alive because the cause of death looked to me like drowning. I doubt he was in the water for more than a day. I saw no nibble marks on him that would likely be there if he had been in the water longer. Are you with me so far?"

Heddy broke in. "Don't those men have boats to go to and fro from the beach?"

"Yes, they do," Van agreed.

"So why climb up and down a dangerous cliff?"

"That's a good question," David commented.

Ava perked up. "Don't you think it remarkable he only had that piece of paper with 'Billy had a grumpy pig' on it? He had no ID on him, just like the other drowned man, and he also had a mysterious message on him. There!" Ava sat back in her chair and sipped the last of her tea.

David said, "It sort of fits together, but not quite." He stood up. "We have to move on. It's time to ask Robert Heath to join us. It will be best if Heddy and I see him alone."

Van took Ava's hand, "Come on, we'll take stroll in the garden before it's quite dark."

They walked along a gravel path to where a wooden foot bridge spanned the river Nevern. They stood at the center of the bridge and looked down at the flowing water. There was a pool just down river and they watched as trout came to the surface to snatch at small black flies.

"We'll ask James if we can come and fish here," Van said.

"A nice fellow, isn't he? If I know anything about women, I'd say Laura is taken with him."

"It looks reciprocal to me. Ah! The joys of first love - before life gets serious again."

"Van! Don't be such a cynic! It might be just the thing for them. Incidentally he seems to have a pot of money. You once told me the English gentry were known as 'the stranded gentry.'"

Van smiled, "That's mostly true. James is the exception, much due to his father, George Owen. Before the war George Owen moved much of his British holdings overseas, most of it to America. While England was virtually bankrupted by the war, America thrived. But James himself is no dunce. When his father died he retired from the army and took over the estate and all its holdings. He told me he is on the Board of Directors of some big companies here and has his own brokers and finance people advising him in London and New York. I believe he could be worth a billion."

"Wow! He certainly is a good catch!" Ava exclaimed. "I hope Laura doesn't know. It could screw up her thinking."

"They'll have to work it out if and when the time comes," Van said as he looked down at the pool. "I'd like to do some fly fishing again. I did it here a long time ago. It's fun once you get the hang of casting your line." He lapsed into thought. "You know, you catch fish by giving them a false bait to go after. It's rather like what David and Heddy are setting up with Robert Heath, a false friend. It's a good tactic. The trouble is, if we can do it, the other side can do it too. It's often difficult to sort out a real event from a staged one. Waging war, which is really what's happening now, is full of clever tricks to try to deceive the other side."

Ava frowned. "I don't like deceit much, even when it's needed. I have an idea, Van. You've told me what a great walk it is along the path at the top of the cliffs. Let's do it and have a look where that farmer saw the man. Who knows? We may find something - real or deceitful!"

Van was enthusiastic. "Pity we haven't a dog. I loved to run up there with Topsy. We can take a picnic and hike the rest of the way to the Witch's Cauldron. You'll see the cauldron from the top and I'll show you where I had my canoe misadventure."

"I'd love that. You know, you're sometimes too damn perfect, Van. But you weren't then! It makes you another tiny bit more lovable."

"To err is human, my love, and I've done my fair share, I assure you. I'll have a car from Cardigan pick us up at Ceibwr bay, a little further along. I'll work out our ETA there, estimated Time of Arrival, that is. We will have the car take us to Cardigan to see the old market building there and do a bit of shopping. I had a Welsh wool blanket. Somehow it got lost. I'd like another one."

"What about a Welsh witch's costume for me?"

"OK. As long as you promise to be a good witch!"

Chapter 19

You Start with a Good Welsh Breakfast

The next morning at Llwyn House, on James' invitation, Van and Ava joined Laura and James, and David and Heddy, to enjoy a Mrs. Evans breakfast. That is to say, a groaning sideboard of juices, cereals, milk and cream from the home farm, breads, ham, eggs and bacon, kippers, with kedgeree on the side, and coffee, tea, or chocolate. Ava exclaimed, "God! I'd blow up like a balloon if I did this every day! And whoever heard of rice with bits of fish and sliced hardboiled eggs for breakfast?"

Van laughed. "It's what you've missed by being an American. It dates from British days in India. Kedgeree is best made with smoked haddock, as Mrs. Evans has done here. You add curry powder and butter; then top it with parsley. I'm very glad to see it done so perfectly. Historically it's one of many dishes made from the left-overs from the day before. That was the practice all over the world before refrigeration. In principle it is the same dish as hash. Just thought you'd like to know."

"All right. Just remember, you lost the colonies. I'll try a tiny bit. I still think I would blow up if I ate like this all the time."

"Actually, you probably wouldn't," Van told her. "The life style here is full of exercise. This morning, for example, you have to fuel up for our trek along the cliff path. So eat up!"

James cautioned, "Remember not to go too near the cliff edge. At this time of year, with vegetation growing over the lip, it's particularly dangerous."

"I remember that well," Van assured him.

James left them to go to the Home farm. That morning, he told them, the vet was coming to artificially inseminate some pigs. James put on his Wellington boots and picked up his double-barreled shot gun. "You never know what you'll find out there and Mrs. Evans almost decrees that I bring back a rabbit or a pigeon or a duck or, possibly, a pheasant."

James left and Laura said brightly, "That's all part of the country life here, isn't it? Sort of old-fashioned, but quite dramatic! I'm going to explore around. There's an old stone bridge up the river with a cottage by it. It's called Pont Newydd, New Bridge. It's ages old, of course. It leads up to Penny Hill farm. James tells me an old cowman, who used to work here, and his wife live there. I bet they have some good stories to tell, if I can understand them. The Welsh accent takes a bit of getting used to. James said I should ask them about the spirits pushing the tide up at this time of year to clean things up. The very top of the tide can reach their bridge."

David had a phone call on his mobile phone and went away from the table to take it. He returned to invite Van outside. They sat on a garden seat by the conservatory, basking in the morning sunshine, with cups of coffee in their hands.

"Remember those condoms Ava and you found on the mountain, Van? I was told just now that we have a provisional DNA match. The match is with yesterday's drowned man, Ernik Kristol. It's something of a surprise to find him here. He's usually around Hamburg and Scandinavia. The Copenhagen police tell us he goes to Oslo because he has a girl friend there, a bar girl. Probably he takes in some hash. If he does, it's a small amount, just enough for his girl and her friends. He's not a major carrier. Rather he's the guy who does the heavy work. He's one of the men we keep track of, rather than bringing him in. We hope he'll lead us to something or somebody big."

"Why do you think they brought him here?

"Probably to help build the hut or whatever it is that Major Howe did with all that hardware and planking." David paused. "Slight as it may be, it does make Oslo another place to put on the spider's web, along with the other cities on the Baltic Sea. Whatever else, it confirms that boats seem to be central to whatever is going on. Kristol, the man who drowned, had a mother in Copenhagen to whom he wrote postcards. The Danish police knew he was in Newport. They were monitoring his mother's mail. He had written a postcard to her and mailed it from the post office here. They had alerted Interpol to his whereabouts."

Van sipped his coffee. "I bet Major Howe would be mad if he knew that. One way and another, Kristol made his 'splash' here, didn't he? Just his size made him noticeable. Actually any strangers, like these men of Major Howe, stick out like sore thumbs."

"A good thought," David agreed. "Heddy told me she had put you onto my idea about the xenophobia asset. It certainly is the case here. Everyone knows about them. My other bit of news is about that pencil you found. It had been used as a weapon."

"Really? A weapon?' Van exclaimed. "How does a pencil become a weapon?"

"We have the latest in forensics. In spite of having been in the sea for a number of days, there were microscopic molecules of blood and human tissue still on the pencil, mostly under the metal band of the rubber eraser. The lab in London has extracted DNA from these fragments. It's preliminary, but the DNA suggests a man known to the French police."

"Yves Mateur was French," Van recollected.

"Yes indeed. We know there is a French connection, similar to the one unearthed some time ago. A pretty good film was made about it. But this one's even smarter, thanks to the person running the show, whoever and wherever he is. So far he has outsmarted us. But that's going to change. We are slowly unraveling things. As in any operation we have our share of setbacks. We lost that undercover man who was fished up out of Newport bay. He was a resourceful fellow. I told you that pencil you found had been used as a weapon. We are virtually certain he used it for escape purposes. He killed someone with it before he went overboard."

"How come? Was there something special about the pencil?"

"No. It was just an ordinary pencil. He was undercover on a yacht out of St. Malo in Brittany. He was about to give us, we think, good intelligence about the organization. Those scratched words on the pencil gave us the name they use for their boat, *Mother Hen*, and he confirmed that it was in the dope smuggling business."

"So he didn't drown entirely in vain?"

"That's right. We and the French police suspected the boat. Now we know. We have not claimed our man. We want to keep them guessing whether he was a genuine mole for us or not."

"So what was the yacht doing precisely?"

"As of now, we think it was doing a reconnoiter for the run from St. Malo to the Welsh coast, possibly carrying people on board to land here. However, it turned round and went back to St. Malo, we think soon after the killing incident on board. There's another yacht that started out from the Persian Gulf. It stopped at Gibraltar and received a clean bill of health from our people there. But they didn't search the boat more than to have a cursory look around. After sailing through the Mediterranean, it went up the coasts of Spain and France and into the Irish Sea. We think it a sister boat. It may be docked somewhere around here. We ask Harbor Masters to report any suspicious boat, but these days there are so many boats cruising around that we don't have too much luck in that direction."

"So what about the drowned man, your agent?"

"We can only speculate. They must have begun to suspect him. He'd figure he was about to be killed, probably tortured first. He could have lured his guard into the place where he was being held. We teach our agents all the tricks, like simulating an epileptic fit. He found a pencil and thrust it forcefully through the man's eye into the brain. We teach them that; all the way in. It's part of the training in how to use ordinary objects to kill a person. We also teach them to take it out and take it with them. That can leave the other side guessing about what exactly had happened. Our man evidently found a life jacket and must have hoped to swim to shore. But people don't last long in cold water. A tough customer."

"He must have been."

"An important reason why I've told you this, Van, is I don't want you to be under any misapprehension. What you are doing is not without risk. So be careful!"

Van chuckled. "You know, David, I came here for a spot of R&R on my sabbatical. Now I'm caught up in an international plot, with myself, and Ava too, being told we might be at risk! Well, David, I'm thrilled! Nothing quite like risk to stir up my warrior genes! And what little I can do to stop a gang of thugs, I'm happy to do. Yes, I'll be careful, don't worry."

They returned to the dining room where Ava and Laura were lingering over their last cups of coffee. Ava told Van, "Laura has arranged with Mrs. Evans to send us off with a picnic lunch. You can carry it in your backpack."

"That's fine. We'll need some water, too."

"I'll put a bottle in my backpack."

They went out the front door and onto the gravel driveway. Now they were alone. "Hey, Van! Have you seen what's happening here? It's pretty obvious. Laura is taking over being the mistress of the house and James is loving it. I predict weddings bells in the not too distant future."

"You love playing Cupid, don't you?"

"H'mm … maybe … I think Eros suits me better. More sexy."

"Don't be too sure about this, Ava. Why hasn't James remarried by now? He's an obvious catch, as you've said before."

"That's totally unromantic of you, Van. He just hasn't met the right woman, until now."

* * *

Having been back to their cottage to change, put on their hiking boots, and pick up their hiking poles and backpacks, Ava and Van walked down to the Parrog. There they found Thomas, the boatman. Thomas had a row boat and, when the tide was far enough in to float his boat, he would row people across the estuary to the sands. When he had started he charged sixpence in the old currency; now he charged one pound and people were glad to pay for the convenience. In the summer time Thomas made a tidy bit. Another advantage of having Thomas row you across, was that Thomas knew everything that happened in and around Newport Bay. So when Ava asked him about the lobsters, Thomas knew a thing or two.

"I see them at Morfa Head with my telescope."

"You can see the lobsters with your telescope?"

That made Thomas grin. "*Naddo*, my lady, no. At dark, on the water, like ghosts; *ysbrid*, we say." At that his English seemed to desert him and Ava was afraid he thought they were making fun of him.

To disembark, as they had boarded, they walked along a plank over the edge of the water between the boat and the shore. They descended, somewhat precariously, onto the sands and set off toward the dunes where they would pick up the cliff path.

"Do you think the boatman really saw something out there, Van?"

"I'm sure he believes he did. What the facts of the matter may be, who knows? Down here, when I was a boy, I learned that the difference between fact and fancy lies in the mind, not in objective fact. It was one of the insights, I guess, that led me, eventually, into being a psychologist."

The cliff path was a steady climb up from the low lying dunes to the top of the high cliffs. Once up there, the path followed a more or less flat course, with some ups and downs coinciding with the inlets and coves below.

In a while they were near Ffynon farm, with Seal Cave on the shore line below.

"I'm going to have a look around," Van said, letting his back pack slide off his shoulders.

A slope of earth mounds, short grasses, and heather led to the lip of the cliff. Van edged forward gingerly. The grasses on the slope were slippery. As he neared the lip, he tested the earth with his pole, feeling for the edge of the underlying rock. When he found it, he dropped first to his knees and then onto his stomach so that the center of his weight was well back. Ava was on the path, clenching her hands, fearful for her husband. It looked so damn dangerous.

"Come back, Van! Please come back," she cried.

Van edged back until it was safe to stand. "I saw it. It's just along there."

"What is?"

"The top of the climb up from the cove."

Finding the place, Van descended a sufficient distance to see down to the shore line of Seal Cave far below. He had his binoculars on a strap round his neck and, after finding a firm place to lodge himself, examined the stony beach.

The beach was the one they had seen from *Daisy*, where the surly man had met them. Van saw nothing new. There was the same mound covered by a shiny black sheet. Van scanned as far to the back of the beach as he could see, having to lean out from where he was to bring it into view. The back of the beach was in the shadow from the cliff and was sheltered by a rocky promontory running out at an angle from the base of the cliff. At its inland end was the mouth of a cave. They had not seen the cave when they were there before. It was hidden from the sea unless you were at exactly the right place to sight round the curve of the cliff and look up the line of the promontory.

Van moved gingerly to find a better position to see to the mouth of the cave.

"What do you see, Van?"

"The beach, the whole beach now, the one we saw from *Daisy*. There's nothing going on. No. Wait a minute. There are two men down there at the entrance to the cave. They are doing something. They seem to be moving stones about. I can't really see. Now they've stopped. They've sat down and lit cigarettes. I'll just wait here, Ava, and see whatever else may happen."

"OK, darling. I'll sit up here and find out what Mrs. Evans has packed for us."

A few minutes passed. Ava was looking along the coast and out to sea.

"Hey, Van! Can you hear me?"

"Yes, but speak up."

"Look to your right along the coast. Isn't that one of the rubber boats coming toward us?"

Van looked in that direction and saw the boat. He inspected it through the binoculars. "There are a couple of men in it. I rather think, from James' description of him, that one of them is Major Howe."

Van followed the boat and saw that Major Howe had his camera out. He was stopping at coves along the coast and taking photographs.

"He's taking photos. If for nothing else, it will bolster his story about observing seals here."

After a while the boat turned into Seal Cave. The two men got out and walked up the beach to be met by the two men already there. One of the men was showing Major Howe, as Van was sure he was, the place where they had been moving the stones about. Then

Major Howe pointed up the cliff and seemed to be angry about something.

Van could hear nothing of what was being said. However, it seemed that Major Howe was giving the men explicit instructions, thumping one hand into another, at times pointing to the stones, at times pointing to the top of the cliff, and then to Carn Ingli. When he was finished, he shook the men's hands and left them to walk down the beach.

Major Howe and his man went to their rubber boat, floated it out from the cove, and headed it across Newport Bay toward the boathouse.

Van climbed back up to where Ava had set out their picnic lunch. "That was quite a show," and he related what he'd seen. "Major Howe, I'm sure it was him, seemed impassioned about something. Heaven only knows why the men were moving the stones about. Possibly they were covering something. Then Major Howe was pointing up here. Maybe there's something up here. Let's have lunch and then we'll scout around."

"What sort of thing, Van?"

"I haven't got the foggiest. We'll just look."

They sat on a grassy ledge and feasted on the lunch Mrs. Evans had prepared. "This is one of the best picnics I've ever had," Ava declared. "Or is it just the sea air, my nice company, and the excitement of the chase? Aren't the views something? You can see for miles and miles."

They packed up the leftovers from their picnic into their backpacks, following the rule to take out what you bring in, and then started searching around the area at the top of the path for "something."

Van was about to give up when Ava cried, "Van! Van! Come here."

Ava was on her knees by a ledge, covered on top with a froth of grasses, and with an undercut looking toward the sea.

"What have you found?" Van asked, coming to kneel beside her.

"Two bottles, empty I'm afraid, of Bass Ale. And that's not all. Here are eight D-size batteries, the big heavy ones."

"You found them right here?"

"Yes, right here. The batteries look almost new to me, all shiny. I'll say the same for the bottles. I turned them upside down and a few drips fell out of them."

"OK. Someone was here with something that needed electric power. I'll take a look under the ledge here. See if there's anything else to find. Lift up this grassy stuff, will you?"

Van peered in, but saw no other objects. However, moving along the underside of the ledge and peering at the dirt, he made out the indent of a sharp corner, two lines coming to a right-angle, like a heavy case would make.

"I think we are striking gold, Ava," he said, kneeling beside her. "Someone had a case up here. Something in the case used batteries. The old batteries, the ones we have, gave out and, presumably, whoever it was, put in replacement batteries. So what, my dear, is a reasonable guess at what was in the case?"

"Well, it couldn't have been one of those sex toys. They don't use big batteries like that. So ... let's see? A huge flash light! There!"

Van chuckled. "I think you're right on, except for the wavelength. Light has too short a wavelength. I think the most likely thing to have been here is a radio receiver/transmitter, maybe a transponder, if they were communicating with another. The eight D batteries would give the twelve volts that most equipment like that use. A big flash light could have been here too. But it would have to be unbelievably bright, like the one on Strumble Head, to be used in day time, and a light cannot be seen over the horizon. My bet is a transponder receiving and transmitting to a boat just at or a bit over the horizon. That's why they had it up here. To achieve extra range compared with sea level. The higher you go the more range you get."

"If it's important, you'll explain to me sometime what a transponder is; but not now. In any case, none of your brilliant deductions would have been possible without my finding the two beer bottles."

"Very true. You know, finding those marks under that ledge means they were concealing it there. They must have been coming up here periodically to use it. That could explain why Rees saw his apparition here, why that big man was climbing the cliff and then, on one of his excursions, had fallen off the cliff, sustaining many broken bones, and then drowned."

"I agree. It all makes sense that way, my big brain," Ava declared.

They gave each other a hug. "We make a good team, don't we?" Van said.

"Sure do. Now what do we do?"

"Go on to the Witch's Cauldron and then to Ceibwr Bay where there'll be a car waiting for us."

Seeing the Witch's Cauldon from above was even more enthralling than being in it, Ava thought; at any rate, more intimidating. The wind had got up and at low tide the sea was crashing into the bottom of the cauldron making it look like a huge saucepan boiling over. To one side, at the end of a tunnel, was where Van had brought his canoe many years ago. The path led them down to a spot only fifty feet above the turmoil of waves. When they went further on, the spray from the rocks at the sea's edge came flying at them. They were glad to climb the steep path on the other side and reach again a level 400 feet above the sea.

It was blowing hard. "Whew!" Ava exclaimed. "A boat sure doesn't want to be caught anywhere near here when it's stormy."

"Bet your life on it. There are wrecks all up and down the coast."

The car was waiting for them at Ceibwr bay and they thankfully fell into the back seats. Ava loved the Market House in Cardigan with all its Welsh stuff. Van bought a woven Welsh blanket that he declared would keep him warm at the North Pole.

"Oh, I didn't know you were going there, dear."

"It's closer than the South Pole," he replied, matter-of-factly.

"You're impossible," Ava cried. "That's worth loving you a tiny bit less."

In an hour they were back at their cottage. They relaxed in steaming hot baths to ease their stiff muscles and, tired but refreshed, they went to the Red Dragon for dinner.

Halfway through his serving of pork chops, Van raised his knife and fork in the air. "Aha!" he cried. "I know why Major Howe was pointing to the top of Carn Ingli ... because it's higher. They need extra range!"

Myfanwy came over to chat with them. Like the rest of Newport she had heard about the drowned man and Ava's valiant defense of his corpse. Yes, she confirmed, he was one of the men staying there; one of Major Howe's men.

"They've calmed down a bit, I'm glad to say. But I've had enough of them. You wouldn't believe the trouble I've had with their boots on the floors. I don't know what they are doing out there, but they were coming in with their clothes covered in sticky stuff. Most of those clothes couldn't even be laundered! They just put them in the garbage. Now that's stopped, thank goodness."

"Did you find out what it was and what they were using it for?"

"Not exactly. I showed the boots to Rhys. He knew what it was, resin. So I asked him what resin is for. He told me it's most often used for waterproofing. But what are they waterproofing? That's what I'd like to know. Then they came in here and left their sticky tracks on my floors. It's a devil to get off, I can tell you. I'll be glad when they are gone. Even though they have brought in a very pretty penny. Money seems no object to them. And that is strange, I think, very strange."

Back in their cottage, Van was going over in his mind what Myfanwy had told them.

"You know, Ava, they could have been using that resin to waterproof a roof, though it seems an unusual way to do it."

"And they would have it all over their boots?" Ava shot back, "Hardly! I bet you it's flooring. Sea water! They're keeping out sea water! What else could it be?"

"Goddammit, Ava. You could be right. That would mean they are down close by the shore line. But why should they do that? If they are putting a hut in there somewhere, they could easily stay above the high water mark and be high and dry." Van scratched his head. "Any ideas, Ava?"

By this time Ava had jumped into bed. "All I know is that water goes down. So I think they are in some 'down' spot and they don't want to get their feet wet."

"But they were wearing boots. It doesn't make sense." Van got into the bed beside Ava. "Why should they build something where they would have a wet floor, when they don't need to do that?"

"Put your head down, Van.   They may have built a submarine and it leaks. Good night."

"Good night. A submarine, eh!"

Chapter 20

Turnings and Country Gentry

That evening, David and Heddy were working on what Robert Heath would say when reporting to Derek. That was the name Robert was given to use when calling in. It was all Robert knew about the organization, a man named Derek and that they were into information gathering. From his voice and the way he talked, Robert thought he could be from some European country. Robert's mobile was a simple one. David would pull audio off it with a stick-on mike and play it into his super mobile. That way he and Heddy could listen to the conversation and record it. He would send the recording on to London for analysis.

Heddy had no experience in this particular type of work. David filled her in.

"You remember that Van was talking about how German spies were turned in the war. The intelligence services learned a lot from that. You never make the other side suspect you have turned the source. They must think he is sending them honest *intel*. At the same time, you must assume they will suspect a source has been turned. Therefore, you do things that allay that suspicion. The game is up if they question and then disprove a message content. Basically we send them true but benign stuff, until we are ready to use them against themselves. That's beautiful when it happens. Our first purpose here is for them to show themselves to us. You learn from them what they are up to and then you track them down at the right moment. It's a game with many wrinkles." Heddy was following what David was saying closely. "You have a thought, Heddy?"

"Would our best course be to make it appear we know nothing and aren't suspicious at all?"

"Yes, that's exactly right, Heddy. That's the way we'll go. When we are sure they are accepting what we say - rather, what Robert says - then we will move on. But we can hope they will give us something up front. That can happen by the way they ask questions."

After writing down a series of points, David called Robert in. He carefully explained what they wanted him to do. "Tell me, what it's been like so far?"

"It's mostly, sir, that I say a few things and then he asks me questions."

David directed him. "I want him to talk to you as much as possible. Whenever appropriate you, Robert, ask for guidance and instructions. We will be listening and will cue you when to ask for more information. I'll move my hand like this," and David showed him the circular motion he would use. "You've been talking to him before. Don't do anything very different. Be as natural as possible. Start your report by talking about the second drowned man."

"Yes, sir. It's been reported in the press. They will know about it, won't they?"

"Oh, yes. We can be sure of that. Don't say more than has been in the papers. Now, just relax, Robert. You have us and the British government on your side."

"Thank you, sir. I will do my best."

"I'm sure you will."

The time came and Robert dialed the number on the mobile phone. He was nervous, but self-collected. The phone clicked at the other end.

"This is Robert Heath. I wish to speak to Derek."

"This is Derek. Tell me what's happening."

"There was a second man found drowned in Newport Bay. I can only tell you that he was one of Major Howe's men. Sir James was shocked to hear of it and, I believe he phoned Major Howe or left a message at the Red Dragon where Major Howe is staying. I gathered it was a message of sympathy about it happening."

"Nothing more?"

"Not so far as I know."

"What about his American cousin and the wife?"

"They've been here, to the house and they've gone sailing together. They had lunch in the Witch's Cauldron, a feature on the coast here, and they had looked in at a place called Seal Cave, but hadn't landed. It's where Major Howe has his camp, I suppose you would call it, to photograph the seals."

"I see. Tell me about the people coming to the house by helicopter."

"It has happened before, you understand. Sir James has rich friends. The lady is the daughter of an old friend of his."

"And the man?"

"I really don't know. A polished gentleman; the sort of man the daughter would have as a companion."

"Find out more about him, if you can. Who else is there?"

"A lady from London, a Laura Manners. She writes books. That's all I know."

"You are doing well, Mr. Heath. I believe Major Howe has been to the house to meet Sir James?

"Yes. A very congenial visit. They got on well together. Major Howe is keeping his boats down by the boathouse owned by Sir James. I believe Sir James has told the authorities that Major Howe's project is proper and not to be interfered with."

"I see. Have you heard anything about the shooting on the train from Fishguard?"

"Only what's been in the papers and that Sir James was anxious that he couldn't make his trip to London on the night train. I gathered he was going to London to do things connected with the queen's visit to St. David's. He's having a new dress uniform made for the occasion."

"What have you heard about the queen's visit?"

"Well, it certainly is a topic of conversation and many people are preparing for it, including Sir James, of course. We are to have a number of guests staying in the house here."

"Have you heard anything about extra police and security during the queen's visit?"

"No, I don't think so. Is that something you wish me to be on the lookout for?"

"Yes, Mr. Heath. We want to know about all the activities."

"Very good. I know Sir James has been to Haverfordwest to consult with the police chief there."

"Find out what you can."

David and Heddy, who had been listening in from the start, looked at each other. David gave the sign to Robert for "more."

"What exactly should I be looking for?"

"Security is always important on these occasions. Get any details you can, so we can stay clear of it. If you hear of any threats made against the queen, you'll tell us about them."

"Oh, yes," Robert said. "As you know, I'm no lover of the government. But I'd hate to have anything bad happen to our queen. Is there anything else I should be on the lookout for?"

"Just be alert. People hear things and I'm in a position to pass it on to the proper persons. Has there been any talk of a boat, a yacht, coming up the coast?"

"Not that I've heard of."

"All right, Mr. Heath. Your weekly money will be paid in the usual way. Report again in three days time. We need to keep track of events. So keep alert. That is all. Good bye."

Robert put the mobile down. "Did I do all right, sir?"

David was ecstatic. "Excellent, Robert! Excellent! You are working for your queen and country now. Indeed you are!"

Robert left and David turned to Heddy. "Holy shit, Heddy. We are striking the mother lode! Do you realize what that man told us?"

"I'm not sure. Is there a plot against the queen?"

"Damn right there is. That man as good as said so. Maybe not against her personally, though that's possible. We know his name and his phone number. Having his phone number is huge. If our people can't track it immediately, they will be able to when Robert talks to him again. They'll set up their tracing chip, as they call it."

"How close can they get?"

"With the new satellite system, they can get as close as the best GPS locators can, within a few feet."

"What do you make of the talk about a yacht, David?"

"It confirms our intel that there is a major smuggling effort taking place. We now know for sure there's a boat up this coast. It's not unusual for smuggling to be associated with terrorism. It's one way they get their money to do their strikes. We saw that when those bloody Irish IRA's were attacking us."

David sat down in one of the comfortable chairs in the room. "It's time to put our thinking caps on, Heddy. I'm beginning to be sure we have two things going on here in parallel, smuggling and terrorism. The terrorism is apparently directed toward the queen on her visit here. They may have chosen this place because it's out of the way. Terrorist targets, usually, are in big cities. Therefore, they may think they will have an easier time out in the provinces and, of course, the queen is a highly symbolic target. If they are planning something like a car bomb, they may be thinking to use fertilizer nitrate as the bulk ingredient. There must be plenty around here with all the farms. Heddy, get going pronto on whether there has been any unusual buying of nitrates at the farm stores. If necessary, I'll get help down here. But see what you can do immediately."

"OK, David. Will do. I wonder where the farm stores are. But I can find out easily enough."

David sat back and stretched. He sort of chuckled. "The security people will be all over themselves when I tell them what's up."

"I'm sure," Heddy agreed. "You do remember the queen will be here in fourteen days?"

"Christ! That's right! Thanks, it had slipped past me. This whole thing has to be on the front burner."

"Should Van and Ava be let in on what we've learned?"

"A good thought. On balance I think they should. When they know we are battling a two-pronged thing, smuggling and terrorism, they'll be alert for a wider set of clues to what may be going on."

As if in answer to that thought, Van called.

"David. I hope you have time to listen to this. James and I have a cousin, Fiona Stuart, who lives outside Machynlleth. Is James there?"

"Yes. In the next room. Heddy - ask James to join us, will you? I'll put the phone on speaker so we can all hear. What's happening Van?"

"An interesting observation made by Fiona and . . ."

"Hold on, Van. James is joining us."

When James was in the room, Van said, "James, I have Fiona Stuart on the line. I'm going to make this a conference call ... as long as I can press the right buttons on this thing David gave me." Van succeeded. They could all hear each other and join in on the conversation. "All right, Fiona. Say hello to James. He's at Llwyn House."

"James! You've been having some excitement down there with dead bodies," Fiona said.

"Oh, yes," her cousin replied. "Van and Ava have been in the thick of it. I expect you've read about it."

Fiona exclaimed. "Van, your Ava must be some woman to have thrown a stone like that. We read about it in the Western Mail."

"You must meet her, Fiona. Before we go on, I want you to meet David Crick from London. I'll let him talk."

"Hello," David said. "I'm down here with Sir James and Van on official business. I gather you have something to tell us."

"I hope you are not going to laugh at me. It's only a little thing I saw at the railway station in Aberystwyth a week ago. I was there overnight. I've got to the point where I don't like driving at night, so I took the afternoon train. We had a meeting of the Garden Society at the university and then I stayed at a friend's house. I wake early and I don't like wasting time. So I had a bite of breakfast and walked to the station to catch the morning train back to Machynlleth. I know the station master at Aberystwyth because some of my friends and I put out the flower pots in the station and look after them. I was having a word with him when I saw these three men. One was a blonde and he seemed to be leading the two other men who looked like Arabs; at least, they did to me. They were pulling big suitcases behind them. The blonde man was carrying a long thin case. It reminded me of the cases you put fishing rods in after you have disassembled them; but it was heavier than that. There was just something about them that struck me as odd. Why should two Arabs be catching the seven thirty-five train? And not the blonde man? I thought them a bit furtive, but perhaps that was just my imagination. I'm sure there could be a thousand good explanations."

"Quite possibly, Mrs. Stuart. But what you are saying is very interesting. Please continue."

"Well, I told my husband, Neal, and he told me about the big posh yacht that had come in from the Mediterranean. The Harbour Master at Aberystwyth had told Neal it was a big boat for their harbour. So when Van phoned me and knowing about the work he does in America, I told him, almost as a jest, that we had strange things going on up here with us as well as in North Pembrokeshire. He said, 'Hang on'; I want you to tell the story to someone. That is you, I suppose."

"Yes," David said, "that's right and I'm most obliged to you. I work on security matters, Mrs. Stuart. Would you be willing to work with a police artist to create sketches of the men?"

"My goodness!" Fiona gasped. "I don't know I looked at them that closely."

"We would only ask you to do the best you could. It might be very important. I can't say more than that."

"Well then, I can't refuse, can I? You'll let me know?"

"I'll arrange to have our Mary Odell with you tomorrow morning. She's our sketch artist. Please give me your address and phone number."

Fiona gave him the information. "Thank you very much, Mrs. Stuart."

"I'm glad to do my bit. If that's all, I need to talk to James about something quite different. James, are you there?"

"Yes, Fiona; I'm here."

"It's about the queen's visit. You remember, I'm involved in the floral decorations and the gardens around the cathedral?"

"Yes, I know."

"I should have asked you before, James. I was going to stay down there near St. David's. But every hotel and B&B is booked. Can you put us up for three or four nights? It will make it a reasonably easy drive to and fro for us."

"Of course, Fiona. Neal and you can have the South Room. I've remodeled it so you will have your own bathroom. There will be three other couples in the house, you'll know them all, and Laura Manning, a charming person who writes romance books. I'm sure you will like her. I suppose you are buying the flowers. But the garden here is in full autumn bloom and you can help yourself, if you need to."

"That's wonderful, James. Thank you so much. I will look forward to meeting your guests. It's going to be quite hectic at St. David's. These things are. What are you going to wear, James?"

"Oh! That's prescribed! The dress uniform of the Lord Lieutenant of Pembrokeshire, with the sword, too. I'll try not to trip over it," James laughed.

* * *

After David had phoned London with all the poop, as he called it, he let go of his tensions and laughed.

"That boat and the men coming off it didn't stand a chance. We're in the land of the country gentry, Heddy. They all know each other, and the trades people too, and they know their countryside better than any stranger could hope to do. You have as much chance of hiding down here, as a fox in a chicken coop! For strangers it's like being in a land of spies, though these people don't seem to know it. That works in our favor. A smart cop knows that. We'll be smart cops, Heddy."

Chapter 21

Preparations

The next day was busy for all.

* * *

James had given Laura the guest list for the queen's visit. Besides Fiona and Neal, there were two couples, cousins, from London, and an old army friend and his wife.

"They are the Mountjoys, Laura; you know, one of the lines coming down through the Saxe-Coburgs and cousins to the queen. Mark Mountjoy, the son, is in the social swim in London. The Mountjoys will have their car and a chauffeur. Gosh, the chauffeur has to be put up somewhere. The rooms over the stables should be all right. I'll have to check them; we can put overflow people in there."

"Heavens, James! There's a lot to be done."

"There always is. Malcolm Fitzroy, another of my cousins, will be down from London. That side of the family dates from the Norman Conquest. They have a house down on the estuary. A great chap. And it's all happening on top of whatever skullduggery is going on with this Major Howe and David Crick down from London. He hasn't said so, but I'm sure he's MI5. Oh, my! Forget it, Laura. I shouldn't have said that."

"It's all right, James. I'll be as quiet as a church mouse about it. Is there more?"

"I'm afraid there is. I've planned for the usual garden party where I'll have in people from the county and at least a couple of dinner parties. For the garden party I want the tennis court in first class trim and ... . Oh, heavens! ... There are so many details. For a good bit of my time I'll have to be down south with the program manager, the committees, the police, the security people and God knows who else. Thank God Fiona is a super person and I won't have to be worried about the grounds and the flowers. Robert keeps the Bentley in good shape, but I would really want Mr. Mathias to invite a Bentley man down here to go over the car. I think the security people go over it, too. It would be perfectly awful to have something happen. As the Lord Lieutenant I drive after the Royal car with a security fellow in the front seat. Oh! That's another thing. Will they let Robert drive?"

"James! Stop! It's absolutely ridiculous you don't have a secretary! It's quite obvious what you need. Me! I'm a good planner. Let me work with your housekeeper and the others. You must have a marquee on the front lawn. Have you thought of that? And a decorator for the house and garden. We'll have to fly flags. A caterer too. Otherwise Mrs. Evans will be overwhelmed. And we

have to think about bathrooms and lavatories. They have
very good portable ones these days. I saw them when I
did a tour of Buckingham Palace. We have two weeks to
work in. Right? It should be just enough time."

* * *

With help from Roberts of the Home Farm, Heddy discovered that the focal point for farm supplies in the region
was Crymych, a small town lying ten miles inland. Sir
James had Robert drive her there and, on the way, Robert
taught her how to pronounce the place, *crim-uth*. Heddy
had her Police and MI5 identification with her and, at the
Davies Farm Store, she was soon talking with Mr. Davies
himself. Mr. Davies told her his Farm Store was the big-
gest for many miles around. It seemed to Heddy they sold
everything that any farmer could ever want.

Heddy told Mr. Davies they were worried about the
wrongful use of ammonium nitrate for explosive purposes.

"Well now. We do sell a lot of it as fertilizer and I know
it can be used as an explosive, like it was in America to blow
up that government building and kill all those people and
kiddies. My Dad worked in the mines and they used what
they called ANFO, that is ammonium nitrate mixed with
fuel oil. It has additives in it to make it easy to use. Any
strong detonator will set it off, especially when it's mixed
with TNT. We sell TNT to the quarries round here. My
father knew all about it. He showed me how to make fulmi-
nate of mercury, it's a powerful detonator."

Heddy was impressed. "I certainly have come to the
right place to learn about it. You say you sell a lot of ammonium nitrate?"

"Tons of it. Most of the farmers round here use it, I'd
say especially for their oats and barley."

"Have you noticed any larger than usual sale of it?"

"It's funny you should ask that. Bryan Jones was in here the other day. He has a small farm, down Brynberian way. He wanted a lot of the stuff, more than usual. I asked him what he wanted it for. He said he had cleared some land and wanted it for that. I sold it to him. It's none of my business what he does with it. But if you go down that way, I'm damned if you'll see any newly cleared land."

"Is he a good farmer? Does he make his farm pay?"

"I suppose. But only barely. He has had troubles paying his bills. I know that."

Heddy went back to Llwyn House. "We could need a search warrant," she told David after recounting her conversation with Mr. Davies.

* * *

After their long day exploring the length of the cliff path and the rim of the Witch's Cauldron, Van and Ava slept the night through.

In the morning Ava put on the coffee and looked out the window. "Are we really going up the mountain today? It looks like rain," she told her sleepy husband.

Van stretched himself. "Rain? That's what we natives call Welsh sunshine. As my father used to say, 'Pay no attention; just do what you want to do.' It's still good advice. We'll take our rain gear and have another day of healthy exercise, rain or shine."

"Your Pembrokeshire healthy exercise is going to kill me! No, not really. We'll just not sprint up the mountain. OK?"

"I'll take you a different way so we can pass the Wishing Well. We have to take pins."

"Why pins?"

"There's a small cleft in the rocks, always with water in it, into which you throw a pin. The pin is supposed to stick your enemies and spur a spirit to make your wish come true. Something like that. These Welsh superstitions don't always make much sense."

"OK. Two pins. One for you and one for me. I don't like making bad wishes, so I'll just wish for a fairy tale outcome for - well, I won't tell you."

Van smiled. He could guess Ava's fairy tale wish.

After going astray amidst the winding paths through the heather on the mountain slope - it had been a long time since Van had been there - they eventually found the Wishing Well.

"At all wishing wells, Ava, as I'm sure you know, you can't tell your wish to anybody. Then it would never come true!"

Ava looked at Van with a grin. "Hey, my super rational scientist. You sound as if you believe this stuff!"

He laughed. "Well, our Welsh Nanny believed in it when she brought me up here as a baby and wished me well, and look how well I've turned out!"

"Hey, Nanny! Wherever you are!" Ava cried as she threw her pin into the little well, "make our wishes come true!"

They resumed plodding up the mountain in their rain gear. Misty rain was falling. The way was steep as they neared the summit. Van said, "If we tack a bit to the left, we'll come to that little cave I told you about. I've brought a flashlight, so if there is anything to see in there, we'll see it."

They could make out the entrance to the cave as they clambered upward. When close to it, Van exclaimed, "Hello! Look at the footprints around the entrance. They weren't there the last time we were here."

Van stooped down to enter the cave. He turned on his flashlight. "Crikey!" he cried. "Come on in, Ava. Mind your head."

Ava came in and squatted beside Van. "Crikey, indeed!" she gasped. "It's either Treasure Trove or a suitcase atomic bomb."

Van chuckled. "Nanny has made my wish come true! I asked her to find some way that we could do in the bad guys. She's made a good start. If I'm not mistaken, it's the case we saw traces of above Seal Cave. It's about the right size and has sharp corners. And look! That clinches it." Van pointed with his flashlight to a set of D batteries discarded onto the sandy soil of the cave.

"What is it, Van?"

"I can guess, but the only way to know is to open it. Let's drag it out a bit more into the daylight."

In the mouth of the little cave they saw the case had snap locks and straps around it so a person could backpack it. "Someone carried it up here and it's quite a weight," Van said. "They must have thought it worth their time and effort."

Van undid the straps and looked at the snap locks. "They either locked it or they didn't. We can but try," he said, lifting the levers of the locks. The lid loosened. "That's a bit of luck. Here goes," Van continued, opening the lid.

"Well, it sure is something," Ava announced, peering at the switches and dials on the panel that Van had revealed. Van was feeling around the case. "Ha!" he cried, stretching out a long telescoping aerial. "It's definitely some sort of radio." Van looked over the front panel. "Yes. It's a transponder. I'm not going to turn it on yet. I have to think about it."

"OK, my love. Tell me now what a transponder is."

Van continued to examine the panel as he explained the purpose of the equipment. "A transponder, Ava, is a radio that both receives and transmits. This type of transponder, I'm pretty sure, is used to create a private communication channel between two transponders. When this one is turned on, it transmits a signal to the other transponder. That transponder sends back a signal to which the person with this transponder replies with the correct signal. Otherwise no communication is created. You have to have the right return signal. That way both know that it's legit. Do you understand?"

"I think so. You turn it on. The other guy knows you're here. He says 'hot' and you say 'cold'; then each of you knows who the other is and it's OK. Is that it? Sort of like a tennis game."

Van smiled. "I don't know about the tennis game, but you have the idea. Now you can understand why I didn't want to turn it on right away. If and when we turn it on, and have the headphones on, we will hear a security signal. If we don't respond correctly or make no response, they will know we are intruders. For all I know there's a bomb in this thing that would then explode," Van added, not too seriously.

Ava sat down on a nearby rock. "Tell me why it's up here. You said something yesterday about getting better range."

"It's probably communicating out to sea and this is the place to do it from, high up."

"The other guys are in a boat out there?"

"I think so. This transponder, and the one they have, is the way they communicate in private to one another. Much more private than a mobile phone or just simple radio."

"Have I got this right? If we turn it on, they would know someone is here?"

"That's right. As I think about it, and with a bit of luck, we might be able to masquerade as one of them. It would be a gamble. But perhaps not a bad one. Anyone could have found it and simply turned it on, not knowing what it was. They wouldn't know what to say. Probably the thing turns itself off automatically."

"That sounds pretty innocuous."

"It would be, assuming I'm right. If I was at the other end, I really wouldn't know what had happened. Let's give it some thought. If we can do it, that is be in contact with them without arousing suspicion, we could be sitting on a gold mine way to find out what's happening. That's the high side."

"And, if we can't get through, we may have done no damage because they won't know who is at this end. Is that what you are saying, Van?"

"Yes, but we're doing a lot of guess work."

Ava was enthusiastic. "Oh, let's have a go, Van! When we hear their signal, we'll think like mad what the return signal could be. Perhaps it's really simple and we may get lucky."

Van paced up and down at the mouth of the little cave. "I'm just going through our thinking and making sure it makes sense that this is the best thing to do. If we get through, we will hope they suspect nothing. After that, we'll simply leave it here. I can't help thinking that time is going by and that whatever these guys are about to do, they will do soon. I'm pretty sure the queen's visit is a marker for them."

"Doesn't that say we should give it a try, Van?"

"Yes, on balance, I think we should."

They both knelt by the case. Van said, "If I can figure out what to say, I'll do it in my best English accent, without any Americanisms. I'm thinking it could be Major Howe up here and I'm sure his speech is very British."

"Good thinking, Van. I'll take notes. I have my little note-book with me. Take some deep breaths before you start."

Van sat back on his heels and did his best to relax. He continued to examine the front panel of the box. "Here's the power switch," he said, pointing to a swivel switch," and this must be the send button. There are two head-sets. You put one on, Ava. But don't say anything. Bend the mike away from your mouth. As far as we know, all Major Howe's people are men and I will want to make it see I'm alone up here. You OK? "

Ava nodded, "Yes", tense herself,

"Here goes then," and Van hit the power switch. A little red light came on and then turned blue. "OK. We have power," Van said. "Here we go," and he pushed the send button. Two small signal lights began flashing. "It looks as if we are getting through."

There was a pause of about five seconds. The signal lights went steady. They listened on the head phones. Then a male voice said, *"Mary had a little lamb."*

Van and Ava looked anxiously at each other, first with blank looks.

Then Ava's face lit up. "I've got it," she whispered to Van. *"Billy had a grumpy pig."* Say it, Van, say it now."

"Billy had a grumpy pig," Van recited into the mike.

There was another silent pause of five seconds. They hardly dared blink. Then they heard, "Lief here. Sounds like you, Trevor?"

"Goddam!" Van muttered under his breath, hardly believing he was through.

"Yes, I'm up here," Van replied, trying to keep his voice steady.

"We're way out here," Lief said," but your signal is coming through quite well, just a bit muzzy. That moun-tain top spot was a good idea of yours. Are you alone?"

"Yes. There was no need to bring anyone else."

"Good thinking. The more the people, the greater the chance of leaks. We're all set. All that is necessary right now, Trevor, is to confirm the schedule. Climbing that mountain, I'm sure, is not your favorite occupation. So, unless something goes awry, you won't need to be up there again anytime soon, perhaps not at all."

"Thanks," Van said.

"OK. As planned, the dummy run is on, but we'll have to delay it. Without Oscar Flavio we're having trouble with the keel compartments. I'm going to make a quick run back to St. Malo to try to fix the problem. We have to be able to open and then close the compartments properly. We'll be back here in four day's time and that night I want one of your boats here at one thirty in the morning. I gave you the position before; but just to make sure I'll give it you again. This is it in decimals. Write it down. North 52.17393 West 5.05096. Repeat back."

Van repeated the lat and long numbers. Ava had her little notebook out. When she was a teenager, she had taken some shorthand. Although not expert at it, it came in useful now. She wrote down what she'd heard, particularly the numbers.

"OK, Trevor. If there is any change, I'll give you it by normal mobile. No need for anything elaborate, just a change in meeting time and date. Understood?"

"Understood."

"Trevor, about that clumsy Dane of yours who fell off the cliff and drowned. The Boss knows about it and is not amused. No more slip ups. You hear?"

"Yes, Lief. I hear."

"As you know I'm planning on three runs after the dummy run has proved out. They will be on the following three nights. Everything the same, place and time.

We have a lot of stuff to move. You will store the stuff in the cache and leave it there, until the night before the queen's visit. Make sure about it. The two events must coincide. Before your run up the coast, you will secure your boats on the beach in the space under the covering. That was a good idea of yours to do that and leave it empty. Anyone who has been looking will not see any difference. After that you will take the stuff up the coast in your boats during the night. There will be transport vehicles at Ceibwr Bay to take it on. Do you have any questions, Trevor?"

"No, I don't think so. Is that all, Lief?"

"Good luck to you. Over and out."

Van switched the machine off. "Whew!" he exclaimed, wiping beads of sweat off his forehead. "I'm not sure I'm cut out for this type of work. That was nerve wracking. I tried not to say more than I had to."

Van drank from their water bottle. Ava told him. "I'm so proud of you, Van. You were awesome. Just awesome! I made notes in my notebook. I've got the numbers and the dates. Did you understand about the boats? We have to remember every word while it's still fresh in our minds. Let's go through it," and she read back her notes.

"That sounds perfect, Ava. You got it all. You were awesome yourself with that *'Billy had a grumpy pig'*. Thank heavens you were here. I would never have got it."

"It really wasn't difficult, you know, Van. My drowned man had the grumpy pig thing in his pocket. That was because, I'm sure, he didn't trust his memory. He had been up on the cliff above Seal Cave and must have been using this transponder thing up there. So he needed the return signal. *Voilà!* So there it was, lying in my head. They had the same sing-song sound. *Mary had a little lamb, Billy had a grumpy pig.* Piece of cake!"

Van had to laugh. "Some cake, my dear! Amazing! You would be the sideways thinker of the year, if there was such a thing!"

They closed the case and left it in the cave as they had found it. Feeling exhilarated with their success, they swung down the mountain path in the mist and rain, like happy children, to where Van had parked the car on the Cilgwyn road.

Back in the cottage, Van got hold of Heddy, now back in London, on the phone. Using the speaker phone so Ava could chip in and provide details from her notebook, Van told Heddy what had happened.

Heddy was astonished. "You two are something else! You have filled in nearly all the details we need to know on their smuggling. It's amazing. You know, we are taught to not believe intelligence until it is verified, just in case the other side is purposefully deceiving us, like we try to do to them. But I can't see how they could be doing that here. I think they are confident they have this thing taped down. "

"Do you know the man Lief I was talking to?"

"Oh, yes. He's Lief Foss, a Norwegian. His boat is called *Mother Goose*. It's a sea-going yacht, with big powerful engines. It's registered in Copenhagen. We know about it and its travels. You should know, Van, we've picked up a few more messages in the code you broke. Thanks again. Lief has a sister in Oslo. She's in the loop, we're sure. I'll tell you about her later."

"What do you want me to do now?"

"Just hold fast. We'll have a decision session here to figure out what's best to do. I'm pretty sure we'll let the dummy run go through while observing it closely."

* * *

Rhys had Taf by the ear as they sat in the Llwyn Arms over a pint.

"I'm damned if I will sit around any longer while those men steal our lobsters, Taf. I'm sure that's what's happening. Old Thomas the boatman has seen them out there in the early evening. They stay out there for a while, then go back to their cave. After that they come back to the boathouse and put their boats on the grass there. I suppose they think that their supplies and equipment are safe out there at their beach during the night. And they would be - except for us, Taf. If you'll come with me, we'll go out there after midnight and see what we can see."

Taf put down his pint of beer. "Well, now, there's daring of you, Rhys. And what if they have left a man there?"

"I'll take my good old walking stick and conk him on the head!"

"You don't think we should tell our constable about it?"

"No, no. He won't do anything. I heard that Sir James has been to Haverfordwest to tell the people there to let this Major Howe have his way. So we can't expect any help from them. We have to do things for ourselves or else we're stupid buggers who don't know how to tie our own shoe laces. What about it, Taf?"

"Well, now I'm tempted. What would you have me do?"

"We'll take *Daisy*. No lights or anything; just torches, for when we get there. We'll put *Daisy* on a short anchor and you stay with her while I wade ashore. When I find it's safe on the beach, you make sure *Daisy* is good on her line, and come ashore with me. It's going to be calm tonight, so *Daisy* won't be in any danger. Though there are storms forecast for later in the week. The usual storms.

As we know, they happen every year at new moon time in the autumn. How does that sound?"

"Indeed, it is an adventure. I'll have to slip out of the house quietly without the wife hearing me. You can be sure she would have a fry pan on my backside if she knew."

"Mine too, no doubt," Rhys grinned.

Taf finished his pint. As he put down his glass on the table, he gave a good burp and told Rhys, "I hope we don't find another dead man. I've had enough of them!"

Chapter 22

Another Discovery

Rhys and Taf drove the short distance from their homes to the Parrog at midnight. Not a soul was to be seen.

"That's good then, no one knows we are about," Taf said. "My missus was safely in bed and asleep when I left."

"Mine too," Rhys told him.

They walked along the Parrog shore-front to the boathouse and trundled *Daisy* down the slipway in the mist and light rain. There was hardly a breath of wind. Rhys pulled the outboard to life. It was a dark night with a finger nail moon breaking out from behind scattered clouds. Patches of mist floated on the water. Knowing the coast so well, Rhys had no trouble in steering a course for Seal Cave.

"I have brought my new digital camera, Taf. Just in case we find something."

"That's good, as long as the men who may be there don't mind having their portraits taken."

"That's true," Rhys chuckled. "We have to chance it."

They approached Seal Cave cautiously. When 100 yards out, Taf turned on his big torch. They approached closer. Nothing stirred on the beach. "There's either no one there or they are fast asleep."

"We'd best be cautious, Rhys, boy."

"I'll be careful. Put the anchor down. Keep *Daisy* close in."

Rhys had his waist-high waders on. When he got out of the boat the water was only up to his thighs. He had his stick with him and used it to steady himself as he waded ashore over the stones. On the beach he proceeded slowly, keeping the promontory of rock between himself and the cave entrance. He used the torch to light the rocks and stones in front of him. He didn't want to fall or twist his ankle. To his side he saw the mound covered by black polyethylene sheets. The ends of the sheets were held down by large stones placed a foot apart. Rhys reached the promontory and peered around it to the entrance to the cave. He shone his torch here and there and, seeing that nothing stirred, he shone it into the cave itself.

A little way in he could see rubbish on the sandy floor and some upturned boxes. He went nearer. The stones felt different under his feet. He didn't know why. Then he saw what he had expected to see; a big pile of lobster shells. "The buggers," he muttered under his breath. There was a camping stove there and some pots and pans. A pile of emptied food tins was beside the lobster shells. He shone his light further up the cave. The floor rose so that the far end of the cave was above the recent high water marks. Rhys could see small mounds under tarpaulins and some boots and clothing. They had better clear their stuff out, Rhys thought to himself, the highest tides of the year were due.

He had gone far enough. He would go back and bring Taf in with him so they could make a thorough search of the place. He went back to the boat. *Daisy* was secure on her short anchor chain. The two men left her in the little bay.

On their way back to the cave, Rhys lifted a corner of the black polyethylene sheets and shone his light in. There was nothing there! Just poles and planking to keep the sheets up. Otherwise it was empty and no sign that anything had been there.

"That's peculiar, now," he said to Taf.

"They must be planning to put something there, don't you think?"

"I suppose."

Again the stones felt odd to Rhys as they approached the cave entrance. He almost felt he could feel them bounce, like he had sometimes felt when going over small wooden bridges. They examined all the items in the cave. Rhys took photographs of everything including the empty space under the sheets on the beach. They were going to and fro when Taf stumbled over some stones piled near the cave entrance. One fell with a thud.

Taf stopped. "Did you hear that?" he asked Rhys. "That stone made a funny noise, like an echo. I'll try it again."

Taf lifted up a fair sized stone and let it drop. They both listened. Rhys was puzzled. "That is not a usual sound, Taf. Let's try further down the beach. Perhaps it's the cave here catching the sound."

Ten yards further down the beach they dropped big stones. The sounds were quite different. They were what they expected to hear, more a clink than a thud.

"It must be the cave then," Rhys said. "But I've never heard a thing like this. As a boy I used to throw stones a lot."

"The same with me," Taf said, picking up another stone and dropping it and then another and another, then stamping on the stones near the cave.

"Taf, it sounds hollow to me."

"I hear that too. There's something under these stones."

"Here, Taf." Rhys was shining his light down through a crack between some stones near the mouth of the cave, "What do you see?"

"It looks like a board covered with that black sheeting down there. I'll move these stones to have a better look."

Taf lifted a dozen stones. Rhys tapped his heavy stick on the top of what seemed a board. They both heard an unmistakable hollow sound.

"There's a hole under there, Taf. Sounds like a big one to me."

"It isn't natural to have a hole here. The sea would fill it in with just a few tides."

They fell silent. "What's that?" Taf whispered. They were both hearing the distant sounds of an outboard motor.

"Quick, Taf; put the stones back. They may be coming."

They hurried to put the stones back in place. Rhys doused his light. They made their way back to *Daisy* as fast as they could and lifted her anchor. Rhys, looking out toward Newport, dimly saw a boat out by the lobster pots.

"The oars, Taf. Be as quiet as we can."

They put the oars in the rowlocks and, taking small strokes, rowed *Daisy* out of the little bay toward a patch of thick mist. *Daisy* moved forward slowly. They heard distant voices and then a light was shone in their direction. They entered the patch of thick mist.

"Did they see us?" Taf asked anxiously, keeping his voice low.

"Maybe. I don't know. Listen."

They heard voices, but there was no sound of an outboard.

"They seem to be staying with the pots, Taf."

"There's lucky, now," Taf breathed, a little more easily.

"We'll row on, up the coast, Taf. They'll be going into their beach there. When we are far enough away, I'll start the motor and we'll head out to sea and then make our way back. That's the best thing to do."

They rowed on, now pulling strongly on the oars.

"Hey, Taf! We're good at this," Rhys called out.

"Oh, we had that practice when we ran out of petrol, remember?"

Rhys laughed. "I knew that was good for something!"

They rowed on for five minutes. "Let's take a spell, Rhys. I'm puffed," Taf said.

They pulled their oars in.

Taf recovered his wind. "It was good we put the stones back. Think you they will know we've been there?"

"We didn't leave much trace of ourselves. I doubt they will notice anything."

"What do we do now? Shall we tell the constable?"

Rhys didn't think much of that idea. "No, we don't know they are doing anything wrong, except stealing our lobsters. Though that is serious enough! But we couldn't prove it. My opinion is, Taf, that we tell Sir James. He will know better than the constable what is best. Do you agree?"

"Yes, that's best, tell Sir James."

"We'll keep quiet about it until then. You know he's put out that Major Howe should be left alone to do his seal watching?"

"I heard that."

"Yes, Taf, that's the best thing for us to do. Tell Sir James what we've seen and show him the photographs."

Rhys brought their outboard back to life and, made a course out to sea, then back to the boathouse. He brought *Daisy* safely back to the slipway.

Thankfully, both men found their wives more or less still asleep when they crept into their houses. "I had to go to relieve myself," Rhys told his wife. Taf said much the same.

It was only later that the wives found out the truth. Then they were in two minds about whether to give their husbands a good scolding or to join the rest of Newport in hailing them as heroes.

Chapter 23

Review

The Deputy Director of MI5, known as DepD, a brusque and direct man, had called an 8 a.m. meeting. The group was in the same room where Van and Ava had been. They were serious people with serious responsibilities.

"Good morning," DepD greeted them, his face grim. "This is a MI5 restricted meeting. Assets will be informed on a strict as-needed basis. This afternoon you will receive a transcript of this meeting and supporting material. Level of document security is red. Any questions as to security?"

Someone said, "It sounds bloody serious."

"It is. I'll come straight to the point. A domestic terrorist attack is highly likely, the threat level is 'Severe', and we may bump it to 'Critical.' The threat is this: Muslim operatives, identified as Al Qaeda Jihadists, are setting up a strike against our head of state, the queen."

The people around the table were visibly shaken.

"Our intelligence verifies their intention to a very high probability. Our Head and I will be briefing the Buck House people and, later, very possibly, her majesty herself."

DepD sat down at the head of the table. "All right everyone. It is serious, but we've been in serious situations before. It is our lot to live in this particular age and we have to cope with it. Al Qaeda's hostile intentions are well known: to destabilize our political and economic systems and, from there, our western culture. To defeat their designs is our counter-terrorism challenge.

A little history. This is not the first time the queen and the royal family have been targeted. Recall the Jihadist conspiracy against the royal family in 2006. That conspiracy reached the conceptual planning stage, but no further. They had no operational plan. Our counter-terrorism units were successful in aborting the scheme. This new conspiracy also has the queen and other royals as their targets and, in this case, their planning is well advanced, as you are about to learn.

Also recall the recent attack against the Dutch royals. The attack was made by driving a car at speed through the crowd, aiming to crash into the vehicle holding the royals. No royal was hurt, but eight people in the crowd were killed. The people we are dealing with today are, in my estimation, unlikely to resort to anything so haphazard. We must assume their attack will be well planned and will be well executed, if it reaches that stage. That would be their plan A. However, if things go wrong for them, they may have a more reckless plan B in waiting."

The DepD stopped to drink from a glass of water and to look around the room. He had everyone's full attention.

"As I've said, the conspiracy is quite advanced. David Crick and Heddy Stridewell will tell you what we know to date which, I'm happy to say, is considerable.

The Jihadists come from the Near East and are now in this country, no doubt forming up with and training and financing some of our home grown bastards. We know where most of these cells are, embedded in places with high concentrations of Muslims, such as the city of Leicester, where thirty per cent of the population are first and second generation South Asian Muslims. I spot Leicester because we have indicators this new lot may have gone there, following a route from Aberystwyth, where they came ashore, through Shrewsbury, and on to nearby Leicester.

These new people may be fanatic, but they are not simpletons. They have an ingenious scheme. They have inserted themselves in a major smuggling operation and thereby made use of the smuggler's know-how for getting themselves and their stuff into the country and dispersing once here. The smuggling activity provides their transportation and gives them protection and screening for their devilish purpose."

"I imagine the smugglers are being well paid," a man commented.

"Undoubtedly. The two Jihadists started their trip from the Persian Gulf and the bad guys there are swimming in ready cash.

Much of the activity to date has been centered on a small seaside town called - er - ," DepD consulted his notes, "ah, yes, Newport, a small coastal town in Pembrokeshire, southwest Wales. Incidentally the Welsh name for the region is Dyfed. Don't be thrown off, you Anglo-Saxon English people, when you come across it. I must admit this is the first I've heard of this Newport. We think it was chosen because it's an out-of-the-way place, where nothing much happens. That, it now seems, may have been a mistake on their part. They hadn't counted on the curiosity of the people there.

David and Heddy have been in the thick of things. The two of them, with some valuable help from outsiders, have made rapid progress. Be clear in your minds that the conspiracy is two-fold. The first is smuggling drugs and illegals into the country and the second, interwoven with it, but distinct from it in terms of purpose and outcome, is to strike at the royals. The time and place of the planned attack, we think, is during the queen's visit to St. David's cathedral in Pembrokeshire in ten days time. If we can find and arrest them beforehand and nip the whole thing in the bud, we will, of course, do so. But without something radically changing, we can only mount our precautions and defenses. We don't have any time to waste. Each of you, in your own sphere, must give this matter your highest priority. That must be completely understood. The damage done, if they were to be successful, would be monstrous and heart-rending.

All right. David and Heddy. Bring us up to date on what has happened so far."

DepD stepped aside to let David go to the head of the table. "I will give you the big picture, and then let Heddy fill you in.

First, *Security* and *Counter-Terrorism* have been fully briefed about the planned attack. They are on the job. We are in support to them, giving them intelligence of the other side's intentions, capabilities, and actions.

The itinerary of the royal party to St. David's has been published in the Gazette, so it is public knowledge. The train leaves Paddington in the evening. The queen and her immediate party will have a carriage to themselves with sleeping rooms. Attached will be a restaurant car and lounge. Invited guests will occupy other cars of the train and may be invited to the queen's carriage. The train arrives at Fishguard, Pembrokeshire in the early morning.

The queen leaves the train at nine o'clock. The Lord Lieutenant of Pembrokeshire, Sir James Owen, will welcome her to the county and she meets local dignitaries.

Next is the drive to St. David's. Because we fear a car bomb attack, similar to the attack in Oklahoma, the attempted attack in New York, and the IED attacks in Iraq and elsewhere, surveillance and clearance of the route and any vehicles on it are primary considerations.

At St. David's the queen is met by the church dignitaries and enters the cathedral. After the service the queen is escorted outside by the Lord Lieutenant. She will then be presented to the line of people chosen by the county. No more than twenty people, I understand. She may then wish to meet the townspeople making up the crowd.

The Lord Lieutenant and her personal equerry escort her to her car. The line of cars drives through the small town of St. David's and continues on to Haverfordwest, the county town of Pembrokeshire. There she will have luncheon at the County Hall. At about three o'clock she will board the train at Haverfordwest station and return to London.

Working with *Counter-Terrorism* makes me confident about the precautionary measures. They will bring practically every sniffer dog in the country to sniff around southwest Wales and St. David's for explosives. Security will bring the latest detector machines down from London to screen for density differences at the security gates. The new DDD's are the best yet for explosives.

Clearly we fear explosives but, about equally, we fear firearms and sniper fire. The Kratos option will be operative. For those of you who may not be fully aware of Kratos, it is this. To fire at the head and effectively decapitate anyone with strong indications that he or she is a suicide bomber or about to fire a weapon. If someone does fire a weapon - and hopefully misses their target - we have the latest American technology, called *Boomerang*, to locate the actual spot from where the weapon was fired. That means we can see it visually, locate it by radar, or pinpoint its GPS location. *Boomerang* will be mounted on a military patrol car and manned by trained men from the Welsh Regiment.

The customary crowds of people will be lining the streets and there will be flags and bunting everywhere. The local police, supported by others drawn from the region, will be posted in the usual way. Squads of the Royal Welsh Regiment will be the Honor Guard.

There are many points of vulnerability. We think the most likely place for the attack is at St. David's itself - if successful it would be highly symbolic for them - and at any time the queen and other royals mingle with the crowds. About all that can be said is that *Security* lives with this condition day in and day out and have been a hundred per cent successful in keeping the queen and other royals safe.

As the Deputy Director has suggested, they may be planning multiple attacks and *Security* is fully alert to this contingency. Now I will ask Heddy to review events to date."

Heddy took David's place. "I have pictures, so we will close the curtains." She turned on the projector and hooked up her laptop to it. The first slide appeared on the screen.

Slide 1. Photos of Lief and Kari Foss; Sketches of the Jihadists

We have called the illicit organization responsible for the smuggling and bringing the Jihadists into the country, Q. We now think it is based in Norway. It is run efficiently and ruthlessly. A high-up in Q, possibly the boss, is Lief Foss. He was born into a good Oslo family, thirty-four years ago. He has an older sister, Kari Foss, who runs a shipping line out of Oslo. Interpol has no indication that these ships have been involved in smuggling or any illicit activity. But we know she is implicated in the smuggling business.

These photos of Lief and Kari Foss were taken at the inauguration of the new opera house in Oslo to which Kari Foss had contributed generously."

A hand went up in the room. "May we ask questions?"

DepD took the question. "Only about a specific point in the presentation. Anything more general we'll discuss later."

"All right. I just wished to ask, Heddy, whether you are thinking that the shipping line and, being generous and prominent, are a cover for their smuggling?"

"The short answer is 'yes'," Heddy told him. "Hold onto that idea; we'll talk about it later.

Here I want to show you a sketch that a police artist made of Lief Foss. You will see its strong likeness to the photo. The sketches of the other two men were made at the same time, on the basis of a Mrs. Stuart's remembrance of them on the platform at Aberystwyth station. As the sketch of Lief is accurate, we felt the sketches of the other two men were likely to be equally accurate. In addition to our own resources, we sent the sketches to Washington and the CIA were the first to come up with a positive ID. The two men are Abd-Al-Qadir, which means in Arabic, 'Servant of the Powerful' and the other is Faruq, which means, 'Who knows Right from Wrong.' We think these names are cognomens to demonstrate their dedication to the cause. We have not publicized the sketches or the names of the two men. Perhaps the Deputy Director wishes to have a word about that."

DepD walked over to the microphone.

"Publicizing names and sketches is always a matter of judgment. One balances the possible gain of someone identifying the targets against the downside of the targets knowing they have been spotted. Then they will go to ground even deeper. In this case, we have decided, the option of leaving them alone and letting them come forward into the open is best. We know about them and, in due course, we expect to be able to bag the whole lot."

Heddy resumed her presentation with the photo of the first drowned man on the screen.

Slide 2. The corpse of "Claude" at autopsy. Dead by drowning.

"This man, Claude had been recruited by Q. He's a Frenchman. The French police had recently successfully placed a mole, a man named DeBouef, into a French component of Q. We call this group, Q-French. DeBouef infiltrated Claude into Q-French. Claude had been in the rackets in Marseilles and must have seemed to Q-French to have good credentials. However, he had been a police double-agent for some time.

Claude was put on a boat, *Mother Hen*, a seemingly innocuous yacht operating out of St. Malo on the Brittany coast. This boat sailed up to the southwest coast of Wales to be in the vicinity of Newport. Newport is situated on a rugged, lonely coast with only a few farms set back from the tall cliffs. We now know that, probably as a result of *Mother Hen* reconnoitering the coast, that this is the place where Q plans to land a large load of drugs. They have another, larger boat that actually carries the stuff and this larger boat, *Mother Goose*, is the one the two Jihadists were transported in.

Evidently the people on *Mother Hen* began to suspect Claude. He went overboard after, we think, killing a man, probably his guard. He used the pencil method, making use of his training; that is, thrusting the pencil into the man's eye and deep into the brain, and then twisting it around. It's a wholesale lobotomy which, when performed ruthlessly, kills instantly.

The pencil later washed up on Newport Beach. On the pencil Claude had scratched the name of the boat, *Mother Hen*, and the word 'dope.' He did his best to confirm our supposition that the boat was a smuggler.

After the body of the drowned man, Claude, was recovered in Newport Bay, a search of his clothes revealed no ID, not even tags on his clothing. However the Medical Examiner in Milford Haven discovered a scrap of paper with letters in code on it. We think Claude had somehow copied the message and thrust it into his pocket before he went overboard, not knowing what it meant.

Slide 3. Recovered code message.

These were the numbers and letters.

52Y017   04M832   161216   072018   040707 201809 240716 260000

As you see, it is a typical cipher, spelled out in six digit blocks. A Dr. Bentham, now one of our assets, gained a copy of it, actually through a lapse in our security fence. In this case it happened to turn out well, but our security fence simply did not work. That has to be seen to. Remarkably quickly, Dr. Bentham decoded the cipher while we were still struggling with it. Here's the message.

Slide 4. Decoded Message

YM = Yves Mateur. Message reads: *'Newport aware correct Irak'.*"

It's very cryptic. The import of the message, when understood in context, is that Yves Mateur, who was a minor dope carrier for Q, is to be killed. It also says that the boss is aware of what has happened and that everyone needs to sharpen up. We now know, almost certainly, who the boss is, but we are being highly restrictive about it to avoid any chance of warning that person.

We have found other messages in this code. Q communications extend across Europe and into the Near East. For the here and now, we are concerned with the operations in Wales.

Slide 5. The Smuggling Operation

This map shows a location on the Pembrokeshire coast called Seal Cave. Here are a series of photos taken the night before last of the cave and what was found there. How we acquired them is an interesting story that can be told later. We are fairly sure the smugglers have dug a hole in the beach in front of the cave They made it waterproof and covered it over with stones so that it looks like a part of the beach. They are going to use the chamber as a cache for their stuff. Rather remarkably, we know when the smuggling runs are due to be made and other data about their *modus operandi*. Our knowledge is partly due to having turned one of their field agents. I will come to him in a minute. The penetration into their communications is primarily due to Dr. Bentham and his wife. He is a consultant to the FBI in Washington and has worked with Dr. Phillippa Crest, who some of you know, on profiling. We're currently asking Dr. Bentham, a Ph.D. psychologist and a medical doctor, to profile our two Jihadists in order to anticipate their actions and behavior in the various scenarios that may develop. He will consult with our own profilers.

The actions of the two Benthams have been most helpful to us. A second drowned corpse was found in Newport Bay. The corpse was brought ashore by the same two lobster-men who found the first corpse. This corpse had a written jingle on him. This jingle enabled the Bentham's to penetrate their transponder communications. Here is the drowned man, Ernik Kristol, at the time he was brought in.

Slide 6. Pictures of Ernik Kristol when brought in to Parrog beach

Ernik Kristol was a member of a Major Howe's team, that is the smuggling team, and he also had no ID on him when fished out of the sea. The photos were taken by Ava Bentham and have helped to positively identify him. She happened to be on the Parrog beach when the two Welsh lobster-men brought in the corpse. She realized that having photos could be important. She also realized the importance of handing over the corpse to the police and not giving anyone access to it before it could be examined. Police are few and far between there and it would take time for them to appear.

A part of this story has been published in articles in the Western Mail and these articles will be attached to your transcripts. I cannot resist, if the Deputy Director will forgive me, to call your attention to the defense of the corpse by Ava Bentham against three of the smugglers. She was approached by these three men in a threatening manner. Ava Bentham had been a softball player in her college days in America. Now she picked up and threw a stone with such force, speed, and accuracy as to half kill the lead man attacking her. Don't ever underrate us, you men!

Slide 7. Pictures of Sir James Owen and butler Robert Heath

Now we turn to the Lord Lieutenant of Pembrokeshire, Sir James Owen, who has become an important player in the situation. It wasn't any of his doing. But since he has found himself involved, far beyond his normal activities as Lord Lieutenant of the county, he has been another vital cog in our counter-measures.

I am pairing these two men together because they form a sub-team for us.

Robert Heath had been recruited by Q-Brit, a sub-division of Q.

I digress for a moment to tell you about Q-Brit. We are learning about it by interrogating one of their operatives, a man called Oscar Flavio. He is in our custody. We know where their safe house is, a somewhat seedy hotel near Paddington station, and that a senior operative of Q-Brit is a Mark England. Q-Brit is a primary target for us. We have infiltrated it by means of a Robert Heath, the butler to Sir James Owen.

Robert Heath had been dishonorably discharged from the Royal Welsh Regiment on, what now seems, a bogus charge. He was bitter about it. Q-Brit learned of him and, rather cleverly, had him employed as a butler to Sir James Owen, the Lord Lieutenant. Heath was now in a position to likely know about any discovery of the smuggling operation and provide information concerning the queen's visit. He reported back to Q-Brit by mobile phone, his handler being a man called Derek. We have located Derek in the safe house near Paddington.

Robert Heath's conscience was troubling him, in part due to his fair treatment by Sir James Owen, himself a retired brigadier of the Royal Welsh Regiment and, perhaps in greater part, to his realization that he was being used in a plot against the queen. Now Heath is 'turned.' He is feeding Q-Brit innocuous information and learning from them items of their intentions and activities. David has been supervising the handling of this valuable double-agent.

Robert Heath has stayed in the employ of Sir James as butler, valet, chauffeur, handyman, etc. and the other side seems to be accepting him as a genuine asset for them and have suggested he play a role in the attack against the queen, though what that would be they have not told him, as yet. However, they have wanted him to describe some back roads in the county. We are not sure what the significance of that is."

Heddy paused and looked around the room. "There is considerable detail that I have not mentioned. You will find many of these details added to the transcript of this meeting that you will receive." Heddy turned to the DepD. "Sir, may I hand it back to you?"

The Deputy Director came to the head of the table.

"As you can all see, we are on top of this thing and I want us to remain there. We need strong teamwork to do that. The code name for our counter-terrorism operation is *Tom Thumb*. The plum we are going to pull out is the whole Q operation.

We will meet again at four o'clock this afternoon for questions, discussion, and planning. Department Heads will talk with their immediate staff concerning the measures they will employ to maximize the outcome. The Liaison Group will work with the Navy, Coast Guard, and Customs and Excise, on their dispositions to round up the other side's vessels when told to do so. The Liaison Group will also work with the Pembrokeshire Constabulary and others in securing the arrest of any and all Q-Brit people on the ground in Wales.

You, Heddy, will organize the activities of the Metropolitan Police here with respect to the safe house at Surrey Gardens and the people there. I will say again, security must be absolute. If it is, they will fall into our trap as innocent babes in the woods. Tom Thumb will have pulled out the plum! That is all."

In the later meeting that day, Heddy briefed the group on the surveillance of Q-Brit and their safe house. Her team had been planted in an opposite building. Equipped with the latest in visual, auditory, phone, and electronic snooping gear, they recorded a minute by minute account of the comings and goings and who said what to whom.

Heddy almost felt sorry for the Q-Brits. They had taken the simple precautions that any clandestine group does, but clearly had no idea their every action, utterance, and intimacy was being revealed to MI5. So much the worse for them. They deserved everything that was coming to them, the treacherous bastards. She had made certain the evidence against them was so incontrovertible that they would spend the rest of their lives in prison.

The knowledge they had gained would allow MI5 and the police to program their counter-terrorism maneuvers to maximum effect when the time came to act.

A small gap in their intelligence was the use by the other side of the code name, *Voltaire*. It was a worry. Whoever or whatever *Voltaire* was, it could be used by them in Wales. That was all they had learned.

Chapter 24

Foresights

Heddy reached her office early in the morning on the day after the MI5 meetings. She took care of the routine stuff, examined her e-mail, and sat back with a cup of coffee. Her phone rang. It was a standard call, unscrambled. She had left her card with Mr. Davies of the Farm Store at Crymych and asked him to call if anything unusual happened. His name and number came up on the phone panel. "Good morning, Mr. Davies."

"Ms. Stridewell, we've had a burglary here," Mr. Davies said in his strong Welsh accent.

"Oh, I'm sorry. I hope it wasn't too serious."

"That's just it, it wasn't serious. They took very little. It's what they took is why I'm phoning you."

"Hold on, Mr. Davies. Do you mind if I record this conversation?"

"No, no, not at all. You remember I told you we sold explosives to quarries? It wasn't that we were being careless about it. The two of them, they left two sets of footprints in the mud by the outer fence, broke in during the night. They cut through the second fencing around the TNT and the detonators. They had good tools to do that cutting. The alarm went off and the police arrived in about ten minutes. But it was too late. They had gone."

"What did they get?"

"Just one box; that is six charges and six detonators. They could have taken much more, but they didn't. That seems strange to me."

Heddy's brain went into overdrive. Why? Because that was all they needed, enough for their bomb. Goddam!

"Is there any indication who they were, Mr. Davies?"

"No, no indeed. They left no finger prints, the police tell me. The only thing I could think of was that a stranger to these parts was in here looking around a couple of days ago, a swarthy man with an accent. Then he bought a portable electric drill, a big one. He paid in cash with fifty pound notes. It's just that we don't see many men like that down here. I gave the police a description of him, but they are saying the robbery could have been done by anybody or some lads out for a prank."

Heddy felt a sense of urgency. They had to be making a bomb. Maybe they wanted a hefty drill to prepare a car to hold explosives and to do the wiring for the detonator. Time was running out. They had less than a week before the queen's visit to St. David's. Some persons at MI5 were advising postponing the visit. But the queen had said, "I refuse to be deterred from carrying out my duties."

"All right, Mr. Davies. Hold tight. It's nine-thirty now. I should be with you by about five o'clock this evening. Don't talk about this to anyone. OK?"

Heddy hurried down the corridor to David's office. She had an appointment to see him later that morning to be briefed on project status; but now she burst in. David looked up. "All right, Ms. Fireball. It must be important."

"David, they are assembling an ANFO bomb. I'm sure of it. They have detonators and the trigger explosive and, and I bet they have the ammonium nitrate, too."

David listened to what Mr. Davies had told her, then, without pause, phoned DepD. After telling him the news, David listened intently; then put the phone down.

"All right, Heddy. Whatever you or I think, DepD remains adamant we stay under cover and let them remain confident we know little to nothing about them. London is fine for now. You've done a good job. Congratulations again."

"Thanks. But the job is only half done. We've got to get into them in Wales."

"Exactly. Get yourself down there and see what you can find out. Listen. Major Howe and his gang are still at the Red Dragon in Newport. Whatever you do, don't raise their suspicions. Stay somewhere else. Now, about the nitrate. There's that farmer you told me about. You should visit him. Probably he's just a go-between."

"Yes," Heddy flipped through her notebook, "Bryan Jones at Brynberian."

"See what you can get out of him."

Heddy had risen and was by the door, about to leave.

"Wait a minute, Heddy. Let me fill you in some more. I want you to be in the know so you can make better sense of whatever you find out. We are continuing to intercept their communications traffic. We've confirmed that the boss of Q is Kari Foss in Oslo. You remember we have Ava Bentham to thank for first spotting that Irak spelled backwards is Kari."

"Van and Ava make a counter-terrorism squad all on
their own," Heddy commented. "Kari - Irak. I suppose
it amused her, but not too smart."

"True. In any event Kari Foss has been hitting the air
waves to Lief about being drawn into the terrorist crowd.
She tells him they are in the smuggling business, not aid-
ing and abetting terrorists. She is blaming him for getting them involved. So there's some falling out there.
Kari Foss had threatened to pull out of the arrangement
with the Jihadists and betray them to us. That's a little
amusing. Her caution was trumped by money. Her price
to the Jihadists to stay in the game was two million dollars. They've paid up."

"Well, I'll be gobsmacked!" Heddy exclaimed. "Two
million dollars for the queen's life!"

"Believe it," David told her. "Their smuggling effort,
that is to bring the stuff ashore and begin transporting it to
cities, is scheduled for the night preceding the queen's visit
to St. David's. That will be when the royal party is on the
train to Fishguard. They are thinking our security will be
occupying themselves with the queen's visit and, therefore,
less likely to be alert to their smuggling operation and that
we won't be around to intercept them. That's what we want
them to believe and DepD won't give that up."

"OK. I get the message."

"The other side has become increasingly careless.
That's why DepD believes they suspect nothing and that
we're really going to get them - hook, line, and sinker.
Interpol has been working with the police forces of
the countries involved. We can get the whole shooting
match, Heddy!"

"That's great!"

"Mark England of Q-Brit has been using an open mobile phone. God knows what he's thinking. Our guess

about Leicester has held up. We know they bought train tickets to go there from Aberystwyth. That's been their home base. We know they've been recruiting there. Faruq and the other guy came in with a lot of money, so it's not been difficult; and they have that crazy Iman there promising seventy-two virgins for martyrs. No doubt the ordinary Muslim is OK, but they sure have a nutty fringe. I suppose that could be said for all religions, but we are dealing with this one.

Another source has been Oscar Flavio. The interrogators have done well with him. He started by telling them: *'You torture me - I don't speak - have a good time. You kill me - OK - have another good time.'* Some character, eh?"

"So how did our people break through?"

"By conversation. It turned out that Oscar comes from an old Serbian family, very traditional in its thinking and politics. Oscar would like to see their monarchy restored. That was the opening. Our people gave him proofs that what he had done was to facilitate an attack on our queen. That horrified him! He spilled all the beans he had, including everything we needed to know about the boat, *Mother Goose*. By the way, they conceal the drugs in compartments in the keel of the boat, only accessible from the outside. Oscar confirmed what we had learned from the transponder intercept made by Van and Ava."

"These people go to a lot of trouble."

"Yes - and successfully up to now. We are sure they have moved tons of stuff by *Mother Goose*. In any event, Heddy, the upshot is that we know their schedule. They will do their dummy run the night after next. You will be among the observers along with Hedrick Lines, the fellow who has been helping you at Surrey Gardens. He'll contact you."

"Good. I like him."

"Fine. In the following three nights they will transport their bulk stuff and stash it in the cache they've dug in the beach at Seal Cave. On the night before the queen's visit to St. David's, they will transfer the stuff in a run up the coast in their rubber boats and transfer it into waiting ground transport at Ceibwr Bay. Any questions?"

"Oh, about two hundred! But I'm anxious to get going to South Wales and talk to Mr. Davies."

"I'm sure you are. Get yourself down there and learn all you can. Go to St. David's and scope it for a car bomb or other attack. Security has done it, but they're not infallible. Where could they put a bomb where it could hit the queen? What else might they do? Give me your own assessment of that."

Heddy had a 270 mile drive in front of her and that distance always seems longer in Britain than elsewhere. Getting onto the westbound M4 out of central London was slow going. She was impatient and cursed the traffic.

Once past Reading, her pace picked up. The miles spun away beneath her wheels. She crossed over the Severn on the new bridge and stayed with the M4, passing the major cities of South Wales: Newport, Cardiff, and Swansea. She stopped for petrol at a filling station, had a pee and a bite to eat before going on to Carmarthen, hurrying all the way. One side of her knew that hurrying did no particular good, but it was some comfort to her feelings that she was doing all she could as fast as she could.

She picked up the A40 road leading on toward Haverfordwest. She checked her watch. She was making good time. Following her GPS she turned off onto the country road A478 and went through the town of Llandissilio and thence curved around the east side of the high moors of the windswept Preseli Mountains. She arrived in Crymych just as the church clock struck five. "Hey! Not bad!" she said aloud.

Heddy was almost certain her hunch would be right, and it was. Mr. Davies had no trouble in picking out Faruq from the two sketches the police artist had made.

"Yes, that's him. No doubt about it."

"Thank you. Now I must ask you not to tell anyone about this identification, not even the police."

"Oh, yes! Don't worry yourself," he assured her. "You cannot explain anything to me?"

"No. I'm sorry, Mr. Davies. You'll just have to be patient. In due course your contribution to this important case will receive full recognition. Now, Mr. Davies, can you advise me where to stay near here and have dinner?"

"Oh, yes. I will phone the Salutation Inn at Felindre Farchog to see if they have a room. They have good food, too." Mr. Davies used his mobile phone, speaking in Welsh. "There, Ms. Stridewell, you have a nice room waiting for you."

"Where is this inn?"

"Oh, no distance at all and simple to find. Just continue on this road to the sign for Llanfair-Nant-Gwyn, turn left and continue on to Eglwyswrw until you come to the big road coming down from Cardigan. You turn left there and soon enough you come to Felindre Farchog at the bottom of a hill. A very nice place. Quite modern now. Gwarw Denley is the lady there. Oh, a lovely lady!"

As Mr. Davies spoke the Welsh names, his accent became more and more Welsh. Heddy's English brain was reeling. Thank heavens for her GPS. With its help she managed to find her way along the lonely high roads of the moors and the narrow high-hedged roads of the valleys. She was rewarded by a fine dinner and a soft bed to curl up in.

She told her anxious brain to stop and, after a time, it did.

At breakfast the next morning, Heddy asked Gwarw Denley whether she knew of a Bryan Jones at Brynberian.

"Oh, yes! He's a bit of a character is Bryan. He spends a bit too much on his beer and whisky and never seems to have a penny to his name. He gave me a rubber check once. It bounced at the bank, as I suspected it would. But it's hard not to like him and it's sad his wife died. She made the best Welsh cakes. Is it that you wish to see him?"

"Yes. I have some business to do with him. But I don't know where his farm is."

"Not far, not far at all. I have a map and will show you where it is."

Heddy's trusty GPS got her there after a couple of wrong turns along the lanes. She found Bryan Jones in his cow barn. She had her mini digital recorder in the pocket of her jacket and turned it on. She told him she had been talking to Mr. Davies at Crymych.

Bryan Jones exclaimed, "There's a thing for you, now; stealing explosives from Mr. Davies. We'd all better look out!" and Bryan Jones laughed heartily. "Anyhow it's not the hydrogen bomb they stole!"

"Have you any idea why someone should do that?"

"No doubt about it! They will go fishing!"

"Fishing?" Heddy was incredulous.

"Now, I don't say I have ever done it, see. It started during the war, with the Home Guard. They had these hand grenades and food was scarce. So they threw the hand grenades into the river, where there's a pool with fish in it. The fish are trout too, you know. Bang! The trout are stunned and it's simple to gather them in and then eat them or sell them. They brought a good price, too! That's what my father told me. Oh, yes! It still happens. They'll make their bombs from what they stole from Mr. Davies and have fish for supper."

"That's very interesting, Mr. Jones. I didn't tell you before, but I'm from the police in London and I'm interested in people getting hold of explosives when they have no right to them. Mr. Davies told me you have bought a fair amount of fertilizer."

"Oh, yes. Indeed I have. To put on my land, not to make bombs like that fellow in America did. I wouldn't know how to do that."

"Were you going to use it yourself?"

"Some of it, yes."

"Some of it?"

"That's how it was. This foreigner came here with a story about buying a farm in the south of the county and wanting to fertilize the land. But he had to do it on the quiet because of some legal thing. It didn't make much sense to me. Then he said, if I would buy the stuff he would give me double the price as long as I didn't say anything about it. So I bought the nitrate from Mr. Davies and sure enough this man paid me twice the price, in cash, too. I did nothing wrong, it was a fair deal, and I'm not so rich as to turn down an easy bit of business like that."

Heddy showed him the sketches of the two Jihadists. Bryan Jones recognized Faruq immediately. "That's one of them. He was the talker and making the deal with me. The other just kept quiet."

"They came back to pick up the stuff?"

"Oh, yes. I had to leave a message at the phone number they gave me. But I knew the number, the Red Dragon in Newport. So that was no secret for me."

"Then they came to pick up the stuff?"

"Yes, in a van they had. I helped them load it aboard, seeing as how they had paid me. Fifteen bags it was."

"How much is in a bag?"

"Fifty pounds, close to. They have it in kilograms now. Twenty something kilograms, I think."

"Did they say where they were taking it?"

"I think they said the farm was in the south; nothing more."

Heddy gave him her card and asked him to tell her if anything else happened and, after thanking him, drove out of the farmyard picking up splashes of cow dung as she went.

She returned to the Salutation Inn and phoned David. "They have seven to eight hundred pounds of ammonium nitrate, David."

"Good work. If they detonate it, it would make an awful big bang. I'll let DepD know."

"David, what do you think I should do now? I thought of swinging by Van and Ava's cottage in case they have anything new and then drop in at Llwyn House."

"Sounds good. Do that."

Chapter 25

A Rush of Events

The preparations being made at Llwyn House remained frantic. Megan Lloyd and her maids were going through the large house, cleaning and sprucing up everything as fast as they could.

A Floor Management company had arrived to take care of the floors and the carpets on them. A plumber was dealing with some recalcitrant drains. Electricians were stringing wires for the outside lights and the marquee. James circled around the activity, trying to keep out of the way.

Laura had taken over a space in James' study as their Command Center and brought in a bright young woman from London, Penny Williams. Penny normally handled publicity appearances for Laura in connection with her books. Now, joining forces with Laura, she was keeping track of the people coming and going, the scheduling of who was doing what when, the laying on of the afternoon Estate Party the day before the queen's visit, and the multitudinous particulars of the queen's visit and the subsequent fete at Llwyn House.

Men from London, accompanied by the county police from Haverfordwest, arrived in black cars. A senior man confirmed that the princes, accompanied by their group, would be visiting Llwyn House in the afternoon and evening of the day of the queen's visit to St. David's.

The men had to be shown around the house and grounds. Penny Williams and Megan Lloyd acted as their guides for the house and Robert Heath for the grounds, the buildings behind big house, the garages, and the old stables.

The senior man remained with James and Laura in the study. "Following our usual practice, Sir James, we'll sweep the grounds and buildings. All outside personnel, such as those putting up the marquee and those serving in it, will have security checks run on them. We will have four security personnel here for as long as the royals are present. We believe the risk of some form of attack happening somewhere is 'severe', though, of course, it may not be here."

"Let's hope it isn't," James said, with some feeling.

"Quite so. It would be best if, in this world of ours, there was no threat of attack and no attacks at all, as I'm sure you'd agree. But we must take precautions. What we ask of you is to be cooperative in whatever is required."

The Chief Inspector from Haverfordwest said they would have two cars and eight police there from headquarters, as well as a dozen men from the local constabularies on the road. They would be around the lodge and elsewhere for crowd and traffic control.

"The people around here will be very curious to see

what's happening, Sir James. We can be sure of that. We'll do our best to keep them off the grounds."

When the men had left, Laura plonked herself down on a sofa and exclaimed, somewhere between a gasp and a moan, "James, we're in for it!"

"God, I hope we can manage. This is growing more like a military operation everyday!"

"No faint hearts, James. We're going to do it. I've done what I can to help Slippery Sue, the parlor maid, in the dining room. I have taught her she must walk more slowly and I've bought her a pair of rubber sole shoes to rein in her skating on the parquet floor. Having solved that problem, everything else will be simple! I hope," she laughed.

"You're a wonder!" James cried. He fell down beside her. She turned toward him and closed her body to his. She didn't say anything, just opened her lips. She drew his head toward her. They kissed. Suddenly, out of the well-mannered, usually restrained, body of Sir James Owen, there erupted a burst of energy. He flung his arms around her and smothered her face with kisses and caresses. She returned them, both of them releasing their tensions in what, as Laura thought, a joyous release of the affection that had been growing between them.

But James pushed her away. He covered his face in his hands and, with tears streaming down his cheeks, sobbed, "Oh, God! Oh, God! Forgive me, forgive me."

Laura tried to comfort him, stroking his head, finding one of his hands and clasping it. "There is nothing to forgive, James."

James found his handkerchief and blew his nose.

"Oh, Laura, how I wish that was true."

"James, James. There's nothing that bad. Truly."

"Oh, yes, there is. I...I...I... "

James could hardly speak.

"Yes, James ... "

"I killed my wife, Eira. I killed her, Laura. I know it. And I won't kill another. I won't kill you. You mustn't let me," and sobs again wracked his body.

Laura took him into her arms. "James, stop. Please stop. You can tell me. I promise, you can tell me. Whatever it is, you can tell me."

James slowly brought himself together.

"Eira was younger than I, and still young enough to be pregnant. We had one child, a daughter. Yes, we're estranged, ever since Eira's death. I - I've tried ... but ... "

"I'm sure you have ... "

"We were in Uganda. I was a military attaché there for a short time. Complications appeared in the pregnancy. Some awful infection when she was at the end of her first trimester. The infection spread from the baby to Eira. It all happened so quickly. The medical people there were just not up to it. I flew back from Brussels where I'd been at a NATO meeting. I arrived on the day the baby died inside her, and the next day Eira died."

Laura held his hand tightly.

"But how could that be your fault? Do you blame yourself for taking Eira with you to Uganda?"

"No. She wanted to come. She liked adventure. Nothing much stopped her."

"So what was it then?"

James got up and walked away. Standing alone, looking as if the weight of the cosmos was crushing him, he told Laura, "I had - I still have - herpes."

James knees buckled. He knelt on the floor. His head hung low. "I betrayed our marriage vows. I betrayed Eira. I had sex with a prostitute when I was away from her. The usual story. Too much to drink. Other men doing it. I did not know I was infected. There were no symptoms. But the virus had got into me. I gave it to Eira. Usually that's not serious. But it is when a woman is pregnant. The virus goes everywhere, into the baby, and infects it. That's what happened. Eira and the baby died. I had killed them. It's no use. I killed them."

Laura knelt beside him and they cried together.

"It's all over, Laura. You should go. I have been at great fault to have you here."

Laura struggled to her feet. "Give me your hands again, James, and stand up."

James slowly came to a standing position.

"James, you invited me here and, if you will let me, I will stay and we will bear your burden together. I love you. It's not a girlish fancy, but a deep down true feeling as a woman, in my bones as much as in my head. I believe - no, I'm sure - we have the combined strength to weather the storm that is going on inside you and trying to wreck your life. I cannot speak for Eira but, from what I know of her already, she loved you and would not wish you to live out your days alone and in bitter guilt. I feel a kinship to her. She was your woman and I wish to become your woman."

It was good they didn't have to dwell on it or analyze it. They were too busy. They were partners now and their mutual understanding and affection grew from doing the small everyday things together and from tackling the hectic myriad of problems, great and small, that had descended on them.

Chapter 26

The Meaning of Voltaire

Having phoned Van and Ava and received an invitation to lunch, Heddy drove to their mountain-side cottage. It was another fine day and the view over the bay was sparkling with sunshine.

"Let's eat outside," Ava announced. "You two can clean off the table on the patio. We'll have salmon for lunch."

Mr. Browne had set aside steaks for her from a locally caught salmon. The people in the grocery could hardly take their eyes off Ava. A young girl in a pretty dress asked her for her autograph. Mr. Browne could not do enough for her. "The salmon was only caught yesterday, Mrs. Bentham. It's an honor for me to have it for you. Please accept it as a tribute to your bravery." The people nearby, a small crowd by now, burst out clapping.

"You are going to enter Pembrokeshire mythology at this rate," Van chuckled.

"The people down here are something else. I love them," Ava declared. "They are quick onto anything and are as generous as they come. If you want an answer to anything, they will tell you, true or not; and they joke and laugh and drink enough beer to fill the bay."

Van began to laugh. "I have a memory. When I was a boy, down from my English school here, and thinking myself very smart and superior, I was helping a carpenter and other men put up a shed. The carpenter picked up his level and declared, 'My God now, I have lost the bubble. Van, boy, go and ask around and see if any of the men has seen my bubble.' All the men played up to the joke being pulled on me. It was hilarious for them. It took me down the peg or two I needed, and taught me that I didn't know everything. A useful lesson in life, especially for a smart-ass kid. Someone at last helped me out of my misery and, when the work was done, they took me to the Llwyn Arms and slipped me a beer or two, even though I must have been years under-age."

They finished the salmon steaks and turned to the summer pudding with whipped cream that Myfanwy of the Red Dragon had given Ava. "And I only had to throw one pitch!" Ava exclaimed. Ava had never had an English summer pudding and declared it even better than a trifle, which it resembles.

Over their coffees Van asked Heddy whether she could share anything new about the smuggling or the queen's visit.

"Frankly, Van, we've all been warned not to say anything to anybody and I have to respect that."

"Of course," Van nodded.

"However, I rather suspect you may be able to help me with something. My question is: why should someone or something be called Voltaire?"

"That's a new one on me. I don't think I have ever known or heard of a person with that name."

"Well, that French writer had that name. Tell me about him. Why did he have that name?"

Ava sank back in her deck chair. "Look out, Heddy, you are about to be deluged. Van is quite the scholar on French history!"

"It's all right, Heddy," Van assured her. "You have asked a sensible question and I'll give you a sensible answer."

"OK. But spare me. I was never any good at French in school and I must have skipped the class on Voltaire. All I know is that he wrote Candide and Leonard Bernstein set it to music to make a delightful musical. I saw the show."

"There you are!" Van cried. "You do know something about the man. The show, and the play it's drawn from, is a satire on the laws and practices of his day. Voltaire was continually belittling their sacred cows and pricking their hot air balloons. The French aristocracy couldn't stand him. They had him shut up in the Bastille prison. It gave him time to write one of his more pointed plays. But you asked about his name. He invented it himself! His real name was François-Marie Arouet. He decided that name wasn't good enough for his brilliant self. He wanted a name to match the caustic daring of his speech and writing.

There are many theories about the name and how it came about and many people have puzzled over it. Rather than get bogged down in all that, I'll tell you what I make of the name.

Any interpretation of French is always chancy because many words have multiple meanings. However, *vol* most often means flight, that is, flight in the air. Forget about the *t* and come to *aire*. *Aire* means a place. So we have a place of flight. If you broaden the meaning of a place, it can mean a person. So we have a place for flight or a flying person. Much the same interpretation comes from dropping the last e and coming to *air*, the same word as in English. So, in one way or another, we have flight through the air. I think Voltaire thought of himself as a bolt from heaven, though he was no believer in such things," Van chuckled.

"Wait a moment," Heddy cried. "Voltaire could mean flight through the air?"

"Yes, it could, with a bit of imagination."

"Jesus Christ! I don't think we have thought of that yet, but we should. Goddammit, we should!"

"What's this all about, Heddy?"

"First of all, Van, you may have been a bloody genius all over again. I have to let you in on this, in spite of the Deputy Director. The word *Voltaire* has turned up in their communication traffic. It has been very difficult to even guess what it refers to. Now you have suggested it may mean an aerial attack."

"I have?"

"Well, sort of. We will have to empty the airspace around St. David's."

"Heddy!" Van cried, "It's a very thin thread to go from Voltaire to an aerial attack. Wait, let's go through this again. Ava, you've been listening, what do you think?"

"I would say, dear, you've given up pure reason and come to play in my backyard, putting two and two together and coming up with any number you like. On the other hand, your intuition may be dead on, Heddy. After all, they do have this attack planned. Right?"

Heddy had sat back. "Damn it, it doesn't fit together. They would have to have a big plane to move a ton of explosives. Ava, you could be right. We may be just conjuring stuff out of thin air."

Van chuckled, "There's that *air* again, thin or not. I'll tell you what. Voltaire is a French name. Somewhere along the way, David suggested I look into the French connection. I could ask my friends in *La Sûreté* what they think it could possibly refer to."

Heddy thought it a good idea. "Please follow up. But you'll have to wait until I can get you official clearance to talk to them. Even in a case like this, we have our bloody bureaucracy to go through. You will excuse me. I have to make phone calls."

Heddy rose from the table and found her scrambler phone. Van and Ava could hear: "yes, an aerial attack … we can't rule it out … no, as I told you, they have the makings of a big, I mean big, ammonium nitrate bomb … tell David … it's the primary risk, I'm sure … "

Heddy left. Van was frustrated that he had to wait before he could talk with his pals at *La Sûreté*. On the other hand he didn't know who to talk to about the case. He reckoned it could hold for a day or two without harm. That's what he thought. He got up from the table.

"Hey, Ava. What about driving up the coast and see if we can catch some shrimp in Ceibwr Bay?"

"Would I have to kneel again?"

"Absolutely!"

Chapter 27

The Dummy Run

Lief was angry. Trevor Howe must have been drinking too much and the damn man needed to be on top of his game. In the clear, Trevor had asked for instructions. Lief had told him they were following their schedule.

"What damned schedule, Lief?"

"The one I gave you, on the trans."

"That's news to me. We can't wait around forever, Lief."

"Jesus Christ! Get up the mountain and talk to me on the transponder from there."

Trevor said, "fuck you" under his breath, but plodded up the mountain. He found the cave all right and saw the many footprints around it. He looked inside. The transponder was gone. Shit!

* * *

Actually he was only just too late. Some boys from the Gwaun valley, a soccer team, had run up the desolate eastern side of the mountain on a training run with their coach. They explored around and came across the box in the little cave. They shouted to their coach to come and have a look. He opened the lid and could figure out it was a radio. But why up there?

"We'll take it down and show it to the police in Fishguard," he told the boys.

The coach had it in his house that evening. His friend had an appliance shop in Fishguard and the coach invited him to come round and have a look. They opened the lid.

"It's a radio of some sort all right, but nothing ordinary," his friend said.

"Shall we turn it on?" the coach asked.

"You found it, so I don't see why not. We'll turn it on and listen on the headphones."

They flipped the switches and then, very faintly, they heard, "*Mary had a little lamb*."

The coach's friend sat up. "Did you hear that? There's a surprise for you. It must be a call sign of some sort."

"I am thinking to take it to the police tomorrow. I don't want to be accused of stealing it."

"No, indeed."

The next day the police at Fishguard called the Navy at Milford Haven. They sent up a technician. He told them it was a radio transponder. "I'll take it back to Milford. The people there will know better than I what it is."

That's how it was that the Intelligence Division at the Admiralty contacted MI5 and that David now had his technicians analyzing the equipment. They even raised some latent finger prints from it, those of Major Trevor Howe.

* * *

Trevor Howe had to resort to a mobile phone to talk to Lief. Now, fully alerted to Q's phone traffic, MI5 was happily listening in.

"The transponder has gone, Lief."

"What?" Lief cried.

"It's gone."

"What do you mean, gone? Somebody took it?"

"They must have done. Not that it would do them much good."

"*Faen!* (Devil). But you were talking with me on the transponder a few days back."

"We've talked two or three times, Lief. What's all this about?"

"*Helvete!* (Hell! Lief was regressing to his native Norwegian.) "I may have talked to someone else. I don't know. It could have been one of your men. Who knew the code?"

"I don't really know. Perhaps all of them. They were amused by it."

Lief did not reply at once. He was burning up. "If things go wrong, Trevor, we'll know who to blame. Listen, we'll go forward as planned. The dummy run will be tonight. I'll come ashore and speak with you. Things had better go right! It's your head, Trevor."

Lief disconnected, muttering to himself, "That fucking idiot with his superior English bullshit."

* * *

They were a party of five secreting themselves in an undercut ledge on top of the cliffs above Seal Cave. Be-

sides Heddy and Hedrick from MI5, a police inspector
from Haverfordwest, and a Customs and Excise man,
who worked closely with the navy and coastguard, were
there. Van was with them.   He would act as their guide.
Hedrick had equipped them all with night vision goggles
and he was going to shoot video through a night lens.

They had come there in the afternoon, walking the
cliff path like hikers, before disappearing into their hiding place.   In the interests of secrecy they had not ap-
prised local officials or anyone else of what was happening.   They had just warned Rhys and Taf to stay away.

Hedrick had stressed they had to be utterly unknown
to the people on the beach. They were all wearing dark
clothing and had blackened their faces once they arrived
over Seal Cave.   Van warned them about the deceptive
lip of the cliffs and the importance of not loosening any
stones or dirt to fall down toward Seal Cave.

There was a slight wind and a waning crescent moon
that evening, large enough still to give a fair bit of light.
Soon there would be a new moon and the tides would be
high. Van had noted it would be a "spring" tide, the highest tide that autumn. A funneling effect occurs between
England and Ireland for the tides coming in from the Atlantic. This results in the southwest Welsh coast having
among the highest spring tides in the world. With a good
westerly wind the tide could be 30 feet. The water could
come to and even over the causeway and low bridge at
the mouth of the Nevern river estuary. Sightseers came
there to see it.

Chatting about it in low voices helped to pass the time.
But they didn't have to wait long for the action to start.

Van was looking over the bay toward the boathouse.
He saw one of the rubber boats being launched. It seemed
to be the only one there.

The low boat with its powerful outboard made short work of reaching Seal Cave. Van could see Major Howe in it and another man. They pulled up on the stony beach of Seal Cave. Major Howe got out. The boat turned around and put out to sea with two men aboard. "It's what I saw them doing before, Hedrick," Van said. "They must be going out to rendezvous with whoever is out there. They're making at least 15 knots in that thing. They'll soon be over the horizon. I would guess they'll be back in less than two hours."

As Major Howe walked up the beach, Van could see men emerging from the cave. They greeted each other as dusk descended on the scene. Major Howe evidently gave some orders and the men began picking up and moving the stones back from the trap door that Rhys and Taf had discovered. To see more, Van realized, he would have to go down over the edge of the cliff to where he had spotted the cave entrance before. He explained this to Hedrick.

"I'll take you down there. I think we can both be there. Bring your video. I have my baby Sony digital. It takes a good picture even in dim light."

They gingerly clambered down to the spot from where they could see the cave entrance and the men moving the stones back. They were still close to 400 feet above the cave and Van was satisfied they were virtually invisible to spot from the beach.

Some gulls chose to quarrel over the remains of a fish over their heads. On the cliff edge, when they landed, they sent loose gravel over the rim and down toward Seal Cave.

"Get down, Hedrick, get down. Hide your face," Van urged.

They flattened themselves against the earth and rocks of the pathway. Out of the corner of his eye Van could see Major Howe's white face looking up to where they were. He called one of his men over to him. They both looked up. The major seemed to be telling the man to do something. The man seemed unwilling. The major had him follow behind him along the waterfront to the place where it was possible to start climbing the cliff.

"Damn it!' Van muttered. "Hedrick, it looks as if that fellow is going to climb up here. We'll wait and see if he's really going to do it."

"It looks bloody dangerous to me. Didn't you say the other drowned man had probably fallen off this cliff? Perhaps this man will do the same," Hedrick said, with a spot of black humor.

They waited and watched. They saw the man start to climb and, then, to their relief, he evidently thought better of it. He started to descend, but he lost his footing and slid down to the beach where Major Howe was standing. There ensued an altercation between the major and the man with the loudness of their voices being carried up on the wind as far as Van and Hedrick. Howe stalked off, back to Seal Cave. The man followed, now with a limp.

"So much for that," Van said, "I don't think they'll try again. But we'll still be careful."

The men below had cleared the stones off the top of the trapdoor and lifted it away. Shortly a light appeared in the chamber beneath. Through his binoculars Van could see a ladder beneath the trapdoor and a man inside the chamber.

The tide was half in. Van's eyes swept up the beach, looking at the high water marks on the rocks through his binoculars.

"Interesting," he whispered to Hedrick. "The highest tide will be in three or four days time. They could have misjudged where to put their cache. That trapdoor could be underwater if we have a good westerly blow. If everything is maximized, the water could reach and pretty much fill that cave."

Hedrick whispered back. "I'm glad you are along, Van. I would have never realized that. Perhaps they don't either. What would happen?"

Van scratched some sand off his chin. "It all depends. If the tide is high enough, it would flood that chamber. With the trapdoor on, perhaps not too badly, depends on how well they have constructed it. But I sure wouldn't want to be inside it when the water begins to come in. You know, there's an old wives tale round here that the very high tides are caused by a Moon Goddess to clean out the shores. Perhaps she'll do her stuff with theses rascals."

Darkness fell over the scene. Van and Hedrick gingerly crept back to the others. "You can come out. No one will be along the path now. Crawl to the edge of the cliff and you can get a pretty good view of everything. For heaven's sake don't go too near the lip or we won't see you again. Follow me. I'll show you what to do."

Heddy, the Police Inspector and the Customs and Excise man, following Van's directions, crawled to the cliff edge. They lay down and were able to see down to the beach over the lip of the cliff. Through their night vision goggles they saw most of the beach and the open trapdoor of the chamber.

Though the wait seemed interminable, and made more dreary and cold by the misty rain that was falling, the watchers were rewarded by the return of the boat from over the horizon. Three men were in it. Van trained his goggles on the third man. Yes, it was Lief. Van could recognize him in spite of the green color and fuzziness of the image given by the goggles.

Lief jumped out of the boat onto the stones and was met by Major Howe. Another altercation ensued,

punctuated with much waving of arms and angry ges-
tures. Then the men seemed to cool down. Lief put his
arm around Major Howe's shoulder. They walked together to peer into the underground chamber. Two crew
men brought cartons from the boat and the team put them
in the cache.

All these activities had been faithfully recorded on
Hedrick's video. Van had taken pictures too, using the
lowlight setting on his Sony.

As best as they could tell from the top of the cliff,
Lief and Major Howe were holding a parley, seemingly
about particulars, drawing diagrams in a patch of sand.

In half-an-hour they were done. With another man,
Lief returned to the boat and they roared out to sea.

The men on the beach retreated into the cave and
Van saw a sleeping bag being unrolled and taken back
into the cave.

They had seen enough. They walked back along the
cliff path to the parking lot by the sands and piled into their
cars. They all went to Van and Ava's cottage. In spite of her
mild protests, Heddy was given first dibs to the bathroom.
She warmed up in the hot shower and soaped off the black-
ening she had put on her face. The men followed suit. They
all sat down to eggs and bacon prepared by Ava. "It's what
they used to give us," Van told them, "when we returned
from dropping bombs on the bloody Hun."

"Now, now, Van, "Ava gently scolded him. "I'm sure
that is a politically incorrect thing to say."

"Maybe, my dear. But it's historically correct. Enjoy
your eggs and bacon, people, and give a thought to the
thousands of airmen, Brits and Yanks, who died to make
our lives here possible."

Heddy said, "Thank you for reminding us, Van. I
wasn't born then. All I can add is that we are going to

catch these bastards now and stop them ruining the life you guys gave us."

"I'll drink a toast to that," Hedrick said, raising his cup of coffee. "Down to all bastards!"

Having sipped his hot coffee, along with the rest, Van smiled, "I'm not sure if I agree with 'all.' A cousin of mine is Malcolm Fitzroy. He's descended, so he claims, from a bastard son of William the First. Fitzroy in Norman French means 'the bastard son of', so he's probably right. So here's to all good bastards and not the bad ones!" and Van and all raised their coffee cups again.

They went over the notes they had taken and the photos Hedrick and Van had recorded. The Police Inspector reminded them to sign the notes, witnessing each other's signatures, and for Hedrick and Van to make out brief affidavits concerning how and when the photos and videos were taken.

"They will have to stand up in a court of law," he reminded them.

The others had left. Van and Ava were alone.

"Ava, I'm almost too old for these shenanigans. I'm going to bed even though it's ten o'clock in the morning. Do me a favor will you? Visit Myfanwy at the Red Dragon and find out whether Major Howe and his gang have checked out."

"No problem, my dear. I was going into town in any case to visit my most gallant admirer, Mr. Browne, the grocery. You see, I'm almost speaking Welsh. They don't say at the grocery shop or store. They're more economical. They just say, 'the grocery'."

"Very good, Ava. Off you go to Myfanwy, the Red Dragon, and Mr. Browne, the grocery."

Van awoke in time for tea. Ava was back and told him, "They checked out, Major Howe and the men. The vans they had are gone too."

Van nodded. "I thought so. They're on schedule. I'll let Hedrick and Heddy know."

Chapter 28

Deliberations

In the days before the rapidly approaching queen's visit to St. David's, a variety of deliberations were taking place.

* * *

"Are you telling me, Lief, that a conversation you had over the transponder was with a stranger?"

"Hold on, Kari. Not exactly. It could have been with one of Howe's men. No one else knew the reply."

"So what did your precious Major Howe have to say?"

"He doesn't know."

"*Faen!* Doesn't know!" Kari bit back her anger. "All right, Lief. And now the transponder has been lost? Is that right?"

"Yes. Howe left it unguarded on top of a mountain. He put it there to get a longer range to us. Heaven knows who took it."

"How much are we compromised, do you think?"

"That's a tough question, Kari. In the best case, I would say, not at all. Only one attempt has been made to use it and that drew a blank, of course. That's the safe guard of transponders. Unless you get the right reply, there is no communication."

"So it may just be sitting in someone's garage?"

"Very possibly. On the larger picture, Kari, there has been no sign in Pembrokeshire or London or, even, Leicester that the Brits are onto us."

"What about the worst case, Lief?"

"That's always the unknowable, isn't it? They may have planted an agent who we haven't uncovered, or broken into our communications, or just sat tight, waiting for us to reveal ourselves. It's a guessing game of who knows what about the other side. As I see it, there's always a worst case that, if you take seriously, would stop you doing anything at all. There's no such thing as zero risk. All I can say is that I haven't seen anything saying we are in trouble."

Kari got up, walked to the window, and looked out over Oslo harbor. Many times, she had found, doing so helped her think straight. It was a risk/benefits game. The weak link in the chain appeared to be landing the stuff on the Welsh coast. But there was always a difficulty in getting the stuff ashore, no matter where. She had chosen the Welsh site because it seemed to offer low risk and Lief was now confirming that was so. Once they had the stuff ashore and in the hands of the carriers and distributors, the risk went sharply down. The police could catch the small fry, but not penetrate anywhere near her. "Lief, are you still there?"

"Yes."

"You have made your dummy run?"

"Yes. It went smoothly."

"No sign of the opposition?"

"None."

"In the next three nights can you get the stuff ashore and hidden?"

"Yes. We already have some of the stuff out of the keel and topside. It's not easy, but we are doing it. Our cache is in good shape and well hidden and the stuff won't be there for more than two or three days. Kari, we should go ahead. We're too far into it to turn back now. We'll be successful, I'm sure, and will be able to retire and live in luxury for the rest of our lives."

Kari laughed. "What a terrible prospect, Lief. We'd die of boredom! Before you go, what's happening with the queen's visit to St. David's?"

"Well, she's coming and, as you know, we are scheduled to move the stuff ashore and for it to be on its way during the previous night. Their security forces will be focused on the visit, giving us a clear field."

"I hope you're right. I have to trust your judgment. Those two men you put ashore at Aberystwyth. Any news of them?"

"Howe has acted as a phone link for them. That is all. It seems quite innocuous."

"Maybe. Our man in Paris has picked up a sniff from the French police that the Jihadists are planning some form of attack in the UK. He says the Brits have rated it 'Severe.'"

"My thought is, let them fight it out."

"I don't like you being so flip about it, Lief. If it blows up and they are caught, it's possible the Brits could trace back to us."

"Let them try. I think we are clean. Just giving a couple of tourists a ride."

"All right. I like your confidence, Lief. Go ahead. *Ha det godt* (take care)."

* * *

Laura examined the list of people and events for the Estate Party with Penny. It included the tenant farmers and lessees of James's holdings in the county and elsewhere and then took in an amazing assortment of local gentry, doctors and lawyers, bishops and parsons, mayors and politicos, trades people and shopkeepers. It seemed no one was left off. Furthermore, all wives, husbands, and children were invited to come along.

"Good God! It must be 200 people at least, Penny. And look, there is going to be a tennis tournament!" Laura exclaimed, experiencing something between a laugh and an anxiety attack.

On approaching James about it, he told her, "Oh, yes, it's the tradition. Can't do anything about it, even if I wanted to. We always have a tennis tournament for the young people. We have our own rules and scoring, only one serve and who gets to five first, so that each match is short and sweet. Everyone plays everyone else. Great fun! Perhaps Penny, you can take care of the tournament this year? Don't worry. I'll explain it all to you."

So that was settled.

"James, we have to get serious about the food and drink. For two hundred people, yet!"

"Oh, there may be more. But it's all right, Laura. Not everyone on the guest list shows up, though most do; and down here, people come by, you know, and I hate to turn anyone away. It's worked out pretty well in the past.

We have enough house staff to cope. We have barrels of beer, pitchers of lemonade, and a fruit punch bowl, bread and cheese, lots of fruit and cake, strawberries and cream, and ice-cream for the kids. Nothing fancy. The Llwyn Arms supplies the beer and Mr. Browne, the grocery, does the rest. They do it every year. It's important for me to give the local trades people as much business as I can. And the constable takes care of the traffic and the parking on the front field with a couple of helpers. Everything almost takes care of itself, you know."

Laura had to laugh, along with Penny, when James had left.

"Penny, it's different down here. James tells me he wants it to be a great success, even better than usual, because it's his first year as Lord Lieutenant and because royalty will be visiting the house. We'll go with the flow. Get yourself over to the Llwyn Arms and Browne the grocery. Say you are now Sir James personal assistant. They probably will be able to do it all with little help from us. For Christ's sake get enough of everything. We mustn't try to repeat the miracle of the loaves and fishes."

Laura had asked James for a budget, but all she got was a wave of the hand and a "do-whatever-is-needed" as he disappeared in the Bentley with Heath at the wheel, his brief case stuffed with papers for meetings at Haverfordwest and St. David's.

As Robert Heath told Laura, he knew the roads in Pembrokeshire like the back of his hand and the shortcuts, too. "I can always get Sir James where he has to be and on time, too."

David had mulled over Derek's questions about the back roads. Robert had given away nothing more than could be found on a detailed road map. There was no way they could patrol all the back roads in Pembrokeshire. David had passed on to the local police that there might be some unusual activity on the back roads. That was all he could do.

Laura had to be tactful, of course, with the cook. "Mrs. Evans," she said, "I think Sir James wishes you to reserve your special skills in Welsh cookery for the house guests and dining room. Those Welsh cakes you make are delicious." In other words, though left unsaid, the caterers would take care of everything else.

"Very good, madam. Will you be so good as to look at my menus and lists of provisions? Mr. Bryn, madam, tells me he has twenty thistle artichokes; that's what we call them here. Sir James loves the thistle artichokes. I steam and serve them whole, after Rhoda trims the spikes. She's the scullery maid, madam, and a little on the simple side, but a good worker. I serve them as a savory dish with lemon butter and have Mr. Heath set the table with warm lemon-water bowls. Mr. Heath says they spoil the taste of wine. I'm sure I don't know about that. And then there are the meats and fish, madam."

"Well, Mrs. Evans," Laura smiled at her," I can see we have to sit down and deliberate about these matters."

Mr. Jonas Bryn, the head gardener, and his son, Daffyd, lived in the round 200-year old lodge at the start of the driveway by the main road. An assortment of females came and went and a covey of children, as James put it, whose parentage was a matter of speculation, occupied the little house too.

"I'm a local magistrate, Laura," James had told her. "Every so often a man is accused of incest. The accusation can fall flat because of the difficulty of figuring out the relationships of the people involved. I remember one hill farmer whose wife had died. His defense was, 'I do that with the sheep. I don't need any girls!'"

Laura ventured into the walled one-and-a-half acre kitchen garden and was led around by old Jonas Bryn.

He had known the grandfather of the present Sir James and explained in some detail how he had built up the gardens and the grounds. "And then there was Sir George after that, with Lady Florence who loved the flowers. I'm sure you should be knowing these things, madam, if you don't mind me saying so."

While being introduced to the Owen ancestors by Jonas Bryn and being led from one part of the large garden to another, Laura was delighted to see that there was a conservatory growing bunches of table grapes, peach trees on the old stone walls facing south to catch the sun, raspberry canes, gooseberry bushes loaded with fruit, apple and pear trees, and all the usual vegetables that a proper English garden has.

Laura was informed by Jonas Bryn that Mrs. Evans told him every morning what she wanted from the kitchen garden. He took the fruit and vegetables into the back of the house where the scullery was and then had a sit-down with Mrs. Evans over a cup of tea. Quite often Thomas the cowman would join them. He had his dairy, with its thick slate counters to keep things cool, in one of the buildings behind the house. There he separated the cream from the milk, churned butter, and made cream cheese in muslin bags. "I'm sure he would value a visit from you, madam," Jonas told her.

Laura could plainly see that she was being appraised and tutored by the household staff and, no doubt, being sized up by many more in the county for the future lady of the house.

"Ava," she cried urgently over the phone, "I have to see you. I'm in such a turmoil."

* * *

At Llwyn House the large marquee on the front lawn dazzled the eye with its broad red and white stripes. A smaller one was in the back, with a portable kitchen in it for the use of the caterers. On one side of the lawn was the posh temporary washroom, divided into men's and women's. It was, as James said, rather amazed, "fit for a queen."

Laura said, "It actually has to be fit for the princes. I wonder if they'll bring girl friends? If they do, look out for the paparazzi!"

James leaned back in his chair and clasped his hands behind his head. "I've got to the stage of accepting what will be, will be. We have to leave all that kind of stuff to security and the police. I just want our fete to go off well and then for the queen's visit to be a smooth, hundred per cent success. We shouldn't try to do anything more. We have to trust other people to do their bit."

They left it at that.

* * *

Van had been whisked away by Hedrick to deliberate with the Chief Inspector of Police, a naval commander, and a Coast Guard captain, on how they would apprehend the smugglers on the night preceding the queen's visit.

Hedrick asked the commander to lead off.

"The Weather Service is forecasting quite a blow for that night. A westerly storm is coming in. So we have to prepare for that. We'll have one of our new class of frigates out there, HMS Furious. She's equipped with the latest electronics, is almost opaque to radar, and is very fast when she needs to be. It will be a good exercise for her. She will have Customs and Excise aboard. We hope the smugglers will surrender without incident, but we are prepared to put a warning shot over their bow. As far as their small landing-type craft are concerned, we leave that to the shore people. The little boats will be close to shore. Of course, if one of them tries to make a run for it off-shore, we will be after it."

"Thank you, commander. Chief Inspector, please describe the provisions you've made on shore," Hedrick said.

The Chief Inspector had a map of the coast and the inland areas on a large easel and pointed out the geographical features as he talked.

"They have three boats at Seal Cave and they're putting them under the black polyethylene sheets on the beach along with some other supplies. They are camping out there, living and sleeping in the cave. I have our men watching them with powerful telescopes from Dinas head, and they report four men there including this Major Howe. You have been seeing them too, Dr. Bentham, with your telescope."

"Yes, that's right. I can't see right into the cave; it's around the corner. But I've seen their boats going in and out."

"Quite so. And you've been keeping us up to date on what you've seen and their boats going in and out of the Cwm. It's been most helpful. We are, of course, staying clear and I've personally warned Rhys Jones and Taf Jenkins to keep away.

Evidently Howe thinks their three boats may not be enough for their entire load. He has been to Swansea to buy three smaller inflatable craft that, we suppose, they will tow behind them. That way they'll be more sure of making just one passage up the coast.

We know they intend to land at Ceibwr Bay and meet their ground transport there. In any case, the bay there is the obvious place for them to go. It's isolated, deserted, shut off by cliffs, and has a small road going down to it. From the landside it's so sheltered that you have to be right there to see it at all. Its narrow entrance from the sea leads inland to a sandy beach. Dr. Bentham has been along the cliffs as far as Ceibwr Bay recently and, he tells me, there simply is no place between Seal Cave and Ceibwr Bay to land small boats. Isn't that right, Dr. Bentham?"

"Yes. There are small beaches along the coast, but to get off them you would have to be a damn good cliff climber, equipped with ropes and pitons and you couldn't carry any load that way. If they have thought to lift the stuff up the cliffs on ropes, a hell of an undertaking, they would then have to carry it to the nearest road, a half-mile or more away. It would be a lengthy and laborious business, full of chances for things to go wrong. So, I think it most improbable.

Other than use Ceibwr Bay, they could go north into Cardigan Bay. But there they would find more inhospitable coast lines and a few beaches, but with houses down to the waterfront. The chances of discovery would be hugely increased."

"Dr. Bentham," the commander interjected, "in the early hours of that night the spring tide will be at full ebb; then, later, at full flood. Does that make any difference to your thinking?"

"Not to any considerable extent, commander. The weather forecast is for wind and rain. Depending on the strength of the storm, their boats could become swamped, they have very little clearance. Not that it would sink them, but they sure could be in difficulty; depends on how good sailors they are. And they could be cramped on their little beach when the tide comes in. But I judge that, unless things go badly wrong for them, they'll make it"

The Chief Inspector outlined for them how he was going to deploy his men. He would have observers around Seal Cave and a Special Service Squad in and around Ceibwr Bay.

The meeting broke up after the parties had worked out their collaborative procedures and contingency plans.

* * *

In the sunshine on the patio of the mountainside cottage, Ava and Laura sat at the table with a bottle of wine. Laura was agitated. "You know why I'm here, Ava, I'm sure. What should I do? I don't know whether to collapse or jump for joy!"

"Has James said anything?"

"Yes and no. I know why he's as shy as he is. But I can't tell you."

Ava would have none of that. "Nonsense! Of course you can tell me, Laura. That's why you are here with me now. What are friends for? You're so wired. It's either me or you're off to a shrink."

Laura fortified herself with a good swallow of wine. "All right. James believes he killed his wife, and the baby inside her, because he contracted herpes from a prostitute."

"Wow!" Ava sat up straight. "That's a hell of a thing! Van thought he had something in the closet. But who would have thought of that! Is it possible? I mean, can it be true?"

"I looked it up on the Internet last night and it seems to be possible. I tried to reassure him when he told me. He was in such a state. But what can you say?"

Ava grimaced. "I think I'd be struck dumb. You're right, what can you say?"

"It's just eating away at him. It could ruin his life.
He's compensating like crazy. He's always so busy, all
into his fete, the Estate Party, and the queen's visit, trying
to run away from his bottled up secret, but being assas-
sinated inside by grief and guilt. And that's not all, Ava.
He thinks he can't marry again because he's a wife killer.
I know that's rubbish. Herpes can be controlled by medi-
cation and not endanger life at all. Pregnant women and
their babies are the ones at risk. But he only sees that
he's done it once and is terrified of repeating it."

"Well, as to the pregnancy bit - unless I'm very mistaken, you are not under any risk!"

"True," Laura smiled, "I left that possibility behind
me five years ago. I've fallen into a situation, Ava, that
has to be solved, but I don't know how to do it. Just this
morning, I was talking with the gardener at Llwyn House
and, without him actually saying so, like the others do,
he made it obvious that I'm being looked over for being
the new wife and the mistress of Llwyn House."

Ava raised her glass to Laura. "Hey! Couldn't happen to a nicer girl! If you want it, go for it, Laura. You'll
find a way to have James agree and put the past behind
him. He's that type, even though he may not recognize it
himself. But he'll need your help."

"What should I do, Ava, tell me?"

"Right now, Laura, I don't think you have to do anything more than what you are doing. You and he are
working together as a team. The seed is there for both of
you; it'll sprout when the time is ripe. Is James coming
back this evening?"

"Yes, he said so."

"Have Mrs. Evans cook up one of his favorites. Then
have Heath lay a little table for two in that alcove off
the drawing room. Put on a nice dress and then, just

be yourself. Guaranteed something will happen. If not immediately, then a little later, after it has sunk into his male consciousness that he is incomplete without you." Ava grinned. "Poor Van, he never realized what had hit him, once I had made up my mind."

They rose and hugged each other.

"You'll have to choose a color to be married in, Laura. That can be tricky."

Chapter 29

The Preliminaries

Van had turned a deaf ear to the discussions concerning shoes, dresses, accessories, hats - Oh, yes! The Hats! For his part it had been simple. He had sent his measurements for a morning suit to Grenville's, Saville Row, London. It had arrived and fitted him perfectly.

Not that Ava, who operated in the fashion world, was as much at sea as Laura, but she had brought nothing with her that, to her mind, was suitable for the once-in-a-lifetime event of being presented to the queen at St. David's. So Van phoned Patricia. She was Van's second cousin and they had kept up with each other to the extent of exchanging Christmas cards. Patricia Mill was the editor of the London edition of *Toque* and after greetings, explanations, and mild mutual scolding for not keeping up with each other more, Van broached

the subject. Patricia would come to the rescue. "Put
them on a train to Paddington. I'll have an aide meet
them and we'll go from there."

After tripping up to London and back on the night
train, and becoming both exhilarated and exhausted in the
fashion shops in London, the ladies returned triumphant
with box after box of "*la mode*" fit to meet the queen
and, of course, some auxiliary outfits for the evening party, with their etceteras. It was all achieved at incredible
speed under Patricia's supervision, undoubtedly helped by
the say-so from James that she would be in his party at St.
David's and then at the ancestral home. Laura told Van, "I
guarantee Patricia will have her own photographers there
and they'll bring in the paparazzi for sure."

"Oh, God!" Van moaned, "What have I done?"

* * *

Megan Lloyd told Laura that Patricia would have to be
in one of the rooms over the stables. "All the rooms in the
house are taken, madam. I really need another maid. Hot
water has to be taken to those rooms in the morning along
with the tea and biscuits. And the mattress on that bed is a
disgrace; it must have been there since the Great War."

"All right, Megan, have somebody local bring in a
new mattress and hire another house maid. I'll tell Sir
James. Anything else?"

"Some fresh linen and towels, madam," Megan Lloyd
began and then continued with a litany of what should be
acquired for such an important occasion. "I can have it
all here in a day or two, madam."

Laura took a deep breath, looked to the ceiling for
inspiration, though that didn't help, and said. "Very well,
Megan. Just go ahead."

* * *

In the servant's hall in the late afternoon, the staff gathered for their high tea. Later they would all be busy. Downstairs they would be serving the master and his guests and upstairs the maids would be preparing the rooms and beds.

Mrs. Evans, having seniority, presided at the head of the table and said the grace in Welsh. They sat down and Mrs. Evans told them she had a few things to say.

"The house will be full of people, some related to the royal family. In the afternoon and evening of the day of the queen's visit, we are expecting the two princes to be here with their companions. I need hardly tell you, I'm sure, that Sir James expects the best possible behavior from each of you. If you have any doubts about how to behave and what to do, ask Megan Lloyd."

The maids - young, excited Welsh girls who well understood that service at the big house was a passport to making a good marriage in the county - began to chatter in Welsh. Mrs. Evans held up her hand. "Quiet, please. As you know, Laura Manning has been staying here and has been assisting in the arrangements. There is nothing more to be said at this time. Whatever our expectations may be, we will take care not to express them."

One of the maids couldn't contain herself. "Oh!" she cried, "She would be the perfect Lady Owen. She could be a royal. She has that wonderful air about her!"

Mrs. Evans smiled as she picked up the large sized teapot and poured herself a cup of tea before passing it on, "Whatever you or I may wish ... and it's not hard to tell what those wishes are ... we will continue to address her as 'madam.' Now we'll have our tea and talk over what's to be done and whatever problems any of you may have."

A buzz of talk broke out when Megan Lloyd told the maids they would be having new maids' dresses in the latest fashion. "You too, Rhoda, just like the others. We may be having visitors to the kitchen."

Rhoda sat stupefied ... a maid's uniform ... she'd be like the house maids ... and she might see a prince ... then she would absolutely die ...

The next day the driveway was full of cars as the guests began to arrive.

Chapter 30

A Stormy Night

The deck lights of *Mother Goose* were cutting through the driving rain and spray of the storm. They illuminated the crewmen struggling to load the last of the cartons onto the landing craft and then secure the load with buckled straps. Captain Hans Fliegel, with Lief beside him, strove to keep a shelter for the landing craft on the lee side. Even so, the rubber boat was riding precipitously up and down. The men could only transfer the cartons when it rose momentarily to the level of the deck. Already one man had lost his footing and dropped between the two boats. He was hauled back in on his security line, white faced and choking. But, finally, it was done.

Lief risked an open mobile phone to tell Trevor Howe that the boat was on its way.

The captain turned *Mother Goose* into the wind. She was pitching now rather than rolling. That made it easier on the keel. Its structure had been weakened because the doors of the keel compartments could not be properly shut. They had to be locked in place to preserve the structural integrity of the keel. The replacement diver, relatively inexperienced, had not succeeded in closing them properly.

Lief cursed that he didn't have Oscar Flavio with him. Now the man was in police custody. But they wouldn't get anything out of him, Lief was sure. Oscar was too tough for that. The diver had done what he could, but was shit-scared of diving in the heavy sea. He wouldn't go down again. Lief could hardly blame him.

The captain told the helmsman to keep her into the wind and, along with Lief, went down to the bilge. There was no doubt about it. The seals by the keel were sprung. Water was coming in. He turned on the bilge pump. If it didn't get any worse they could manage, the captain reckoned.

Back on the bridge Lief and the captain examined charts of the coast. They had to find calmer water and send the diver down again. They could only hope the keel compartment doors were not too damaged and were still able to close securely. By steering northeast they could place *Mother Goose* in the shelter of the Cemaes headland up by Cardigan. They would still be in reach of Ceibwr Bay for the pick-up operation. After that, they would skedaddle out of there.

* * *

The captain of the Royal Navy Frigate, HMS Furious, looked over the shoulder of his radar man. The target had to be arrested in British Territorial waters, not on the high seas.

"It looks to me, sir, as if that small boat has left the bigger boat and is bound for the shore off Morfa Head. The blip is very weak and will soon be out of range."

"What about the bigger boat?"

"Here she is, sir," the radar-man said, pointing to the screen. "She came up into wind and then, just a moment ago, turned northeast, making about twelve knots, heading up the coast."

The captain turned to the helmsman. "Steer 050 at twelve knots."

"Aye, aye, sir. Zero five O, at twelve knots."

The captain turned back to the radar man. "Report any change in her course or speed. She's probably making a run to find some shelter from the storm."

"If she continues on course, sir, she'll be by that Cemaes headland quite soon," the radar man said, pointing to the screen.

That's what the captain wanted to hear. "Very good. Keep me informed."

* * *

Trevor Howe was cursing everything, the storm in particular.

Goddam this bloody storm! Things had gone reasonably well up to now. For two nights they had run the boats out to *Mother Goose*, loaded them up, brought the stuff back into Seal Cave, and stowed it safely in the cache. That way, even if someone had come by and was curious, their cover story would still have been good. There would be nothing suspicious to be found.

Now, the storm driven tide was threatening to ruin them. For a couple of days it had only come up to the trap door of the cache, not over it. But this tide, driven by the westerly storm, was flooding in like a tsunami.

Trevor watched the water come up. He looked around. He had anchored the landing craft fore and aft, as securely as was possible.

"Batten that trap door down. Put heavy stones on it," he shouted to his men, making himself heard as best he could through the wind and heavy rain flying horizontally at them.

The rising water was inexorable. With each wave, it came higher. They retreated into the cave. The water followed them up the slope of the cave floor. They were about to be trapped. Trevor saw it. He could only hope the tide would peak before it drowned them or forced them to try to escape, and that could well drown them too.

"Pick up your stuff, men. Take it to the end of the cave."

They were crowded like rats at the end of the cave. The water kept on coming. Their sleeping bags became soaked and floated out, then everything else. They were kneeling in the water with their heads touching the cave top.

"If it gets any higher, men, we'll make a swim for it. We'll watch it on the wall. Give it another inch. Then we'll go. Don't give up. I've been in worse pickles. We'll get through yet."

Their faces were drawn and white. No bravado now. One of them crossed himself. They waited, shivering in the cold water.

Trevor made a line on the cave wall with a stone, marking the water line. They watched and waited, each man with his own mortal fear. Perhaps not so oddly, Trevor remembered the Latin master at his prep school teaching that the word 'cave' in Latin did not mean a cave as in English. It was pronounced *kay-vee*, at least by English school boys, and meant "Beware!" Perhaps he should have remembered that before trapping his men and himself in this cave.

At last! At last! The water came no higher. "Fucking hell! We've made it," Trevor cried out.

Cramped, wet, and cold they emerged from the cave as the water receded. Trevor had them running in place to work up their body heat. They cleared the stones off the trap door. When the water left it clear, they prised it up and looked inside. To Trevor's relief, there were only a few inches of water in the cache, just to the raised floor boards they had put in. The water proof cartons, some four hundred of them, were safe.

The spring tide ebbed quickly from its unusually high peak. Soon the beach was clear. The men retrieved the boats and started loading. The heavy work warmed them up and restored their spirits. By the water's edge they loaded each of the boats and, then, each of the smaller ones they would tow behind them. It was arduous work on the stony beach in the wind and rain, even though the storm was abating.

Trevor knew they couldn't stay there, even if they wanted to. All their gear had been lost, washed out to sea by the under-tow of the waves. At least their life-vests, secure in the landing craft, were safe. They were still going to make it, come hell or high water. High water indeed!

They saw the last boat coming in from *Mother Goose*, being tossed about in the turbulent waves.

"That sea's a bugger," the man getting off the landing craft told Trevor. Not that Trevor needed to be told, he could see it for himself.

"Listen men," Trevor shouted, "These boats were made to cope with all this shit. They won't sink. As long as you keep underway, they're self bailing. Put on your life jackets and tie on your security lines. If you do get washed overboard, haul yourself back in. You've all had experience in the boats since we've been here. Put it to good use and we'll get through."

Trevor went round his small flotilla making sure all the straps were buckled up tight.

"OK, men. You know your instructions. Follow me to Ceibwr bay where our ground transport is. If we get separated find the bay on your own. You've all been there and know where it is. When we've unloaded, you'll take the boats to *Mother Goose*. She will be in view off the bay and will blink a light. They'll take you aboard and the boats too."

One by one, they pushed off and started their engines, each larger boat towing a smaller one behind it.

The passage to Ceibwr Bay seemed to take forever as they fought the wind and the high seas. Towing the small boats behind them made it additionally treacherous. Every boat and its tow were tossed around like popcorn in a fry pan. Somehow they made it and ran up to the beach in the comparative calm of Ceibwr Bay. As planned the vans were there and their drivers helped unload the cartons from the boats. They filled the vans to the roofs.

The vans drove off. "There goes the money coming to you, men, enough to keep you in style for the rest of your lives. Now we get the boats out to *Mother Goose* and have some hot food and dry clothes. Let's do it!"

Mother Goose was not foundering, not yet at any rate. The bilge pump was keeping the water at bay. If only they could make it to Aberystwyth harbor, then, Lief was sure, he could save her. The captain drew *Mother*

Goose in close to shore at Ceibwr Bay. He blinked a light. They saw the landing craft coming toward them. The men clambered on board *Mother Goose* and went below. The landing craft were pulled up the stern slipway and deflated.

The storm was dying. Lief and the captain agreed they would turn north, running with the remains of the storm, up the coast to Aberystwyth.

Trevor and the captain were on the bridge, together with Lief. After all the turmoil of bringing the stuff from Seal Cave to Ceibwr Bay, Trevor was celebrating with a tumbler of Scotch whisky. He raised the tumbler, "OK, Lief! Here's to success in spite of a few difficulties." He jigged a little dance, "We're in the money! We're in the money!"

It was at that moment that *Mother Goose* was enveloped in a powerful beam of light from HMS Furious, making speed toward them. A loud hailer cut through the remains of the storm. "Royal Navy! You are under arrest. We will escort you to Aberystwyth. Maintain course and speed."

Astonished beyond measure, Lief, the captain, and Trevor stood rooted to the floor of the bridge. Lief was the first to recover his senses. "Have we got any stuff left on board?'

The captain told him, "No, no cartons."

"OK. Our only hope is to bluff it out. There is no way, in the state we're in, we can outrun that Navy boat. Go to the naval radio channel, captain, and tell them we will comply."

Mother Goose sailed into Aberystwyth harbor with the frigate shadowing her all the way. At the mooring they were met by the local police and agents of Customs and Excise. They were arrested on multiple charges and taken to the town jail. All were so exhausted that it was a relief to lie down on the cots and fall asleep.

The Chief Inspector and his forces stopped the vans emerging from Ceibwr Bay by the simple expedient of parking a police car across the narrow road at the top of the hill, a mile inland. There was no place for the vans to go. The men were arrested and they and the vans driven to Haverfordwest. The police there, from the Chief Inspector on down, were astounded at finding stuff in the vans worth, at street value, £7,000,000, or $10,000,000 US.

As one of the policemen said to another, with a broad Welsh smile, "That high tide of the Moon Goddess certainly helped us and ruined them tonight."

Chapter 31

Going to St. David's

At Paddington, the red carpet had been laid down between the entrance from Eastbourne Terrace through to Platform 1. A guard of the Royal Welsh Regiment was formed up. A small crowd had gathered to see the queen and the royal party, including the duke, the two princes, and their entourage, board the train. At its front, the train was flying the royal standard. Possibly as an antidote to the national disgust with any and all politicians, the popularity of the queen was high. She had weathered the storms family members had brought on the crown and emerged as the steadfast and beloved mother of her country.

The word was out that there would be certain eligible young ladies on the train. The London press, especially the gushing tabloids, could not miss such a chance. An opportunistic fellow was selling maps of St. David's,

Haverfordwest, and Newport. He had drawn a sketch showing the way to Llwyn House and helpfully suggested its pronunciation.

In the morning the dignitaries were assembled at Fishguard station. Chief among them was the Lord Lieutenant, Sir James Owen, in his dress uniform. He officially greeted the queen to the county with a salute.

"Good morning, Sir James, I'm glad to be here."

A squad of Royal Navy personnel from Pembroke Dock came to attention and presented arms. The band of the Royal Welsh Regiment played the British and Welsh national anthems. A choir of Welshmen sang them enthusiastically in English and Welsh.

After the introductions to mayors, members of parliament for Pembrokeshire, and a Welsh regiment soldier wounded in the current Afghan war, the third war for the British there, the queen went to her car. The Lord Lieutenant went to his. The powers-that-be had cleared Robert Heath to be Sir James's driver following his exoneration from his court martial. The line of cars set off for St. David's.

* * *

Previously that morning, security forces and police had patrolled the road yet again with their detection devices and sniffer dogs. They had not let the dairy farmers put their milk churns out on the platforms on the sides of the road. A terrorist could conceal a bomb in them. All along the route, the hedgerows and the ground behind them had been inspected, buildings along the route had been entered, occupants vetted.

* * *

David and Heddy were there, very conscious of the threat, but unknowing how the Jihadists intended to strike. Always the problem was that the most obvious methods were the easiest to foresee and defend against. The Jihadists would know that. Would they come on nevertheless or would they seek out some novel form of attack? And what would that be?

At their last brain-storming at MI5, David had summarized, "We know their intention, we also know they have a big nitrate bomb. First and foremost we have to anticipate a car-bomb attack. That entails keeping vehicles away from the royal party at all times. That's fairly simple for the police to do.

All persons going anywhere near the royal party, those in the cathedral, for example, will go through scanning gates. All that has been laid out in the police protocols and is routine. Defense against sniper attacks is also a routine matter. Vantage points within two to three hundred yards are inspected and guarded. The Welsh regiment has proposed the deployment of their *Boomerang* system, the latest sniper location device from America. When a shot is fired *Boomerang* locates its range and bearing within milliseconds. We have agreed to have it there in one of their patrol cars.

The security around the person of the queen will be *'Tight'*, as the security people say. The standard four men close to the queen will be amplified to six. Another six will be employed within the nearby crowd to detect any threat, including handguns and suicide bombers.

An attack by air is possible. ATC - Air Traffic Control - will void the low airspace for fifty miles around and armed helicopters will be in the airspace around St. David's. These security measures have been gone through with the people at Buck House. They are acceptable. However, we've been asked to make them as inconspicuous as possible."

* * *

Fiona and Stewart had started off at five o'clock in the morning from Llwyn House so that Fiona could make final arrangements and inspections of the flowers and grounds in and around the cathedral. She had put in some extra flowers from the Llwyn House garden, just in case. The police had told her that the cathedral grounds would be swept by men clomping around with metal detectors that morning. If they dared set foot in the herbaceous borders, she would be after them with the most dire imprecations they had ever heard - in English and in Welsh!

Mrs. Evans, slippery Sue, and Rhoda had been up before five to provide them an early breakfast in the dining room. In another half hour all the house staff were up and attending to their tasks. Soon the guests were stirring. Their retinue of cars would be leaving at seven.

For Laura, Ava, Patricia and himself, Van had hired a "stretch" limo from Cardiff with a driver. Myfanwy from the Red Dragon had been invited by Sir James to be in his party at the cathedral, so she was included in the limo. By seven o'clock they were on their way.

They had all been warned to turn off their mobile phones and other electronic devices once near the cathedral. However, Heddy had told Van, "Have our mobile with you and keep it turned on in the silent vibrator mode. It's possible we'll need to talk to you and, if you see something, don't be afraid to call us."

They were driving along the route the queen would take and saw people and police gathering along the roadway. Here and there bunting, Union Jacks and the Welsh dragon flag, adorned the houses.

Approaching St. David's they had to show their invitation and passes. They drove on slowly in the line of cars going to the west door of the cathedral. Once more they had to show their papers and then each went through the scanners.

At the cathedral they were ushered to their reserved seats near the front, those allotted for the Lord Lieutenant's party.

Chapter 32

St. David's

It was a long wait. The ladies whispered between themselves. Van, seated on the aisle, interested himself in spotting the security men trying to be invisible in the building. Having done that, he played the devil's game of thinking what the other side might do.

A big bomb? He hardly thought so. How would they get it through the police screens and close enough to affect the royal party? A suicide bomber? Maybe. A sniper or someone with a concealed handgun in the crowd? Possibly. As his mind roamed around the possibilities, nothing really clicked. Police and Security were well prepared for such attcks. The chances of success would be very small. Most likely, he thought, if there was an attack, it would be something unusual. That's what would make it so dangerous. He was worried. What the hell might it be?

His musings were put to an end by a trumpet blast announcing the queen's arrival. The archbishop and his minions appeared in their robes in front of the altar. The service commenced, half in English, half in Welsh. Once the singing in Welsh had begun, the whole mass of Welsh people in the cathedral joined in lustily. Then the boy's choir sang an Ode to St. David in Welsh, in their beautiful high voices. It was hard not to be moved.

An usher came silently up to the Lord Lieutenant's party and led them outside to be posted in a line on the pathway leading from the south door of the cathedral. The queen would emerge from there to make her progress down the line, stopping and talking to whomever she chose. Along the opposite side the honor guard of the Royal Welsh Regiment would be lined up under the command of their colonel. By the queen's side would be Sir James and he would introduce each individual in the line. Laura would be introduced as the author of books, some of which, it was known, the queen had read. The queen, from long practice, understood the protocol exactly.

Suddenly there was a commotion about a hundred yards away down the slope from where they were, something was going on in a small parking lot adjacent to the cathedral. Van saw a curl of smoke rising. Even as he saw it, he flipped open the mobile to Heddy.

"Possible pre-explosion fuse smoke," he told her.

"Down on the ground, all of you," Heddy came back in quick reply.

Van put his arms around his ladies, "Down! Lie flat!" he told them urgently. Ava helped him with the others. "Van! Van! What the hell is happening?" she pleaded, as both were lying flat.

Van saw the queen being rapidly drawn back into the cathedral. All the people around were lying flat or fleeing.

"I don't know, Ava. Could be a bomb."

Van raised his head enough to see people rushing away from a vehicle that was emitting smoke. Within seconds a Police Bomb Squad van appeared. Heavily armored men came flying out of it.

Flames began to lick out of the car. A Bomb Squad man with a foam extinguisher doused the flames. Another Bomb Squad man raced to the car. He plunged his hand inside and, within seconds, tore out a clock timer with its wires dangling from it.

Heddy was on the mobile again. "Keep down, Van. They've got one fuse; there may be another. They think it's nitrate in the car. It has a doctor's ID on it. That's why it was allowed there."

Van shouted to everyone to keep lying down, waving his hand downward. He peeked again and saw the bomb squad men around the car. One of them was attaching a tow. The police were shouting to people to get out of the area.

Heddy was on the mobile again. "Van, the bomb was a dud. They hadn't placed the detonator properly. That's what the bomb squad leader has just told us. The danger is past. The car has been towed away. You can stand up and resume your positions. The queen insists on continuing."

Hearing the good news, everyone struggled to their feet. They brushed themselves off, doing their best to restore their looks, the ladies adjusting each other's hats. A pair of medics came along, asking if anyone needed help.

Ava said, "I'm going to postpone my post-traumatic-shock until later. What the hell was all that about, Van?"

Van was even more worried. "I wish I knew. That was damn curious. Their bomb was too far away. I can't help thinking that something else is about to happen. Why would they do that? There must be a reason."

Van's mobile vibrated again. "Yes, Heddy?"

A man's voice with a French accent came on the line. "No, no. I'm not Heddy, you rascal. Van! It is your old friend, Jean-Paul from *La Sûreté* in Paris. We are on the same team again, hunting down the bad boys, eh! I have some information for you."

"Jean-Paul! Great to hear from you, but you've caught me at the worst possible moment."

"But I only take a moment. You wished to know about Voltaire. It is the name the bad men have given to their super sniper rifle, the best sniper rifle ever made. It has killed a man two kilometers away, over a mile in your measures. That is what you wished to know, isn't that so?"

"Oh, my God, yes! Excuse me. I must go."

"Who was that, Van?" Ava asked, looking at her husband's startled, taut face.

Van's brain raced. Voltaire … a flight through the air … Fiona had seen a gun case …

Van looked around frantically. They were in a dip. The close hills had police on them. There was a more distant hill to the south, about a mile away.

The queen was coming down the line, now only ten feet away. She was facing south, in full view.

"James!" Van yelled, "Stand in front of the queen. Put her out of sight. Shield her. Stand in front of her, for God's sake!"

James took one look at Van's frenzied face and did what Van was frantically gesturing him to do. He stood in front of the queen.

There was only the slightest impact sound as James let out a small gasp, "Oh!" His hand flew to his shoulder. He staggered and fell. The 306 bullet, fired from a mile away, had taken a bit over a second to get there. It had gone through his shoulder and, now spent, had fallen to the ground just beyond. If James had taken one second more in moving in front of the queen, the bullet would have hit her head, killing her instantly.

Within another second the security men had enveloped the queen in a cone of their bodies. A police car came up fast. The queen was bundled into it. It took off, sirens screaming. The rest of the royal party was in hurried retreat back into the cathedral.

James lay on the ground, his hand red from the blood flowing from his shoulder.

Laura let out a wild cry and flew to him, kneeling by his side, protecting him with her body. Ava knelt beside her.

Van yelled, "Medics! Medics!" repeatedly, waving his arms above his head.

James looked up at Laura and, quite calmly, said, "This may not be the right time exactly, Laura, but please marry me. I seem to need someone to look after me. Oh! And I love you. I'll be fine." He winced, his face screwed up. "God! This bloody thing hurts!" and he closed his eyes.

"I'm here, darling. I'm here," Laura sobbed, her whole body trembling.

As Ava said later, "Never let it be said that the Brits, when put to it, are not passionate!"

The scene on the pathway by the cathedral unfolded into a fast moving drama. People of every sort were running and shouting as if the world was coming to an end.

A rock in the tumult was the colonel of the Welsh Regiment. He was aiming his swagger stick out to the spot where the lieutenant in the patrol car with *Boomerang* was pointing.

"Sergeant! There's your target! Go, man, go!"

"Squad! On the double, follow me!"

It should be noted that the Royal Welsh Regiment is light infantry and has been famous for its running speed since Wellington's day.

* * *

Around the cathedral things gradually calmed down. Medics had bound James' shoulder and taken him to the Haverfordwest hospital in an ambulance with police car escorts.

It was all being recorded by television crews. They were having a field day.

Van heard from Heddy about Sir James. The bullet had missed the subclavian artery and, miraculously, had done no great damage. The bleeding had been stopped. They had sewn him up, put his arm in a sling, given him antibiotics for possible infection and some pain pills, and allowed him, on his insistence, to go back to Llwyn House with Laura by his side.

"Van," Heddy continued, "You and Ava have played an invaluable role in all this. Don't think it has not been noticed."

"Oh, we just did what comes naturally and are glad things worked out well."

"I see you've retained a talent for British understatement, you old dog. Let me catch you up on some other good news. We've scooped up Q's entire smuggling ring. They're all in jail. The Oslo police have arrested Kari Foss as the mastermind of their organization."

"Well done, Heddy, well done."

In an emergency meeting of MI5 and the police, it was decided that the Jihadists had shot their bolt, at least for that day, and that it was OK for the scheduled party at Llwyn House to go ahead. Indeed both the princes, the younger of whom had been in the army and seen action in Afghanistan, insisted that, like their grandmother, the queen, they would not be deterred.

The fizzling car, they now knew, was a plant; put there to deceive them into thinking the danger was past. The Jihadists had intended that the queen would proceed openly with no fear and thereby give their sniper a perfect target. They nearly pulled it off.

Heddy had asked the question of why they had bought so much nitrate, almost three times as much as was in the car at St. David's. "These people are not stupid," she said. "Now they may think we'll be off our guard and sitting pretty for another attack with the nitrate they have."

David said, "All right, Heddy. Actually, by the same argument, we are more alert than ever. We know they are on the attack and we are well deployed to foil them. We were damn lucky for Van to learn about the Voltaire rifle in time. Luck has been on our side, thank goodness. *La Sûreté* tells me that just one rifle had been stolen and now we have it. The shooter, with the rifle, has been caught. The police say he was lucky to be arrested by them before the Welsh boys found him. They were all set to lynch him.

So we can celebrate, Heddy. We'll keep our guard up and let Sir James go ahead with his party at Llwyn House. We're invited, you know."

Chapter 33

Llwyn House

With the princes declaring their intention to continue with the schedule as planned, the half-a-dozen other young persons in the royal party agreed to go with them.

They repaired to the Cloisters of St. David's cathedral for a buffet lunch. Later in the afternoon, they would all drive to Llwyn House in two cars with two security cars accompanying them. This arrangement gave time for people, including Sir James and Laura, to gather at Llwyn House before the princes arrived.

Llwyn House would be seeing nothing like it, not at least in modern times. The last royalty to be there was Henry Tudor in 1485. He was born in south Pembrokeshire and would shortly be crowned Henry VII. In so doing he founded the Tudor dynasty that continued with Henry VIII, of the six wives, and Elizabeth I, who defeated the Spanish Armada.

At that time James ab Owen gave Henry Tudor and his captains lodgings. The army of 6,000 men camped in the fields. James ab Owen then guided the future king and his army over the Preseli Mountains. Henry Tudor went on to victory at Bosworth Field defeating Richard III and to claim the throne, rightfully his. He knighted James ab Owen for the aid he had given.

The princes had been reminded of this history. Now the present Sir James Owen had served his sovereign in the ultimate way. Once the danger was realized, he had stood in front of the queen and taken the bullet intended for her.

"I rather think," Rupert, the younger prince said, "that Elizabeth One would have recognized what this Sir James Owen did. We should talk to grandma about it."

George, the older prince and the Prince of Wales, surmised, "I think grandma should give him a life peerage, make him a Lord. Actually he is a Lord already, a Lord Lieutenant, so it wouldn't be a big lift. I don't think they have any full Lords from Pembrokeshire in the peerage. It would be a good thing. Put Pembrokeshire on the map more. What do you think? Lord Owen of wherever he chooses."

Shelly Marlborough, of the Churchill family, who was riding with them, chimed in. "That's a splendid idea. Courage and valor, and saving the queen's life, are just as important, really a lot more so, as being a politico, especially as they are making such a mess of things."

Their car, flying the Prince of Wales standard in the center of which are four Welsh dragons rampant, was driving back along the route to Llwyn House that the others had done an hour or two earlier. The news of the attempt on the queen's life had spread like wildfire. The unfolding events had been and still were on all the TV channels. It was known that the princes were continuing their itinerary and hundreds of people in the villages and along the roads lined the route to Llwyn House to cheer them.

In the narrow streets of Newport they were swamped with people and slowed to a crawl. George told the driver to keep a slow pace so that Newport's young people could run beside the car until it reached the gate of Llwyn House.

There they were met by a Chief Constable of the Police. He was in charge of the squad posted there to control the crowd at the gate and in the house grounds. In a line by the round lodge were the head gardener, Jonas Bryn, Thomas the cowman, and Mr. Roberts of the Home Farm. The Prince of Wales got out of the car and greeted them individually to the applause and cheers of the crowd. He waved his brother and Shelley Marlborough out of the car, and Mark Mountjoy and the others out of the second car.

"There's the house," he said, pointing to it. "Let's walk along the driveway through the meadows. My legs could do with a bit of a stretch."

So the group of young people, trailed by security men, set off to walk the half mile along the curving driveway and over the hump-back bridge halfway along it. As they came up toward the house one of them noted that the ha-ha was quite invisible until you were right on top of it.

"It really is a clever way to keep the view open while keeping the cattle out."

By this time they had been spotted and people streamed out of the marquee to stand around on the lawn and the driveway in front of the house to greet them. Word was passed to Sir James and he came out from the front of the house, with his arm in a sling, with Laura by his side.

Often it's a bit abstruse to know how to greet and converse with royalty in these circumstances. The rule is, wait for them to speak to you, on your first reply say 'Your Royal Highness' (to a prince), and after that say 'sir' or 'madam.' Then, after that, you can be on first name basis. It is most *démodé*, especially for people who should know better, to have the prince, or whoever, correct your terms of address.

People made way for Sir James and Laura to go to the gateway at the end of the ha-ha where the cattle grid was. The group walking up the drive reached there. The young ladies took one look at the cattle grid and at the heels of their shoes and were aghast. Prince George, quite unfazed, said, "Pick them up, men." Suiting his action to his words, he picked up Shelley Marlborough and walked across the grid with her in his arms.

The long range lenses of the paparazzi recorded the event in detail, including the two exchanging beatific smiles.

"Hello, Sir James," George greeted him. We are so thankful to you and glad to see you are not badly wounded."

"Your Royal Highness is most kind. I'm thankful too." They both grinned.

"And who is this lovely lady with you, Sir James?"

"Laura Manning, the author. She is my fiancée."

"Congratulations to you both. I didn't know it had been announced."

"It hasn't. We only made up our minds this afternoon. Actually, you are the first to know."

"James! That's wonderful! Are you going to announce it this evening?"

"Yes. We thought we'd do that just before the fireworks."

"What a wonderful idea! Laura, every good wish to you. You've chosen a handsome, brave, and a doer-of-good-things fellow. Will you allow me the honor of introducing you in the marquee?"

Laura felt rather overwhelmed, but managed to say it would be marvelous.

"Good, that's settled then; before the fireworks. You must meet Shelley." He brought her forward. "Shelley, here's the hero and his fiancée. Let's go to the marquee together. I'm dying for a glass of bubbly." In the marquee they drank to each other's health and happiness. Then the princes and the others with them mingled with the people there.

In the midst of all this, Malcolm Fitzroy appeared on the scene, coming up from the footbridge over the river. He was in full evening dress with a double-barreled 12-gauge shot gun over his arm, open at the breech, dangling a rabbit from his hand. The bottoms of his trousers and his shoes were wet. With little ceremony he came up to James. The security men were moving in, but Prince George waved them away.

"Well done, James. I saw it all. Just a knick in the shoulder. You'll soon be as right as rain. What do you think of our Lord Lieutenant, prince?"

James had to chuckle. His cousin was just being his unrestrained self. "Sir, my cousin, Malcolm Fitzroy."

Malcolm, putting aside all formalities, said, "Don't worry, James, George and I know each other. We had a game of backgammon on a train going to Scotland. I expect you remember, George. You won five quid off me. Anyhow, I thought I would come here by walking up the river bank. Maybe bag a pheasant or a duck on the way, but all I got was this rabbit," and Malcolm roared with laughter.

George, Prince of Wales, put his arm round the broad shoulders of Malcolm Fitzroy. The two men went off together, chatting, renewing their male bonding in spite of their age difference. Van and Ava, watching from a little distance, could see the prince was enjoying the break from protocol with the irrepressible Malcolm Fitzroy.

The fireworks were programmed for dusk and would be followed by dinner served in the marquee. In the meantime, some people played croquet on the tennis lawn, others wandered around the garden, finding seats among the flowers and trees. Jonas Bryn led a party around his kitchen garden and allowed them to cut some bunches of grapes in his conservatory and enjoy their sweetness on the spot. A band played in the marquee and couples gyrated on the dance floor.

The time came for everyone to muster in the marquee.

Robert Heath stood at the side of dais. "My lords, ladies, and gentlemen, pray silence for His Royal Highness, the Prince of Wales."

The prince greeted the company and spoke about how pleased he was, as the Prince of Wales, to be in the depths of his principality. He went on to speak about the long association of the Owens of Llwyn House with the crown. "This morning that association took on a special meaning. Sir James Owen risked his life to protect our queen. Everybody stand please and have a glass in your hand."

He waited until that was done.

"I propose a toast to the Queen coupled with Sir James Owen."

All raised their glasses and responded, "The Queen coupled with Sir James Owen."

"Sir James, please step forward with your lady." James and Laura came to his side. "Now I have the great privilege to announce, with their permission, the engagement to be married of Laura Manning to Sir James Owen."

The announcement was met with gasps of surprise followed by cheering and clapping. People crowded around the couple. The band played. The atmosphere was wonderfully festive.

Robert Heath again took the stage to say that the fireworks were about to begin and that the company should proceed out to the lawn and driveway in front of the house.

A security man had his mobile to his ear. He listened in some amazement to a report that two ambulances were being chased by police cars. The ambulances had appeared from nowhere, having taken small back roads to escape detection. The police were taken unawares, but were catching up to them. They were a mile or two away, at Felindre Farchog. He asked if they were a threat. "We don't know," was the reply.

The security man quickly went over to another. "Something may be happening. Be prepared for emergency action."

"That is to take the royals into the back of the house and shield them there. Right?"

"Right."

The two ambulances, now with their flashing lights on and hooters blasting, were approaching the lodge. For a vital few seconds it was undecided by the police at the lodge whether the ambulances were genuine or not. Their minds were made up for them by the ambulances crashing through the entrance by the lodge and starting up the drive.

Police cars, with officers armed with high impact rifles, were after them.

"Shoot their tires out! Shoot their tires out!"

The riflemen could only get a good shot when the ambulances were approaching the hump-back bridge. They got a hit on the second one. It began to swerve. Over the hump back-bridge it was in the air. The police riflemen kept up their fire. The ambulance, swaying giddily from side to side, went over the soft meadow to the right until it was behind and below the rising ground leading to the house. At that point, its wheels bogged down. It rolled over on its side, and exploded with a thunderous clap and boom. The flames from the explosion rose a hundred feet into the air.

The people around the house thought it signaled the start of the fireworks display. They broke out clapping. It certainly was a big bang and highly dramatic. And, in fact, it was beautifully timed. The fireworks display was computer controlled and the man in charge took the big explosion as a signal to start. He pressed "enter" on the key board and the first salvo of rockets soared into the air. The spectators "oohed!" and "aahed!" at the dramatic display.

The leading ambulance continued its hectic way toward the house. The police marksmen were good and punctured its tires. It veered off the driveway while continuing toward the house. Now only the ha-ha ditch separated it from the people in front of the house.

While this was happening the security men had rounded up the royals and hurried them into the house. Megan Lloyd was by the front door. The security men were yelling, "The back of the house, where's the back of the house?"

"This way, this way," she cried and led them through to the back, through the kitchen and down the short passage to the scullery.

The Prince of Wales, the calmest of the lot, looked around. Rhoda was finishing her tidying up. She opened her eyes at the people crowding into her scullery. She had no idea who they were. George smiled at her. "This looks pretty safe. Is there a way out the back?"

Gathering her wits, Rhoda said, "There's my pluck-ing room, sir, just here," and she opened the door to the room where she plucked chickens and other birds. The prince peered in. "And that door, miss?" he asked.

"That leads through the wall to the kitchen garden, sir."

The security man told them, "Everyone into the plucking room."

That's how it came about that Rhoda was in her plucking room with the Prince of Wales, Prince Rupert, Shelley Marlborough and the others.

George said to her, "Thank you for giving us shelter in your plucking room, miss. Tell me your name."

"Rhoda, sir. Rhoda Jones."

"Mine's George. So this is your plucking room? And what do you pluck?"

"Whatever the bird is. I lets them hang for a day or two, depending how hot it is. Then I heats the water to the boil and puts the bird in it for a bit to loosen the feathers. I pulls on my gloves and takes the feathers out. Then I bring them to Mrs. Evans."

"That's very interesting, Rhoda. I never knew that about plucking a chicken."

"It's the small pin feathers, that's what they call them, that takes the time, Mr. George. The big feathers come out easy enough."

"And what do you do with the feathers?"

"I puts them in a bag and sells them to the man. Sir James allows me that. He is a lovely gentleman, sir."

The others, nervous but trying to be calm, had listened to the conversation with a little amusement while helping each other brush off some clinging feathers. All were relieved when the security man came in and told them it was all over.

The Prince of Wales shook Rhoda's hand and gave her a brief hug. "Thank you very much, Rhoda, for your instruction. The next time you are in London give me a call and I'll arrange for you to have a tour of our kitchens," and he gave her his card.

"Thank you, sir. But I don't know when I'll be in London. I've never been there."

"Always a first time, Rhoda. Give me a call and I'll see what I can do."

Megan Lloyd curtseyed to the princes as they left, then put her arm round Rhoda and told her to sit down. Rhoda was utterly amazed and only half-believing the nice young man had been the Prince of Wales. With the help of Megan Lloyd, Rhoda read the card with the address of George, Prince of Wales, on it. It was Buckingham Palace. She had difficulty taking it all in. At that point Mrs. Evans made a pot of tea. It was the only thing to do to steady everyone's nerves.

While Rhoda's plucking room was being occupied by the princes and the others, a wild series of events had happened outside.

The other ambulance had continued its hectic way toward the house, rolling and pitching like a live animal. Whether the driver actually saw the ha-ha was doubtful and made no difference. The vehicle pitched nose down into the water and mud at the bottom of the ha-ha.

When Malcolm Fitzroy heard the big bang, he decided it boded no good. Being Malcolm, he did the natural thing. He grabbed his shot gun and strode outside. He saw the ambulance careening toward him with the police shooting at it and the fireworks going off around it. It was too good a target not to let fly at. Malcolm let it have both barrels of his shotgun in the windshield, smashing it very satisfactorily, and reloaded. The ambulance dived into the ha-ha right under his nose. The passenger side door flew open and a bulky man fell out of it into the ditch. Malcolm leveled his shot gun at him, "Hands up!"

The dazed man, flat on his back, was gasping for breath, gurgling mud and water, and began to move his arms.

"Hands up, I say, "Malcolm repeated, bringing the muzzle of his shot gun within a foot of the man's face. The man, scared out of his primordial wits, in spite of being a suicide bomber, tried to raise his hands from the sticky Welsh mud. A policeman, sprinting from the police car, jumped on top of him, grabbed his wrists, and pushed his arms back over his head. That had the effect of half drowning the man in the muddy water.

The policeman shouted at Malcolm, "Don't shoot, sir. For God's sake don't shoot. He's a bomber."

Malcolm put his gun over his shoulder. "Well I'm blowed. I thought he was just fat."

One of the policemen in the chasing cars had previously been in the Bomb Squad and knew exactly what to do. He extracted the detonator from the would-be bomber's vest with no trouble.

"He's safe now. It's just plastic in that vest. You can give it to a child to play with."

"Good show! Good show!" Malcolm congratulated the policemen. They took the vest off the man and dragged his limp body away.

Malcolm peered into the ditch again. He thought he had seen some kind of animal scurrying away. For a moment, in the half-light, he didn't realize it was a man. Then the light from the fireworks, continuing to go off according to their computerized program, gave Malcolm a better view. He saw it was a man, actually the driver of the ambulance, trying to escape. Reaching the gate by the grid, the man rose up and ran into the garden.

"Tally ho! Tally ho!" Malcolm shouted as he galloped after him as fast as he could, given his portly frame.

It was dark away from the house and Malcolm was losing sight of the fugitive. Before he quite lost all sight of him, he let off his two barrels at the disappearing buttocks.

Malcolm's young son, seeing his father in full pursuit, grabbed a halberd off the wall in the hall and sprinted after him. A policeman added light to the scene with a powerful torch. Shortly, someone was screaming in front of them. They rushed on. The torch illuminated the scene. Malcolm's son had reached the man first and placed the spiky end of the halberd firmly in the man's back, yelling; "Now I've got you!" Whether the man understood or not was beside the point. In the darkness he had run headlong into the monkey puzzle tree and impaled himself on its spikes. He was quite helpless.

The police pulled him clear and shouted for their medic. The man had numerous puncture wounds, some in his buttocks from the pellets of Malcolm's gun, some from the tree, but was more terrified than seriously wounded.

In the meantime the fireworks had continued, ending in a fusillade of rockets and fiery rain. Many of the party hadn't realized that anything untoward had happened. They thought it had been "a jolly good show!"

They all assembled back in the marquee. Malcolm held court at the bar. "I winged him, damme, I winged him! Caught him in the ass! Pretty good shooting in the dark! And my boy was ready to sodomize the bastard with that halberd."

James was sitting in a chair with Laura and the royal party about him. Now that the news of the aborted attack had spread, everyone was relieved that the princes were safe.

James had a glass of champagne in his hand. He announced to one and all, "I feel a bit squiffy. Can't think why. Just a day in the life of a Lord Lieutenant. Laura says I should be in bed and I'm inclined to agree with her. Before I go, I'd like you to notice that my grounds and garden defended us well. The front field snared the exploding ambulance in its boggy patch, the ha-ha stopped the second ambulance and nearly drowned the bomber, and the monkey puzzle tree caught the escaping man in its spiky grip. They deserve a round of applause. Don't fool with Llwyn House!"

Everyone laughed and clapped, including David and Heddy. David said, "Well, as everything has turned out so well, I suppose we can congratulate ourselves, Heddy, and a whole string of other people, too."

"Including a rather unique girl."

"Who is that?"

"*Daisy.*"

"*Daisy?*"

"Yes, *Daisy.* We're all to go out in her to see Seal Cave and visit the Moon Goddess in the Witch's Cauldron."

David grinned. "That's great. Maybe we'll catch another corpse."

"Don't you dare even to suggest it, David! Everyone has had enough of corpses in Newport.

Chapter 34

Nevern Church and Buckingham Palace

There had never been such a wedding in the long history of the old church at Nevern. The newly minted Lord James Owen of Llwyn was marrying. The Royal Welsh Regiment would provide the Honor Guard in full ceremonial dress. George, Prince of Wales would be the best man. On his suggestion the staff of Llwyn house would be represented by Rhoda Jones as one of the six bride's maids.

Laura declared to Ava, "I've never been married before. I don't say I'm a virgin. But I'm as good as one. I'm going to be married in white, Goddammit!"

Van observed, "That morning suit, I think it's the same one, must be used by now to traveling to and fro from London."

Ava exclaimed to Van, holding a hand to her head, "Good grief, Laura wants me to be the matron of honor! I have looked it up on the internet. Have you any idea what that entails?"

"No. You've stumped me on that one. But I'm sure you'll do it splendidly. James has told me the trout in the river are mine, if I can catch them. He's lent me his fishing rod, so I'm going fishing."

"Men!" Ava expostulated. Then she, Laura, and Penny set to work to solve their new set of social and protocol challenges.

"We simply can't do this all ourselves, "Penny said, "We'd be crazy to try. We must find an outfit that does the donkey work."

"I want to find my own dress and those of the bride's maids, "Laura declared. So they went to London, to Harrod's bridal shop.

That was just one of the stops in London for Rhoda Jones.

The story of what had happened in Pembrokeshire had been world-wide news. The media were all over it. The side story of the prince and the scullery maid was lapped up by the tabloids.

Laura put Megan Lloyd in charge of Rhoda. They arrived at Buckingham Palace in a storm of photographers. The executive chef showed them around the kitchens. Photos were taken of Rhoda plunging a dead feathered chicken into boiling water. She was the sensation of the day. Letters poured into Llywyn House addressed to her, including a number of marriage proposals.

On returning to Newport, Rhoda was feted in the streets. However, she had the same answer to everyone. She wanted to return to her scullery in Llwyn House, where she felt comfortable, and serve the new Lady Owen.

The wedding, followed by the reception at Llwyn House, went off splendidly. Malcolm Fitzroy behaved very well until he was into his second bottle of champagne. At that point he began to pinch and tickle the waitresses. He had to be taken in hand by his wife.

In the long hall the wedding gifts were set out, including a complete dinner set, embossed with the Owen crest, from the queen.

Frankly, Ava and Van were glad to escape to their cottage and collapse into easy chairs.

The days went by. They were receiving a ton of mail. The postman had a separate bag, specially for them, that he hauled up the hill to the cottage. Ava had him sit down in the little kitchen and enjoy the cup of tea she made for him. He was full of the gossip about the crowds gawking at Llwyn House and the people coming and going there. Haverfordwest, he informed Ava, had to send two constables to help their own constable.

Van and Ava had been putting the mail in a wicker basket and were going through it bit by bit. Van was dozing when Ava said, "Hello, what's this? Sweetheart, wake up. We've got something from the Lord Chamberlains office, whoever he is."

"Let's have a look. Give me your letter opener."

Van slit open the envelope, took out the contents, and found himself looking at the Royal Crest. He read on: "Her Majesty the Queen requests your presence at Buckingham Palace for the investiture ceremony ... " There followed the date and time and more details.

"Holy mackerel, Ava! We have to go to Buckingham Palace to see the queen. There's going to be some ceremony or other. I don't know."

The queen received them in one of the smaller state rooms. David and Heddy were also there. First there

.ᴜᴛᴇ the formal proceedings to recognize their services and, much to Van's surprise, the award of medals. To Ava's complete astonishment, she was called forward to receive a medal for non-British persons for exemplary service to the nation.

After the awards the queen, with her duke beside her, became quite chatty. She told them she had sent Commendations to the many people in Newport and elsewhere who had participated in capturing the smugglers and foiling the terrorists. She turned to Ava. "I've never seen a softball game. You must throw the ball at very high speed. Show me how you wind up. That's the expression, isn't it?"

Probably for the first time in the history of the palace a demonstration was given of how an American college girl winds up and delivers the ball underarm at high speed. Ava grinned. "It's easier with a real ball."

"Or with a stone. Isn't that right? I understand that knocking down the man helped you know what the code was and say 'Billy had a grumpy pig' at just the right time. I have told the archivist to be sure to record it in the annals. A wonderful story!"

After the queen had thanked them all for their services, they were ushered out.

On leaving the palace they were met by the inevitable barrage of cameras. Van and Ava hurried to their car. Their next stop was the American Embassy in Grosvenor Square. They were to have lunch with the ambassador.

"I guess you have to put up with all this, Ava, when you can throw a stone as you did."

The ambassador and his wife received them in their private dining room. "I'm sure I don't need to swamp you with any more formalities," he told them. "However, I have to tell you, you must fly back to the US, to Washington, tomorrow. We have your tickets."

"Oh, why?" Van asked.

"Well, not too surprisingly, the President would like to meet you both."

Lightning Source UK Ltd.
Milton Keynes UK
12 January 2011

165560UK00003B/3/P